PIRATES of SAUSALITO

Houseboat Wars Murder Mystery

Gordon, Enjoy
Bruce — REPAIR !
John Byrne Barry
☺

JOHN BYRNE BARRY

ISBN: 978-0-9967262-1-4

To my son Sean,
who continues to immeasurably enrich my life.

Cast of Characters

TIN HOLLAND
[First woman chief in Sausalito history]

FENTON FELTON
[Greedy developer, father of Dawn, ex-husband of Alice]

HUCK 'HIC' HENNESSEE
[Sniveling sidekick to Fenton Felton]

DAWN FELTON
[Defiant daughter of Fenton and Alice, girlfriend of Honest]

HONEST ABERNATHY
[Pretend pirate, houseboat resident, brother of Fate, boyfriend of Dawn]

ALICE FELTON
[Vengeful ex-wife of Fenton, mother of Dawn]

BRENDA DIAMOND
[Lonely waitress, houseboat resident, former mistress of Fenton]

LANDER JARRETT
[Oversharing lawyer, representing Aquarius houseboaters]

FATE ABERNATHY
[Forgetful architect, houseboat resident, sister of Honest]

MICKEY MACGILLICUDDY
[Flaky burnout, houseboat resident]

JOHNNY DASH
[TV reporter, *News on the Run*]

JAZZ
[TV cameraman]

SALLY CAL
[Mayor of Sausalito, former brothel madam]

PROLOGUE
The Houseboat Wars

In 1942, as the United States joined World War II, Bechtel Corporation opened a shipyard in Sausalito. Called Marinship, it employed 20,000 workers, who built 93 cargo ships and oil tankers in three years.

Workers came from all over for jobs at the ship factory, but housing was scarce. Marin County's Housing Authority and the federal government teamed up to create Marin City and build housing for 6,000 workers.

Still not enough. Many workers lived on old boats or jerry-rigged them from whatever they could scrounge.

After the war, Bechtel abandoned the shipyard, and boatbuilder Donlon Arques bought 20-plus acres of waterfront property, full of shipbuilding debris. The land was considered worthless.

Arques dragged old boats, like decommissioned ferries, onto the mudflats and rented them to soldiers returning from the war. He charged little or no rent, and his landlord style could be generously described as "benign neglect." Others called it anarchy.

Artists, craftsmen, beatniks, and bohemians built homes on barges and rafts. Out of packing crates, railroad cars, motor homes. These floating homes—most were not true houseboats as they were not navigable—connected to land on ramshackle walkways or floating docks made from styrofoam and plywood.

Residents included British philosopher Alan Watts, cartoonist Shel Silverstein, and singer Otis Redding, who wrote "(Sittin' on) the Dock of the Bay" while staying on a houseboat.

In the late 1960s and early 1970s, after the infamous Summer of Love in San Francisco turned dark, hippies from the Haight arrived, seeking free love and free living.

Arques' property, known as the "Gates," named after the ship factory entrances, became the epicenter of Sausalito's development battles of the '70s. City leaders tried to clean up and clear out the houseboats, citing the lack of sewage hookups. Not to mention the loud parties. Arques was forced to sell. Then the evictions started.

You may have read about the houseboat wars in the *San Francisco Chronicle* or watched news anchors Dennis Richmond or Dave McElhatton reporting live from the Sausalito waterfront as houseboaters in dinghies pushed away police boats with oars and protesters went limp as they were dragged into paddywagons.

But do you want to hear the *true* story? Do you?

OK, then.

This is what *really* happened.

Sausalito • Late 1970s

TIN HOLLAND
[Sausalito's first woman police chief]

1

The Desperate Developer Pressures the Peacemaker Police Chief

Fenton Felton slaps his palm on the tile table and my coffee mug jumps, splashing coffee on his ring finger, where there is no ring, only a band of white skin where the ring used to be.

"You're not *listening*," he roars. "Remove those damn deadbeat houseboat squatters from *my* harbor. *Now!*"

He's in my face, and I back away, flap the air with my hand. *God, does he not know how he smells?*

"You've been through an ugly divorce, haven't you?" I say, hiding behind my mug. I extend a napkin to him, then take another sip of my coffee. He snatches the napkin with a glare. Wipes his hand, then the table.

"Is there any other kind?" he snarls. "How do you know about that?"

Most people appreciate that I ask questions, but not

Fenton Felton. His cologne smells of leather and lemon, not a bad fragrance per se, but he drenches himself in it, and I feel like I'm being deprived of oxygen.

"Sausalito is a small town," I say. "Also, I talk to Alice." His ex.

"Don't believe a word she says." He pauses. "Well, some of it might be true."

"You mean about how you cheated on her with a waitress half your age?" The music thumps through the speakers so loudly I have to raise my voice or lean closer. I choose to speak louder.

"Never happened," he says.

"A waitress at this very establishment—"

"We were talking," he says, "about the eviction raid you're about to execute. That is, if you want to *continue* as police chief."

He thrusts his face back into mine, and I pull away again. Slowly, my eyes on his. He wants me to fear him. I won't let that happen.

We're in the window alcove of The Bar Whose Name We Dare Not Speak, Mayor Sally Cal's establishment, the closest I have to a home away from home. The window opens to the sidewalk, so we can see passersby and they can see us. Not bad for the police chief to be seen talking with big-shot developer Fenton Felton, given his recent tirades against me. I was tempted to show up in civilian garb, because it's Sunday, but this is duty, not pleasure. My uniform pants feel tight today. I'd better lay off the pastries.

When Fenton demanded to meet about the evictions, I invited him to the police station. He countered with his office. We settled on the Dare Not, which surprised me. I figured he would hate this place, because of the hippies and the groovy, laid-back vibes. But this is where he met Brenda, a waitress here, so what do I know? I don't see Brenda here today.

The Dare Not is a quirky mix of café and bar—you can order coffee and breakfast in the morning and booze anytime. They offer a pizza special every night. There's beer and wine on tap. It's early afternoon and the brunch crowd is thinning.

"We're putting together a plan for the evictions," I say, my voice firm.

"Who needs a plan?" he says. "Evict them all now. What are you afraid of, a bunch of no-good hippies and pretend pirates?" He signals for another drink. "I never supported you for police chief. You fancy yourself some kind of *peacemaker*." He spits that word out with contempt.

"I was hired," I say, calmer than I feel, "because the city leaders of Sausalito support my non-confrontational approach to policing. Which means we communicate with—"

"*No*, you were hired because you're a *woman*."

I lean back in my chair and chuckle. "For centuries," I say, folding my hands on the table, "women were *not* hired for jobs like mine *because* they were women. But Sally Cal is mayor now and it's a new day in Sausalito. I've told the Aquarius Harbor residents that they have to get legal and pay rent or leave and—"

"No, no, no," he says. "It's too late for that. I've got a dock to build. They can't live there anymore, rent or no rent. *You* have to clear out Gate 9. *Now!*"

Jenna, the waitress this afternoon, is cheery but cool when she arrives with Fenton Felton's martini. I admire the effortless way she balances her plates and glasses on her tray. Like she can do it on a tightwire and not drop anything.

When I was hired as a police officer here, five years ago, it *was* because I was a woman. The first and only woman officer in Sausalito. You can look it up. Sally Cal, who was a city council member at the time, encouraged me to apply.

I met Sally decades ago when I ran away at fifteen from my alcohol-addled mother and found a job as a maid in her brothel on Nob Hill in San Francisco. I am forever grateful that she never pressured me to be a working girl. I was not pretty, so it was probably a business decision, but I also think she understood me more than I did. I changed sheets, cleaned toilets, and lived in a cramped, but comfortable room in one of the three turrets of the grand house. Up twelve circular stairs wrapped inside a brick wall.

In my twenties, I was a police officer in the Army, during Korea, and I learned to mediate dicey disputes, not just make arrests. Later, I was a trainer at the Presidio Army Post on the other side of the Golden Gate Bridge.

I thought Sausalito was a peaceful and prosperous suburb, like a sleepy Greek island, but I was wrong. I knew about the conflict at Aquarius Harbor, which had been simmering for years. But when Fenton Felton bought the property and announced his plans to build a luxury harbor and condo complex, it erupted into a boiling inferno.

That was a year ago, shortly after I became chief.

"The houseboat tenants are sticking together," I say. "We don't have the manpower to evict them all at once, and we'll have an insurrection if—"

"Not my problem. Arrest them all. Sink their damn

boats. Whatever it takes." He laughs, a deep, loud baritone laugh, like a maniacal melodrama villain, and everyone in the Dare Not turns in our direction.

Fenton Felton is short, with broad shoulders and long arms, and he dresses in black and white, like a penguin, sometimes with a black bow tie, cape, and top hat. According to Alice, he was a magician in his younger years, performing for children's birthday parties, and that's where his get-up comes from. He's not handsome, but he has an undeniable magnetism. His eyes are blue like the sky. Today he's left his tie, cape, and hat at home and the top two buttons of his white shirt are open.

"You must know people call you 'Dastardly Whiplash,'" I say. "That must sting."

"Because I cackle with glee when I crush my opponents?"

He lets loose another demonic laugh. Like he can't help it.

At one time, he was rich and successful, a man about town, or so I've heard, but his new luxury houseboat project has not gone according to plan. He did not anticipate that the houseboaters would put up such a fight. Nor did I. And the more desperate he's become, the more he's turned into a cartoon version of himself. I've never found him likable, but he used to be less combative.

"I can't help how I laugh," he says. "I was born this way. I'm not a *bad* guy, I'm *misunderstood*. Alice has extorted more in alimony than I make and—" He stops and sputters. "It's so unfair—I follow the law and jump through hoops to get my permits and my loans and my eviction warrants, and those squatters *flaunt* the law, and yet I get hissed, and they get cheered. Explain that to me."

The front door opens and here comes Huck, Fenton's sidekick.

He's a large man wearing a gray suit and a Homburg hat with a shiny silver ribbon around it. He hasn't shaved and the gray stubble on his chin looks like sandpaper.

Fenton Felton gestures from Huck to me. "I believe you've met my partner, Huck Hennessee? I call him 'Hic.'"

I shake his meaty hand. "I thought your nickname was Snivel. Or Sniffle?"

"It was," he says, and sniffles twice. "But then," and here he stops, twirls his arm in a theatrical flourish, and hiccups violently, falling to his knees. He gets up as if nothing has happened. He's more graceful than you'd think for such a burly man.

Fenton laughs like it's the funniest thing he's ever seen. It's a different kind of laugh this time, high-pitched and melodic like a young child's.

Huck whispers to me. "He loves my hiccupping schtick, so I indulge him now and then."

Fenton wraps his arm around his partner's shoulders. "Hic is a virtuoso at permits, partnerships, and shell companies," he says. "*Bending* the rules without breaking them. What he specializes in *breaking*," and here he pauses to lock eyes with me, "is people who are *un-co-op-er-a-tive*." He lingers over each syllable and cackles again.

"Yes," Huck says, "but I learned it all from the *brilliant* Fenton Felton." He flexes a wooden ruler and sniffles, then almost convulses with another hiccup. Fenton giggles again.

"Huck," I say, "how are Cath and your daughters?" He smiles, and I suspect that he appreciates that I didn't call him by his nickname. Fenton cuts him off before he can answer.

"Hic is also accomplished," he says, "at digging up incriminating information about the personal lives of public servants who are *un-co-op-er-a-tive*. And leveraging that information as necessary. You are, Chief Tin, an at-will employee of the city."

Huck bends the ruler so fiercely, it snaps. A jagged piece skitters along the floor, and Jenna, holding a pile of plates above her head, kicks it into the corner.

"You're going to expose my personal life?" I laugh. "I don't have a personal life to expose. Unlike you, who—" I give him a silent stare. "Let's just say, I dig too, like Huck, and I've learned a few things."

"Are you threatening me?" he says.

"I believe it's you threatening me," I say. "But you're probably bluffing." I fold my hands on the table again and speak calmly. "I will use my professional judgment to determine how best to enforce the law."

"One more thing, Chief," he says, handing me a photo of a lovely young blonde. "My daughter Dawn has gotten herself mixed up with those damn hippies down at Aquarius Harbor. Follow her and report back to me."

I push away the photo. "With all due respect sir, chasing after your wayward daughter is *not* in my job description."

DAWN FELTON

[Defiant daughter of Fenton and Alice, girlfriend of Honest]

2

The Pretend Pirate Woos the Women's Libber

Today is my birthday and I'm waiting at the entrance to Aquarius Harbor for the handsome and charming Honest Abernathy, who dresses like a pirate and has more than enough low life in him to infuriate my father.

Where I grew up, in the Sausalito hills, I looked down on this colorful houseboat flotilla from my bedroom balcony. My father calls it "a shantytown crawling with deadbeat wharf rats," and I never expected I would one day meet the self-proclaimed leader of those wharf rats.

Despite Honest's looks and his sweet-talking, I am determined to break up with him today, except that he's promised me a birthday present that will "blow my mind." He asked me to meet him here so he could walk me to his houseboat for the "presentation," whatever that means.

But he doesn't respect me. *And* he's late.

I'm afraid the present will be a sex toy, like a vibrator. I tell myself, no, he wouldn't, and then I think, yes, he might.

Up close, the houseboats are more colorful than they appear from the hills, but they also look more rundown and ramshackle. Some are adorable, like the small barge with the old Winnebago painted red.

The whale house is wild too. It started as a railroad car, and on the siding, some artist sculpted a whale breaching the surface.

But many of the houseboats are butt-ugly, lashed together with nails and rope and tarps.

Finally, Honest shows, strutting toward me in his tacky pirate costume, his long, curly red hair tied back with a black headscarf. (I would *kill* for his hair!) His sword bounces against his thigh in a scabbard, hanging from his shiny belt.

"You look ridiculous," I say. He shrugs. He pretends not to care what I think, and he is—in his own mischievous way—rakish and sexy. I don't tell him that. He already thinks too highly of himself.

"Far out," he says. "If it isn't Dawn, my beautiful, bourgeois, *naughty* birthday girl." He leans in for a kiss, but I hold him back.

"One," I say, "I'm not '*yours.*' Two, just because I play golf does not mean I'm bourgeois. And three, I am *not* a '*girl.*' I smile, but with attitude.

"Right," he says, "women's lib. *Right on.* I love how liberated you are, *babe!* I mean, *woman.* But wait, you're too *gorgeous* to be a feminist."

I roll my eyes, but we're walking side by side now on the rickety dock and he can't see my face. Maybe I'll let him get away with *some* sweet talk.

But a real feminist wouldn't tolerate Honest's sexism. "If my father sees me with you," I say, "he will *freak*."

The walkways connecting the landing to the houseboats are treacherous. Rotten piles, unexpected gaps, undependable railings, plus electrical and phone lines strung between posts like linguini. Plenty of places to trip and land in the mudflats.

The stench is tolerable today. It's a warm, hazy afternoon and a gentle bay breeze dilutes the smell. The houseboaters *claim* they collect their human waste in buckets or holding tanks and dispose of it legally at the Gate 7 marina. But I know plenty of them, including Honest, *especially* Honest, who dump their shit in the bay.

There's also the lovely perfume of orange blossoms in the mix, from the dwarf trees in clay pots that line the entrance to the harbor.

Honest starts walking faster, leaving me behind. A speedboat darts across the bay, heading toward Angel Island.

"Hey, slow down," I say, running to catch up. "Maybe it will be *you* my father will kill," I add.

A wave crashes into the wobbly dock and we lose our balance and fall into each other. I'm tempted to kiss him, but I don't.

"I wouldn't blame him." He pulls me to my feet. "Your father."

I brush off flakes of peeling paint from my jacket. "You promised to fix the railing, like, a month ago. What do you mean, you wouldn't blame my father?"

He takes my hand, genuflects, and kisses my fingers. "Because I am not only going to stop your father and his greedy cronies from evicting us and building his luxury marina, I am going to corrupt you *so bad,* turn you into a fire-breathing revolutionary, flying your freak flag high. And, like, mellow out about the railing. I'll handle it tomorrow."

"And you imagine yourself the leader of this 'house-boat resistance?'"

"What's wrong with that?" he asks.

"You think you're Huey Newton, leading the Black Panthers? You think your houseboat protest is like Native Americans occupying Alcatraz? You're not a serious person. You're a hippie goofball pretend pirate. You're a satire of yourself. Plus, you're a lying, womanizing, sexist pig."

Honest tilts his head, as if confused. "I wish you would tell me what you really think."

"Not to mention you pour your foot powder into your boots with a serving spoon," I add. "I know you're dealing with fungus and cracked skin, but I smell that damn stuff a block away."

"I *am* a serious person," he says, "but I *play* a clown. I *play* a pirate. To win attention for our cause. Which I've done."

"You could have fooled me."

I don't get how such a goofball carries himself with so much confidence? If it's all an act, how is he so convincing? In all my relationships at Brown, I was in charge. The boys were all intimidated by me. *Every single one.*

Not Honest.

Could that be why I'm attracted to him? It's more than just because my father disapproves.

But he's not a keeper. I *know* that.

We stop at the "town square" of Aquarius Harbor, where the main dock opens up into six arms that snake into Richardson Bay, like tree limbs reaching toward the sun. No architect could possibly have drawn up such a cockamamie plan. There was no plan.

A brass band practices on a big gray concrete barge, with a cabin on it as tiny as an outhouse. That's where Honest's friend Mickey lives and there he is sunk deep in a lawn chair, waving his trombone.

He whistles at us and shouts, "Hey, hey, Honest, *hubba hubba,* afternoon delight." I ignore him. The seagulls swoop low on the water. An orange buoy clangs in the waves.

"And don't pretend that running for city council turns you into a statesman," I say, once we turn and make our way down the dock toward Honest's ferry. "You have no intention of winning. It's a publicity stunt."

"You say that like it's a bad thing," he says, with a dopey grin, like the golden lab we had when I was younger. I smile, then scowl. He's exasperating. Though I love the carefree way he laughs, like somehow, despite his tragic life story, he gets a kick out of everything and is not tortured like you'd expect.

"You are the *exact opposite* of what my father would wish for me," I say.

He holds up three fingers. "Other than the handsome, brilliant, and ambitious part?"

"You forgot humble," I say.

He slaps his hand on his forehead. "If I were humble, I would never have had the balls to chase you. If I were humble, I'd think you were too good for me."

"I am too good for you," I say. "At last, something we agree on."

"You don't *want* me to be good," he says. "You wouldn't *love* me if your father didn't *hate* me."

When I break up with Honest, *if* I break up with Honest, I will no longer have the pleasure of defying my father. Though I don't have to tell him.

I am smart enough not to make important life decisions *because* of what my father thinks. I will not be like my mother, whose only mission in life these days is vengeance against him. I have such wretched role models. No wonder I'm a mess.

Every day, I wish I were back East in graduate school, but no, my mother begged me to come home after she kicked my father out.

There's Honest's big old wooden ferry up ahead, with two cabins and a garden on the deck. One last rickety section of dock to navigate. I lower my voice, though there's no one around. "Speaking of my father," I say, "I hear he's coming after you, soon, evicting all of you at Aquarius Harbor. Soon as in tomorrow, or Tuesday."

"The capitalists are always about to evict us," he says. "I refuse to live in fear. I just want to groove on good vibes. And wow you with my birthday present."

"You're not listening," I say, "Plus my father keeps pressuring me to work for the family business. He won't let up."

"Just so you know," he says. "I'd be enthralled by you even if you *weren't* your father's daughter."

"Would you?" I lift my chin and sniff. "If you want me, no more dumping your sewage in the bay. And don't give me crap about tides cleaning it up. You know that's industry propaganda."

"But you *love* the tides," he says, "the magical way they move in and out by the pull of the moon." He waves his arms in this woo-woo way, making fun of me again. "And you told me that when king tides wash onto industrial shorelines, they carry pollution back into the bay, and that shit is nothing by comparison."

I do love the tides. And I do understand why Honest loves to live on the water—when I still adored my father, he used to take me out on his yacht, and we would sail under the bridge into the ocean and that hooked me.

But this is a slum. These houseboaters defile the very bay they profess to revere. I know, humans have been dumping our crap in rivers and lakes and bays since forever, but we know better now, and, finally, we have laws like the Clean Water Act.

"Your shit might not amount to much," I say, "but the water is already polluted. Are you part of the solution or part of the problem?"

"Look, you rag on me for my revolution rhetoric," he says, "but look at you up on your ecology soapbox. Oh, I forgot, you're going to be a *doctor* of marine biology."

He raises his fist. "We're pirates. *Arrrgh*. Pirates don't care about sewage."

He lowers his fist and takes my hand. Gently. "Now close your eyes. Time for your birthday surprise."

[Vengeful ex-wife of Fenton, mother of Dawn]

3

The Vengeful Ex-Wife Confronts the Mistress

Today I am going to confront Fenton's mistress at Aquarius Harbor.

I park my Buick in one of the few remaining spaces in the gravel lot. I won't have any problem finding it when I return. It's clean and gleaming and stands out amidst all the dusty and rundown foreign cars.

The private investigator I hired to follow Fenton mailed me a 30-page report, with photos and maps, including the directions to Brenda's houseboat. I was surprised to learn she lives on a houseboat, and not just any houseboat, but one moored at Aquarius Harbor, which Fenton purchased last year and is determined to clear out to build his luxury marina. Or something like that. I stopped listening to his grand plans years ago.

I study the map and survey the harbor. I'm still holding onto my car keys, as if I need to make a quick escape.

stand. I have nothing to be nervous about.
ged party. I'm the well-bred Junior League
ían who stood by her man until she no lon-
ger could, ınd Brenda is a lowly waitress who lives on a
shabby houseboat. And today is a good-hair day and I
look younger than my forty-eight years.

What surprised me about Brenda even more than that
she lives on at Aquarius Harbor is that she is *black*. What
a cliché, Fenton going after a young black waitress. There
aren't many black people in Sausalito. Who does he think
he is, Thomas Jefferson? Fenton has never been the most
open-minded of men, so it makes me wonder. Maybe it's
because she's not like me. Maybe because she's *forbidden*.

Maybe he loves her. I never considered that.

The walk to Brenda's houseboat takes longer than
I expect. The map makes it seem closer. Twice, I step
over piles of lumber. The dock turns left, then right, then
makes a U-turn back toward shore. I don't dare let go of
the railings, even though they wobble.

I've never been into boats. That was something Dawn
and her father had in common—sailing. Back when she
looked up to him. Back before the whole house of cards
tumbled down.

Finally, I arrive at Brenda's. It's a tiny boxy house and
I almost miss it, because the photograph in the investigator's report is black and white and the house in front of
me is bright gold and with a fire-engine red door. When
I raise my fist to knock, I lose my footing on the gangplank, and fall against the door, pushing it open. *Oops.*

I scramble to my feet and retreat to the dock behind
the gangplank. Behind me, I hear a growly saw cutting
wood and hammers pounding nails. Next to Brenda's
houseboat is a brown shingle structure that's shaped like

an owl, with two round windows as eyes.

"Sorry," I say, though I don't see anyone. "I meant to knock, but I tripped."

No one answers. Then I see a pretty young woman with untamed reddish hair peek out from the side of the doorway. She looks startled. Did I wake her? No, it's after ten and she's dressed, at least partly, in loose linen pants and a polka-dotted robe that falls to her knees. She's tall, at least six inches taller than me, so she's taller than Fenton, too. She's not *black* black—her skin is more the color of coffee with milk and her hair is more straight than kinky.

I've been holding my breath without realizing it. Now I exhale.

"You must be Brenda," I say.

She closes the door in my face. She doesn't slam it. She closes it gently.

I wait. Ten seconds later, she opens the door, sticks her head in the opening. She looks at me slowly, from head to toe. "You're still here?"

"So, you're the young waitress who seduced my husband," I say, though I'm sure that's not how it went. I can't believe *she* pursued *him*.

"Your ex-husband," Brenda corrects me, cool as a refrigerated cucumber. "And you must be the bitter, miserable, sadistic wife he cheated on."

She looks me up and down again.

"What did you see in him?" I ask.

She laughs, which puts me at ease. "I can't remember," she says. "What about you?"

"I forget too. May I come in?"

"No."

But she opens the door, steps onto the landing, and

closes the door behind her. She shrugs off her bathrobe and holds it in front of her like a shield.

"Well, actually," I say, "Fenton was *generous* when we first met. He told me I was special. He used to wash and brush my hair. But that was so long ago. It was working with him, working *for* him, for years, that changed everything. It all had to be *his* way."

"Interesting," she says. "He told me I was special, too. And he offered to brush my hair, but I declined."

"Is it true that you're no longer involved with him?" I want to know but I'm afraid of the answer.

Brenda looks at me sideways, as if the question is a trap. "It is true," she says. "I planned to dump him, but he dumped me first, which is *so* unsatisfying."

"Unsatisfying?" I say, my voice rising in pitch. "You want unsatisfying? I wrote the book. I am the *queen* of dissatisfaction." Oops again. That's not where I want to go.

Brenda stiffens her posture, which has the effect of her looking down on me even more than before. "You live an *impoverished* life in the hills," she says, "and you go to yoga retreats and primal scream workshops at Esalen to find yourself. And you want *me* to feel sorry for you?"

"How do you know—?"

"He talked about you," she says.

"You mean ridiculed me," I say.

"You might be surprised," she answers.

I'm a bad feminist. I want my alimony *and* my lovely house *and* my revenge. But it's not like I devote every waking day to making Fenton's life miserable.

I take weekends off.

I still want to kill him, but punishing him is more satisfying.

"You've seen the house?" I ask.

"The outside."

"Not the inside?"

"Once—"

"You didn't—?"

"No, never."

"I suppose I should be grateful to Fenton for that."

"That was not because of Fenton," she says. "I set that boundary."

"Then I'm grateful to you."

I'm not sure what I was hoping to accomplish by confronting Fenton's mistress. I am curious, of course, and there is an element of masochism. Maybe I'm more comfortable punishing Fenton when I'm also punishing myself.

It never occurred to me that Brenda might be likable.

"You escaped," she says. "You could be grateful for that."

"So did you," I say.

"Yes, but I live in this dilapidated houseboat, smaller than any apartment I've ever lived in, I'm on my feet six nights a week working as a waitress, and there's, well, new challenges. But I *refuse* to be a victim."

A speedboat zips across the bay behind Brenda. A gull squawks overhead.

"Oh, you poor little harbor waif," I say, my voice a saccharine snarl. "You sure sound like a victim. But I would assert that, as Fenton's wife of twenty-plus years, I am more *wronged* by that miserable excuse for a human being than you."

"OK, you win," Brenda says. "You're the *real* victim. Now I feel sorry for *you*, which, strangely, makes me feel better about my own situation." She softens. "You poor thing, it must be so hard for you to let go of your anger."

I'm taken aback. Of course, it's hard to let go of my anger. Before I can finish my thought, a choppy wave from the motorboat slams the gangplank and I lose my balance, again, and fall into Brenda, who catches me.

But she drops her bathrobe. *Oh my!* She's pregnant. Or is she?

"Are you—?" I point to her belly.

"Going on six months. I can't hide it anymore." She picks up the robe.

"Is it—? I make a face and imitate Fenton's laugh.

She smiles, and then gets serious. "He promised he would marry me, but then reneged, and I was *furious*. I was also relieved because I didn't *want* to marry him. I want the baby, not him, so I wrung a promise out of him for child support."

I knew my husband slept with this woman, but it hits me now in a visceral way it never did before.

She folds her robe and tucks it under her arm. "He promised he would start support payments last month, so I can cut back on my hours, but now he claims cash flow problems. If I need to, I'll expose him as an adulterer and a liar, but that would hurt you, and me."

"Maybe I'm not the biggest victim after all," I say.

Brenda's baby would be a half-sibling to Dawn and her brother. No relation to me, but that doesn't mean I don't feel a surge of excitement. Why can't *her* baby count as *my* grandchild?

"At least I met a new man," Brenda says, sounding chipper again. "He's handsome and dashing and dresses like a pirate. Would you like to come in? I'll make coffee."

"Ah yes, the pirate," I say. "Honey, let me tell you about your pirate paramour."

4

Houseboaters Hire a Lawyer

"Wait, did you say I never shower?" I must have heard her wrong.

I'm in *my* corner, against the back wall of the Dare Not, under the old photo of Sally Cal on the steps of her grand Nob Hill brothel. Across the table from me is a lovely young lawyer named Lander Jarrett.

"I didn't say that," she blurts. "Or did I? I *was* thinking it. You know how sometimes you say stuff under your breath, like 'pirates don't wash their hair?' I say those things out loud. I was sizing you up for court."

"I will most assuredly wash my hair for court," I say, "and, *ipso facto,* I will wash my hair with this very glass of water, this very minute—*if* I can buy you a drink."

She laughs. "I can buy my own drink, thank you, but if you're as persistent about resisting eviction as hitting on me, you might prevail." She grips the edge of the table and leans toward me, her eyes wide. "These sentences pop out of me, and being a newly minted lawyer, it's not *ideal*."

Lander's honesty is refreshing and I dig her intensity. I know my days with Dawn are numbered, though my inspired birthday present bought me a reprieve. I fooled her all right—all those hints I gave, she thought I was getting her a vibrator. She had no idea.

"You don't inspire confidence," I say. I grab the sheaf of papers on the table and skim the top page.

Lander, with her short brown hair, is not as dazzling as blonde and willowy Dawn, but she's less of a princess. "You expect an accomplished lawyer to represent you for free?" she says. "Your previous lawyer quit because you *embarrassed* her. She felt like she'd been ambushed."

"Our most glorious moment ever," I say. "Until the next one." I'm already sold on Lander. It's freaky the way she tells the truth.

"You should have been there." I say. "Twenty-three of us marched into the conference room of Fenton Felton's hoity-toity banker in our muddy boots and interrupted his meeting, the TV cameras in tow. We humiliated him and delayed the project."

"Pro bono is where they throw rookies to learn," she says. "But you're desperate enough that—"

She's interrupted by the clatter of a busboy plopping a bin of dishes on the bar. "No, no, you're a savvy lawyer." I hold up the papers. "On the first page, you suggest we plead hardship for the children who will lose their homes, get a temporary restraining order, *then* file the preliminary injunction, *then* the permanent injunction—"

"How do you—?"

"Says so right here," I say, reading the top sheet.

"Plead hardship, TRO, preliminary—"

"But you picked up those papers, like, five seconds ago. Have you studied law?"

"I've watched lawyer shows on TV." She doesn't need to know I flunked out my first year at Boalt.

"You read that document *while* we were talking," she says, "and—"

"Actually," I say, "I wasn't listening."

She laughs, then stops. I turn around. My shoulders stiffen.

Fate marches in, carrying her typewriter on a tray, strapped to a harness around her neck, as if she were in a marching band. My sister, the scold, a bucket of cold water you can count on, rain or shine. Mickey waddles behind her, his scraggly blond hair in his face.

"This is Fate," I say to Lander, "my sister, the brains of the operation." Fate likes to believe that's true, and humoring her keeps her from making trouble.

Lander shakes hands with Fate. "We talked on the phone," she says.

Fate points to her typewriter. "Did I tell you on the call that I'm forgetful? That's why I take notes religiously." She types a few words, swipes the carriage return. *Ding.*

It's true that Fate forgets things, though she more than compensates for it with her index cards and rubber bands and colored stickers. Now she's started wearing this typewriter on a harness, which is the kind of over-the-top thing I would do. That's why she's doing it—she's jealous of the attention I get for my pirate act.

But this won't last. It will hurt her shoulders. She'll get tired of it. Still, I take it as a compliment that she's following my lead and understands the importance of visuals.

"Ever heard of shorthand?" Lander asks. She puts her hand to her lips. "Oops, did I say on the phone that I overshare?"

"This is Mickey Macgillicuddy," Fate says, "who was recently served his second eviction notice."

Mickey bows. "Groovy, man." Then he points to me with a grin. "Watch out for this dude. Slippery like a snake."

"So I am learning," Lander says.

Fate launches into her rant before she sits down. "Here's the thing. Honest thinks planning is bourgeois, paying rent is tantamount to treason, and disposing of our sewage in a safe and healthy way is giving in to 'the man.' Which is why we need you and your legal expertise to fend off the developers, who are—"

"We make it more trouble for them than it's worth," I say.

"They own our dock," Fate says. "They—"

"You can't own the bay, man," says Mickey.

"And what law school did you go to?" Fate scoffs.

"Like, I went to college," Mickey says, preening for Lander. "Like, Grateful Dead University. That's where I got my higher education—a *PhD* in *LSD*. Hey, like, how do you know when deadheads have been staying at your pad?" He pauses. "They're, like, still there."

He mimes a drum roll with his hands. Nothing Mickey likes more than a new audience.

"Oh, and what do you call a hippie with a haircut? The defendant. Ba-dum-bump. I'll be here all week."

Gotta love Mickey. But he's a mystery man—there's more to him than meets the eye, though that's true for many of us at Aquarius Harbor. We all came from somewhere else and some of us are more forthcoming than others about why. Mickey told me he can't get arrested in any protest because he has a record. That's all he'll say.

Fate locks in on Lander, launches into pedantic mode. "A bit of background: When California became a state, they mapped out the marshes on the bay with underwater streets, sold the parcels, assuming they'd be landfilled. Most of downtown San Francisco is reclaimed tidelands."

She pulls out a map from her shoulder bag and unfolds it. "But in Sausalito, the streets are still underwater. They have names—Manzanita, Pescadero—"

"Little Miss Encyclopedia, we call her," I say. "You see how *annoying* she is. Private property be damned."

"No, no," says Lander. "I need to understand this. If you want me to help you."

That's all the encouragement Fate needs. She's off to the races.

"During World War 2, where Aquarius Harbor is now, there was a ship factory where, like, tens of thousands of people worked and there wasn't enough housing so some workers lived on boats or rafts or built them from whatever they could scrounge and—"

"A ship factory *here?*" Lander says. "In Sausalito?"

Fate nods and points north. "Half a mile from here. After the war, the property was abandoned and that's when carpenters and junk collectors and free spirits started moving in and then came the hippies and—"

"Right on man," Mickey says. "Like, we've got, like, a groovy community and the ocean is free and we should be able to live here, for free."

"Honest moved us here seven years ago," Fate says. "The important thing is that, because of public health complaints, the previous landlord was forced to sell, and

Fenton Felton, our nemesis, bought the parcel and now he's evicting us."

I've heard all this before, so I tune out and groove to the symphony of voices in the bar. I purposely avoid picking out any one of them—it's like listening to crickets at night.

Fate believes facts will change the hearts and minds of the powers-that-be, and that's delusion. What matters are perceptions, emotions, stories. Plenty of people think my pirate costume is ridiculous, but everyone knows who I am and that I stand for affordable housing and our right to live in peace and harmony. They know that *because* I was on TV last week in my pirate garb after our muddy-boots stunt.

It's not that Fate doesn't understand the power of theatrics, she does, but she thinks they're secondary and the facts come first when it's the other way around.

Fate taps away on her typewriter and shuffles her index cards and blathers away in sentences two miles long. What's crazy is she claims she forgets things, but she never seems to look at her notes when she's talking.

I'm still tripping out about my birthday present for Dawn. She was shaking when I told her to close her eyes. Later, she told me she was afraid I was going to propose.

When I led her to the wooden shack I built next to the cabin and opened the door, revealing the old navy blue steamer trunk with a wooden toilet seat on it, she didn't know what it was. "It's a composting toilet," I said. "For you."

She didn't want me to demonstrate, but I did. "The important thing," I said, "is that when you shit, you have to throw in a scoop of sawdust and give it three turns."

Dawn said she was touched that I took her

environmental concerns seriously for a change. "It's so thoughtful," she said, "it's almost romantic."

Now Fate is talking about how the eviction raids we're expecting will destroy our community.

"Not if we resist," I say. Loud enough that other patrons turn toward our table. I grin and flash a peace sign. "We lie down in front of their bulldozers. Blockade their police boats. Go limp when they arrest us. Invite the TV cameras."

"Civil disobedience *is* at the center of our strategy," says Fate, "but we need *you* to file legal motions, and bail us out and represent us if we're arrested. We're prepared for a raid—we have lookouts and a telephone tree and a foghorn and sirens."

"So, you want *me* to use the law to help *you*," Lander says, "while *you* break the law to help yourselves."

"Exactly," she says. "The police chief is not *on our side,* but she's not on Fenton's side either. She's into peace and harmony and listening and all that hippie stuff, and if we engage nonviolently, she won't bash heads. I told her how we came to live here, about our Mom and Dad's crash—" She stops, turns to me. "Did you tell Lander about that?" There she is, talking about the crash again. It's *always* in her head.

I start to answer, but she keeps going. She's so manic. "We also need to identify, in advance, a *reasonable* spokesperson, the face of the struggle." She points at me with her thumb. "And my pirate brother is *not* that face."

"I wasn't a pirate until Fenton Felton called us pirates," I say, "and I thought, 'OK, we'll be pirates.' The TV cameras, they *love* pirates."

"Pirates or no pirates," Lander says, "there's no legal precedent for living rent free."

"Are we obedient servants of ruthless capitalism," I say, "or are we revolutionaries and harbingers of a new age of cooperation and peace and love?"

Fate ignores me. "I move that Honest is *not* the spokesperson for the Aquarius Collective. That it's me."

Lander looks from me to Fate and back again. "I agree," she says. "It should be Fate."

"Because I don't shower enough?" I remind myself not to lose my cool, but I can't take this power grab lying down. "This is not an official meeting," I say. "Besides, I'm more colorful. We'll get more coverage. Mickey?"

Mickey looks down. "I, like, support Fate, too. She should, like, be our talking head."

"Who cares what you think?" I hiss. "You're a burnout."

I knew this was coming. But no way am I going to sit back and let Fate take charge.

MICKEY MACGILLICUDDY

[Flaky burnout, houseboat resident]

5

Eviction Raid

I spot the police boats through my slot window as they round the sandy spit that hooks into Richardson Bay, a hundred meters from Aquarius Harbor. The length of a football field. The sun is rising behind the hills of Tiburon. I dial Honest.

Three rings. Four. "Pick up, dammit. The pigs are coming."

I stay in character, even when no one is around. It's a good habit. I've been up since an hour before daybreak, on the lookout.

The boats head toward me. In front is a police cruiser, followed by a second smaller police boat and a weathered commercial tug, with strips of bright yellow reflective tape on its hull. The hum of the boats' motors is barely discernible above the slosh of the waves.

I call Fate. She picks up on the first ring.

"Fate, they're here, the bacon brigade."

"Did you call Honest?"

"He didn't answer. A tug's headed my way, and the chief's in a black and white cruiser directing traffic, like, right out of central casting. They're a couple dozen meters away now, the length of a tennis court. Looks like six, maybe seven cops total."

Because most people don't grasp meters and miles, I always communicate distance with examples. From sports, mostly. Tennis courts. Swimming pools. Even when I'm only talking in my head.

"I'll sound the alarm," she says. "Let them tow you, like we planned, but make trouble."

My plan for the day is to go along with the strategy that Honest and Fate and the others worked out, resisting evictions with a variety of nonviolent tactics. At first.

But my case officer, Davis, has encouraged me to discredit the houseboat collective by inciting violence—when the circumstances warrant it, and the opportunity arises. Like today. Throwing a Molotov cocktail into the mix will change the vibes in a flash. *Abracadabra,* no more nonviolence. I don't want to injure or kill anyone, so I'm on the lookout for an empty vehicle or something like that.

Knowing my houseboat will be towed, I've already collected my shit in my backpack, and I've stashed the fixings for a molly in a bucket by the tool shed.

In just six months, I've insinuated myself deeply enough into the Aquarius houseboat community that no one suspects, and I'm not going to do anything today that might blow my cover.

"Good morning, Mickey." It's Police Chief Tin Holland, speaking through a megaphone. I'm startled by how loud her voice is. I guess she sees me through my tiny window.

"We are hereby serving the eviction order on Mickey Macgillicuddy of Aquarius Harbor. If you do not vacate, we will tow your boat with you aboard, and you will be arrested."

Mickey Macgillicuddy? How did I dream up such a perfect name for myself? It was like one of my acting buddies in the Navy said—sometimes your character's name gives you everything you need.

The tug bumps my barge, knocks me off my chair. Barney, Tin's deputy, leans over the gunwale and slips a rope through the cleat on the bow of my barge.

I open my front door and step out. "Where are you towing me?"

Another officer on the tug slips into the shallows in his black boots and cuts my anchor chain with a bolt cutter, its handles as long as his arms. Neither answers my question.

Fate is already on the water in her pint-sized dinghy, poking a long oar like a lance into the tires that are tied to the outside of the tug like fenders on a car. She's trying, with little success, to push the much larger tug off course as it begins to tow my boat from its berth. Jude and Noah, the young artist couple with the girl twins, attack the tug from the other side in their orange inflatable. Noah stands on the bench seat with his legs far apart and his hands wrapped around the shaft of a black oar. He waves the oar theatrically, then jabs it at the tire fender.

The police are not paying attention to me, so I drop to my knees, shimmy on my belly to the bow, and cut the towrope off the cleat with my pocketknife.

Tin, facing Fate, speaks into her megaphone. "We're enforcing the law, Fate. It's nothing personal."

"We're protecting our homes, Chief Tin," says Fate. "It's nothing personal." I snake my way back to my shack and lean against the door jamb. Looks like no one saw me cut the rope.

A white TV van pulls into the parking lot. It's Johnny Dash, the TV news guy who's been covering the house-boat wars since the first eviction warrants were served a month ago. He wears wader boots, a white shirt, and a paisley tie that flaps over his shoulder as he races onto the dock, hopping over rotten planks. He tucks his micro-phone under his arm like a football.

The black cord of the mic is connected to a bulky camera that Johnny's young colleague balances on his shoulder. He wears oversized sunglasses and a Giants baseball cap, and his light brown beard is bushy, so his reddish nose is all I see of him. As Johnny runs, the cord pulls the cameraman along on the rickety dock. But he holds onto the camera and keeps his footing as he films the action on the water.

"This is Johnny Dash, *News on the Run,* reporting live from Aquarius Harbor in Sausa-*leeto!*"

Jude and Noah retreat, then steer their raft directly into the path of the tugboat. Johnny Dash wades into the shallow water and the cameraman sets the camera on the railing of the dock. The tug starts pulling away until Barney realizes the rope is no longer attached to my houseboat. I give the camera my best shit-eating grin.

Two more dinghies line up next to Fate, their oars in attack mode.

Johnny Dash continues. "The police, attempting to serve eviction warrants, have been met by an *armada* of houseboaters in dinghies, pushing away the police boats with oars."

It's no armada, but now another houseboater, a reclusive and wild-eyed mechanic named Dewey, speeds toward the tug in his motorized dinghy at full throttle from the south, trying to block its way.

Tin, standing in the stern of her boat, speaks into the radio on her shoulder. "Protesters are resisting. Send reinforcements."

She raises the megaphone to her mouth. "Drop the oars. Let's keep this peaceful."

Barney, in the tug, points his gun at Fate. "Drop the oar or we'll shoot."

"Stand down, deputy," says Tin. "Put your gun away. And don't rock the boat."

Then, to Fate. "Drop the oars or we'll arrest you."

Looks like I'm not the only one threatening to change the peaceful vibe. I'm surprised Tin hired a badass like Barney, but maybe he was on the force already and she inherited him.

The tug backs up toward my boat again. This time Barney wraps a heavy chain around the cleat and signals for the tug to pull away. He stares at me. I wave at him.

I slip off the edge of my barge into the bay before the tug speeds up. The tide is high, and the water comes up to my crotch. It's cold. My boots sink into the mud. I hold my pack over my head and plod my way to shore.

Behind me, I hear Johnny Dash. "The first eviction is underway. The police tugboat is towing away a small house on a large barge, which will be impounded at a dry dock in Richmond, according to Police Chief Tin Holland." That's my house he's talking about.

I spot Honest shuffling along the dock, in his cork

sandals and boxer shorts, rubbing sleep from his eyes, followed by Dawn, who looks like she's thrown on her dress backwards. From her dinghy, Fate shouts at Honest. "It's about time. Come on."

He climbs into a rusted boat, but Dawn declines to join him. Interesting that she won't join him to fend off the police, but she spent the night with him on his boat, which she never used to do. Honest told me all about the composting toilet he built for her. Maybe that changed her tune.

Honest yells "Cowabunga" and rows furiously towards the tugboat. There's no way he'll catch it, so he turns toward Tin's boat and pokes at it with his oar.

The cop in the cruiser with Tin jumps onto Honest's dinghy, landing on the bench and flipping Honest into the bay.

I sat in on the houseboat collective's planning meetings, so I knew what was coming, but the aggressive resistance to the eviction raid still surprises me. Technically, it's "nonviolent"—the dinghies and inflatables that are "attacking" the tugboat are small and underpowered and the oars the protesters are poking at the police boat and tug are wooden or plastic. But it's quite the spectacle for Johnny Dash and his cameraman to capture for the evening news.

What makes this undercover assignment so different from my last one is the lack of real danger. This standoff today feels more like theater than actual conflict. It *is* theater. Not that there aren't high stakes, like losing our homes. But when I infiltrated the drug gang in Vallejo, I was on edge *every day*. It was the most harrowing six months of my life. In the end, when a gang leader demanded that I kill a rival to prove my loyalty, Davis pulled me out.

I got assigned to Aquarius Harbor because I'd already grown my hair long and I knew boats from being in the Navy. Mostly I'm hanging out and getting high and playing music, as if I have no cares in the world. Now and then I miss the urgency and excitement of my last gig, but there's a lot to like about this laid-back scene.

It's weird the contemptuous looks I get from the cops, like I'm the enemy, a dirty hippie. They don't know I'm on their team. I've come to like my long hair, way more than the buzz cut I had when I was a beat cop in L.A. I can hide behind the hair.

Davis is especially hot for me to identify communist sympathizers among the houseboaters. When I brought him photographs of the *Communist Manifesto* and *Das Kapital* on Honest's bookshelves, he moaned like he was having an orgasm. I tried to explain that for Honest, communism was a costume, like his pirate garb, but Davis hears what he wants to hear.

Honest claims he's a serious subversive in the vein of Abbie Hoffman, and that he has deliberately chosen the role of jester to "speak truth to power." He says he's studied Dario Fo, the San Francisco Mime Troupe, and the commedia dell'arte tradition from Italy. He also says he's studied the role of media coverage and how that changes people's perceptions. For example, he says that because news reports portrayed Malcolm X as a scary black revolutionary, that made the politics of Martin Luther King seem more reasonable. I'm not saying I agree or disagree, but I put all this in my report.

Davis says gathering information is important, but it's my secondary goal, that discrediting the houseboaters comes first. "You don't know how dangerous nonviolence can be," Davis said. "Strike at the first opportunity."

Once I'm on terra firma, I wind my way to the tool shed by the mailboxes. I hide between the shed and a bottle brush tree and change into a dry pair of pants from my pack. It's hard to make myself invisible because there are people and TV cameras everywhere, and gawkers crowd the sidewalk by the parking lot. It's a circus out here, barely controlled chaos. I'm surprised no one has set up a lemonade stand. I'd buy a glass if I didn't have more pressing plans.

Inside the shed, I root through my bucket for the empty Coke bottle, fill it halfway with kerosene from a white can, and stuff a rag through the opening. I push it into the bottle with a twig from the tree, then pour in more kerosene so the rag is saturated. The sirens get louder and closer. Reinforcements are coming. Now is the time to strike.

I knew this morning that this could be the end of my stay here, but now that prospect is real, I'm wavering.

But I have to do the job, no matter what I feel. It's not my place to pick and choose which orders to follow. I don't decide the mission, I execute it.

The fact that I'm second-guessing is all the more reason to strike while I can and get out. When I start caring about the people I'm infiltrating, that's when it starts getting dangerous for me.

Two police cars and another paddywagon careen into the parking lot, and the officers start making another round of arrests. Another punctures Jude and Noah's inflatable with a knife. Honest is now in the shallow water, trying to avoid the police—half-swimming, half-walking, half-skulking.

Now's my chance while the police are busy. There's an empty black-and-white police sedan the width of a basketball court from me. Empty is what I want. I light the wick of the molly and rear back to throw.

HUCK ('HIC') HENNESSEE
[Sniveling sidekick to Fenton]

6

Junk Removal and Healing

I lean on my horn and cut off a Honda hatchback, squeezing into the three lanes heading north across the Golden Gate Bridge. The bridge towers hide in the fog, and Fenton Felton, in the passenger seat, is in full lather, still ranting about the loan officer who stiffed us. Not foaming at the mouth, but on the verge. He waves his arms, shakes his fists, stomps his feet.

"If there's one thing I hate," he snarls, "and I hate *so fucking many things*, it's when someone acts friendly and obsequious as he stabs you in the back. He *almost* convinced me he was going to help. Like some devious English butler before he poisons his master.

"'Of course, Mr. Felton, shuffle, shuffle, we can extend your payment window, of course, Mr. Felton, bow, bow, scrape, scrape. You're such an important customer, you need more time, you get more time. An hour? No, no, you deserve a full day.' *Jesus Fucking Christ.* Go around that damn hippie van. We've got a dock to build."

I tailgate a red VW camper with a tie-dye peace flag flapping from a window vent. There's no space to pass.

"Lazy goddamn hippies," says Fenton. "Of course, they're going slow. They have nowhere to go, no jobs to be on time for. Blare your horn again."

"I'm sure you're right, sir, but the engine on those buses is barely enough to power a motorcycle." Better he rails at a wimpy van than replay our meeting with the loan officer, *again.*

"We are up Shit Creek with no paddles, no life vests," says Fenton. "Explain to me again how the berth deposits are going to keep us afloat."

I pass the hippie van. When did it become *my* job to talk Fenton Felton off the ledge? This is not the first time he's made impulsive and ill-advised decisions, but his financial situation has never been as dire as it is now. As is mine, which is upsetting enough I'm tempted to jump along with Fenton.

Or push him, then step back.

My wife Cath continues to demand that I sever ties with Fenton, or she will sever ties with me. But I can't tell her that we're facing bankruptcy because I invested more than I had, and now the balloon payments are due. She can never know the ruin we face. I should be the one foaming at the mouth and teetering on the ledge.

The thing is, I can't *not* tell her either. All my options are grim.

"It's simple," I say. "We bring in three berth deposits a week, that keeps us even with our debt service. Four, and—"

"*Our* debt service?" Fenton roars. "*You* have no skin in the game. *I know what you're up to.*"

Oh, I have skin in the game all right and he knows it, but he's not capable of thinking or caring about anyone but himself. "But Sir," I say, "prospective tenants must be *confident* we'll clear out the squatters and deliver on deadline."

I used to call Fenton "boss," which is not as demeaning as "sir." But the morning after Cath and I watched some old British movie, I said "sir" by mistake and he beamed. He loves the deference, though he also loves that he's hated and feared. Such a strange man.

Of course, in my head, I call him Fenton Fuckhead, but I'd better be careful or one day that's going to slip out of my mouth by mistake.

But here's the problem. He tells me things. He confides in me. Since his breakup with Brenda, he's got nobody. I didn't sign up for this, but I'm not heartless. I've listened to him because no one else will. I actually feel for the guy, though not at this exact moment.

"Tin's clearing out the harbor now," I add. "At this very—"

"And we're missing out because of *your* lollygagging. Can't you drive any faster?"

I pay close attention to my use of possessive pronouns with Fenton. When flattering him is important, I say "*your* marina." To reassure him of my loyalty, I say "*our* project" or "*our* debt." But today, he's too upset to be reassured.

We'd planned to be there for the eviction raid, but I was able to set up this emergency before-hours meeting with our lender this morning, and that took priority.

I exit the freeway and wind down Alexander into

town. What does he mean, *I know what you're up to?* I'm not going to lie, I am up to things, but how do I sidestep his accusations without knowing what he suspects?

I'm driving my nephew's pickup because we do not want to show up for the eviction in my Caddy. The TV crews love that rich-against-the-poor nonsense. No sense handing them ammunition.

My nephew runs a hauling business, and on the side of the truck, it says "Junk Removal and Healing." The painter was not paying attention and my nephew didn't proofread.

Getting rid of junk is a healing of sorts, I suppose, and my nephew says business is booming.

That's exactly what we need at Aquarius Harbor— junk removal and healing.

We arrive in town and hit the straightaway, where the waters of Richardson Bay splash onto rugged boulders a few feet from my truck. Ahead, a ferry backs into the harbor. On our left, swank and colorful homes cling to the steep hillside, balconies festooned with magenta bougainvillea, purple morning glories, blooming succulents. To our right is Angel Island and the San Francisco skyline. The fog has cleared and the sky is blue.

While the obsequious banker in the City was flattering Fenton, and blowing him off at the same time, I promised myself that today I would sever ties. But Fenton has been blabbering since we left the bank and I haven't had a chance. And I'm still holding onto hope that we can salvage this project.

I finally get up the nerve, but he beats me to the punch. "You're not as stupid as you *pretend* to be," he says, "and I'm not as stupid as *you* think I am."

We pass the Valhalla Inn and The Bar Whose Name We Dare Not Speak, the hotel and restaurant complex owned by Sausalito Mayor Sally Cal, who was a brothel madam in San Francisco for decades before she moved here. According to local lore, she was arrested dozens of times in the City, even though many of her clients were police officers and politicians. There are rumors she runs a side business in her hotel here, but my bet is that she's the one circulating the rumors. I've eaten in the bar plenty of times, but never set foot upstairs. I would *never* cheat on Cath.

"If I may, sir," I say, *"no one* believes *you're* stupid, least of all me—you're a brilliant, creative, confident, charismatic leader. It was your idea to build the shell companies and shuffle the debt around. And I've never *pretended* to be stupid."

Fenton spits out the window. "Oh, you've got your bumbling weak-ass sniveling sidekick yes-man act down to a science. Tripping over your own damn feet, spilling coffee on your shoes, bumping into walls. And of course, the hiccups. *Brilliant.* My favorite schtick is the way you tell a joke and screw up the punchline. I laugh at you instead of the joke. How inventive."

And I thought my sniveling yes-man act was watertight.

"You're no more loyal," he says, "than the seagulls who steal your sandwich from your fingers."

"That's it," I say. "I quit." If anything, I've been *too* loyal.

"You can't quit," he says. "You're a partner, not an employee."

"OK, then, I quit the partnership."

As we approach Aquarius Harbor, I slow down

because people are spilling off the sidewalk and standing in the road.

"Impossible," Fenton says. "You'll lose everything. Drive faster! You're crawling like a turtle. Who the hell are all these people?"

There are police cars all over the place. Looks like every single one in town.

I take the turn onto Gate 9 Road carefully, then pick up speed and veer into the gravel lot. There's police deputy Barney Pike slamming the paddywagon doors, and Johnny Dash in wader boots jogging back and forth on the dock, rehearsing for a live report. Yellow police tape is everywhere, stretching between trees, light poles, and fences.

I squeeze past the paddywagon into the lot, but *Oh God,* someone is lying in the road, legs in front of my tires.

I slam on the brakes, but I'm going too fast, so I wrench the steering wheel right, and swerve toward a crowd of gawkers.

7

An Armada of Dinghies

As soon as I climb out of my dinghy, Larry, one of Honest's goofball followers, who also dresses like a pirate, takes my place, and I race back to the Aquarius Harbor entrance to find Johnny Dash.

After his earlier report, I introduced myself and he promised to interview me later. But we've been mounting non-stop resistance until moments ago. We're still resisting—several people are lying in the road in front of a black-and-white, but the police aren't arresting them.

I'm wet up to my belly button, and my arms ache from pushing away the police boat with the oar for what seemed like forever, but I could not be more thrilled with how brilliant and creative our resistance this morning has been. Organized, too. Larry even showed up early for his shift. The police are clearly not prepared for our coordinated response.

I can't wait to see the news tonight. Everything we've done has unfolded in front of the TV camera—our "armada of dinghies," as Johnny Dash called it. Our colorful skits and songs. Protesters lying down when they were arrested, being dragged to the paddywagon. Someone even moved a rusted old gangplank to block the entrance to the parking lot. That wasn't even part of our plan.

Chief Tin leans against the paddywagon, talking with three uniformed officers from Mill Valley. It's anyone's guess if they're going to try to tow more boats today. The tide is ebbing and the houseboats closest to shore are settling in the mud.

I don't see Johnny Dash. Then again, there are so many onlookers crowding the parking lot, the sidewalk, the rocky shore, it's like a circus. Fun like a circus, though the stakes are as high as can be.

Holding the police back this morning will not be enough. They'll be back tomorrow, with reinforcements. Which is why I need to deliver our message to Johnny Dash. We have to win in the court of public opinion.

Like last week, when we invaded the lobby of Wells Fargo in our muddy boots, and we came off on Johnny Dash's broadcast as scrappy and principled. Honest was on his best behavior that day and he said the exact words I wrote for him—"We demand a moratorium of future evictions, and we demand affordable housing for all displaced residents."

I see Mickey by the tool shed, hiding behind a tree. He's got a bottle in one hand and a lighter in the other. I race over to the shed. My high tops are sopping wet. He leans back like he's about to throw something.

"Hey, what are you doing?"

He turns his torso to hide what's behind his back, but I sidestep him. It's a Coke bottle with a flame.

He glares at me, like I'm the enemy, then cocks his arm again to throw. "I'm firebombing that empty pig-mobile right there."

"*No, no, no!*" I grab his arm and he pulls away, but I hold on tight. The flame gets bigger. "This is a nonviolent protest. You can't."

He twists toward me to break my grip, then he slumps and sighs.

I douse the flame with water from my canteen. He doesn't stop me.

"They towed away my fucking home. I'm so enraged I could, like—"

"You *should* be enraged. They towed away your *home*. But you can't poison our protest. If we engage in violence, we lose our credibility, we lose any sympathy we have, and we lose our homes for certain. We have to maintain the moral high ground. That's the power of nonviolence."

"Where did you come from?" he asks. "You were out in your dinghy a minute ago."

"I was looking for you," I say, though I wasn't. "Larry took my place and the police seem to be taking a pause. I wanted to invite you to stay with us, in the community center."

He balls his fists and clenches his teeth. I've never seen him this angry before. He's always so mellow.

I put my arm around his shoulder, and when he doesn't pull away, I wrap him in a hug.

He shrugs away from me. "I let my emotions get the better of me."

I thought I knew Mickey better. I could see Honest

doing something destructive and impulsive, to get attention, but Mickey seems like a peaceful soul. I'm not good at reading people. Mickey might be at the end of his rope and I missed it. He's such a silly goose that he doesn't seem angry even when he is angry. Except today.

At least I talked him down. Firebombing a police car would be *disastrous.*

Mickey is poor, that must be it. They towed away his shack and that might be all he has. At least I have some paid bookkeeping gigs, irregular and non-lucrative as they may be. And Honest buys and cooks our meals.

Now that I've put out one fire, literally, I run back to the dock entrance. There's Johnny Dash, next to his white TV van.

The camera guy is setting up his tripod in front of a wooden sawhorse police barrier, the yellow crime scene tape taut on one side, fluttering in the breeze on the other. Johnny Dash is admiring himself in the side mirror of his van. I tie my hair back in a ponytail and tuck it under my red checked bandana. From the waist up, I look presentable. I've got my index cards and talking points at my fingertips.

I walk up to Johnny and tell him I'm ready. He says he'll start with an update, then he'll interview me. Honest is nowhere to be seen, so I want to seize the moment.

My wet clothes smell sour and funky. Add to that the diesel exhaust, burning rubber, sewage, and the air is not exactly refreshing to breathe. I also smell sweet potatoes. Who's cooking sweet potatoes for breakfast? I study my notes, bite my lip, and urge my pants to dry.

At the camera guy's signal, Johnny starts running across the parking lot, his tie flapping over his shoulder. That's his thing, I guess, how he starts his reports.

He hops over an overturned sawhorse and stops on a dime in front of the entrance to our harbor. "This is Johnny Dash, *News on the Run,* and we are live in Sausaleeto"—here he pauses to catch his breath—"where this morning, we witnessed a standoff between police enforcing eviction orders and houseboat residents in dinghies pushing the police away with oars. Nine protesters have been arrested. Four houseboats have been removed, one with its resident aboard."

Johnny speaks breathlessly, as if he's still running, but he enunciates all his "t"s and "d"s with crispness and precision.

"We're live with houseboat protester Fate Abernathy. Tell us *what happened.*" He thrusts his microphone in my face, but Honest elbows me out of the way. Where did he come from?

"We showed them not to mess with us," he says.

He has no pants on. Only boxers. Above his waist, he wears his swashbuckler outfit—white pirate frock, headscarf, belt, sword, and scabbard.

I'm livid, but I don't want the TV audience to see us bicker. I rub my ribs and hide my fury. Honest's elbow was sharp like a knife.

"But Honest Abernathy," Johnny continues, "aren't you being evicted because of nonpayment of rent and discharging raw sewage into the bay?"

"It's the ocean," he says. "It's no different than fish shitting in the water. It's—"

Dawn pokes her head in front of Honest. "Excuse me, it's very different. The bacteria that—"

Honest pushes her aside, more gently than he pushed me, and advances on the camera, his fist raised. "No one owns the ocean, man. Private property is theft. The police are stooges—"

Johnny interrupts. "But you capsized the police boat. How is it you were not arrested?"

Honest shrugs. "Good karma, I guess. I was wet so I went home to change."

Now I shove Honest away from the camera. "What he means to say is that the Aquarius Houseboat Collective is an oasis of affordable homes in the affordable housing desert that is Sausalito. And that—"

He tries to get back in front of the camera, but I won't let him. "We agreed," I say. "Remember?"

"No," he says, "I never agreed. You're the one who forgets things."

I slide in front of Honest and stand tall in front of the camera. "Fenton Felton is evicting us to build a luxury marina," I say, "and our houseboat community, a model of cooperation and harmony, will be broken up and we will have nowhere to live. We refuse to leave until the developer finds us a new location."

Honest lets me finish and then elbows me again, but we're interrupted by a blue truck screeching into the lot, past a police cruiser blocked by protesters. My tongue catches in my throat. The truck is going to run over Dewey, who is lying in its path.

But it brakes and veers away and comes to a halt before hitting any of the onlookers on the sidewalk.

On the side of the pickup, I read "Junk Removal and Healing."

Fenton Felton jumps out of the passenger door, curling his lips into an intense sneer. He surveys the scene, his fists clenched.

"Look at all these squatters' houseboats," he sputters. "Why haven't they all been towed away? Where is that damn coward police chief?" He yells for all to hear, fully aware the cameras are rolling. "I will poach her ass on a platter, and I will burn this shantytown down. Don't think I won't."

I forgot to tell Johnny Dash about our compromise plan, only *the most* important thing of all. I didn't look at my notes. I didn't think I had to. But also, I don't have the blueprint with me so it would have only been my words, no visuals. What I was supposed to do, carry the plans with me in the dinghy? The blueprint would be wetter than my pants and shoes.

But Johnny Dash is still here and now Fenton is too. There's time.

I hightail it back home.

I'm not so naive that I expect he'll consider my plan because it saves our homes. But it could save *his project,* get *his harbor* built. We've delayed him multiple times now and my understanding is that he's behind schedule and over budget. Later today, Lander is filing a brief claiming that the city does not have the authority to evict us without a permit from the Coastal Commission. That could force another delay. Fenton Felton *might* have to consider a compromise even if he doesn't want to.

I retrieve the blueprint from its hiding place and race back to the dock entrance, leaping over the pile of lumber by the town square and slowing down only for the stretch where the planks are loose. My shoes feel like sponges that squish with every footfall.

As I get closer, I hear lots of shouting, then suddenly, there's a hush. I elbow my way through the crowd, holding the blueprint close to my chest, so it won't catch on anyone.

When I make my way through the mass of gawkers to the front, Honest is sprawled on the gravel, a circle of blood on his white pirate frock.

He's been stabbed.

FENTON FELTON

[Greedy developer, father of Dawn, ex-husband of Alice]

8

En Garde

Hic stops at the yellow light at Pelican Street instead of racing through it because he's a passive-aggressive sadist dickhead and he knows how impatient I am to see the Aquarius Harbor houseboats cleared out. *Ferchristsake,* he's driving five miles *below* the speed limit, and he thinks I don't know he's a *fraud?* Who does he think he is, threatening to quit?

Finally, we approach Aquarius Harbor, but he keeps driving like an old biddy. I can't see the harbor because clueless gawkers are in the way, clogging up the sidewalk. Over their heads, I spot the corkscrew antennae on Johnny Dash's TV van.

"Can't you go any faster?" I scream.

He turns right on Gate 9 Road, accelerates, and takes the hard right into the parking lot. The tires crunch on the gravel and we pass the police paddy wagon with its back doors open and there's a tow truck, and *oh shit,* there's a goddamn hippie lying in the road.

Hic slams on the brakes, but can't stop in time and he veers to the right and almost plows into the crowd. Everyone screams and scatters. *Jesus, Mary, and Joseph, I am driving next time.* I scramble out of the car and push my way through to the front.

What the hell?!?! The squatter houseboats are all still here. Where is that weak-ass cowardly police chief? Her days are numbered.

Chief Tin was supposed to tow twenty-five house-boats today. She didn't even—No, now I see a yellow tug in the bay pulling houseboats behind it. Four or five, I can't tell, but not enough. The harbor looks even more like a hellhole than usual. Garbage everywhere, diesel slicks on the water, oars bobbing in the waves, a punctured orange raft melting into the mud. *This is a disaster.*

There's the chief behind the paddywagon, speaking into the radio on her shoulder. She is going to regret ever—

Damn, there's my daughter, huddled next to that hippie pirate, behind a sawhorse barricade.

"Dawn," I shout, "what are *you* doing here? I *need* you. To help with the family business. To be on *my* side."

She's such a smart girl, and she could be saving my ass instead of wasting her talents deifying dolphins and sullying herself with these squatters and pirates.

There's yellow crime scene tape all over the damn place. She's got it wrapped around one arm.

She bolts up and struts in front of me, flaunting her height. "I don't need to inform you of my whereabouts," she says.

I laugh with as much menace as I can muster.

She inches away.

"Or the company you keep?" I snarl. "This *pretend* pirate?"

I see Johnny Dash signal to his cameraman. *Oh, you want to put this on TV? Bring it on!*

"You never stop being an asshole, do you?" Dawn says.

I back away like she slapped me. How *dare* she call me out in front of all these people?

Once upon a time, she was sweet and innocent and she thought I was the best father a girl could have, but her mother poisoned her with spite and venom.

Honest moves between us and extends his hand. He's got his pirate costume on above the waist, only his undershorts below. "I want you to know, Mr. Fenton Felton," he says, his sincerity so plainly phony, "that I'm *not* taking advantage of your daughter."

He smirks at me. "That is, except when she *asks* me to."

I refuse to take his hand. "You will pay for that muddy-boots stunt you pulled at the bank."

Honest continues. "I don't *hate* you personally, only your evil, greedy, capitalistic heart, only *everything* you stand for. Like taking away our homes."

I clench. "Those are fighting words. You can't back them up."

Honest whips out a sword from his scabbard and waves it menacingly. "Ah, but I can."

I don't flinch. "Where did you get that sword? Toys R Us? You have no idea how to use it."

"Do you?" he says. He tosses the sword to me, and I catch it by its handle as it passes me. *Whoa!* I'm as surprised as anyone. No way could I do that a second time.

We're surrounded by hundreds of hippies and onlookers. I've never seen so much tie-dye in one place before. It's an assault on my eyes. The sword has heft. It's real, not plastic.

"I was fencing team captain at Stanford," I say.

"Stanford, you say?" taunts Honest. "How stellular! You know why they stopped having parties at Stanford?" He pauses. "The student who had the recipe for ice graduated."

I snort. "I hope your sword is not as dull as your jokes. I would challenge you to a duel, but I won't kill an unarmed man."

Honest puts his hand on his scabbard. "I have a knife."

Another hippie with scraggy blond hair hands Honest a sword, which he waves around in the air as he slips off his sandals. He's going to fence in bare feet on the gravel? He must have thick calluses on his feet.

I remove my tie and jacket, toss them to Hic.

"En guard," I say, my left foot in front, my back foot angled to the side. My knees are bent as if I'm skiing, and my sword points up at a 30-degree angle. If you ignore my shiny black wingtips, I look like I know what I'm doing. Honest ducks under my sword and advances, but I block him with the flat edge of my blade. We hold each other at bay, our faces sweating. I push him away and he trips, but recovers and comes after me.

Johnny Dash runs by, announcing the fight. "Fenton Felton parries Honest Abernathy's attack and feints left," he says into his mic, as if he's been a fencing commentator all his life. "Honest sees the opening, but Fenton twists away from his lunge."

The bushy-bearded camera guy is so close I feel his breath. He keeps prancing around to film at different angles, like he's part of the fight choreography himself. Honest shakes his long red hair and tosses his sword from hand to hand. "They say that behind every great fortune lies a crime," he says. "I bet yours has many crimes."

He has no idea what he's doing or saying. But he's spry and cocky and I'm twice his age and I sit at a desk all day. "It's no great fortune," I say. "It's held together by glue and debt."

"That's what I hear, that you have no fortune. That you're broke."

"Ridiculous." I lunge. "*Allez!*"

The wind whips a strip of yellow police tape across the parking lot and I trip on it, lurching toward Honest and jabbing him in the chest. He goes down. The crowd gasps and then goes silent. All I hear are the gulls squawking.

God, did I kill him?

No, he sits up. His white shirt has a blob of blood, but it looks like the wound is superficial. Like he is. The blood is above the heart, near his collarbone.

Dawn rushes to Honest and kneels by his side, her hands all over him. A police officer rushes over with a first aid kit.

Brenda appears out of nowhere in a bathrobe and runs toward Honest. It's a surprise to see her, though of course, I've been hoping she might be here.

She leans over Honest. "Are you OK?" I haven't seen her in a month.

"Why aren't you wearing pants?" she says. She doesn't even look at me.

She turns to my daughter. "You must be Dawn." Then, to Honest: "You said you didn't *have* a girlfriend."

Honest gets up. "I can explain," he says. He seems to have recovered.

Dawn turns to Honest, then back to Brenda. "Are you and he—?

"No, no, but—"

Dawn and Brenda look at each other, then, at the same time, turn to Honest.

"I know this looks bad," he says. "You see, I thought Dawn was going to break up with me, so when I told you I wasn't seeing anyone, I *believed* that was true. Was *about* to be true."

"Wait a minute," Dawn says to Brenda. "You're the waitress at the Dare Not. You're—"

"That's right. I worked late last night, which is why I'm late—"

"You're the woman who broke up my parents' marriage," Dawn says.

"I think you're angry at the wrong person *and*—

Oh shit!

She unloops the tie on her robe and displays her belly, so everyone sees she's pregnant.

Dawn says, "Are you—?" Brenda nods.

Now Dawn stares at me. "Are you—?"

"I can explain," I say.

The guy with the camera and the shades is filming all this, but I don't care. They never use more than a few minutes on the news anyway. Better that they tell the world about Brenda and me than show the weak-ass eviction raid.

Brenda walks away.

I miss Brenda terribly, and I miss the man I was when we were together. I treated her with respect and generosity. I was a better person. I listened to her attentively. I gave her jewelry to show her how much I appreciated her. I complimented her so frequently she told me to stop, that I was embarrassing her. I was a fool to leave her.

"Wait, Brenda, don't leave," I say. "I want you back."

"No," she says. But I step in her path.

"I'll take care of you," I say, "and our baby."

She swats my sword away. "And my friends here at Aquarius Harbor?" She spreads her arms wide to include everyone in this teeming crowd.

I hesitate.

"I didn't think so." And she's gone.

Before I can follow Brenda, Honest's mousy sister is in my face, offering me a rolled-up blueprint.

"Mr. Fenton," she says, "I've designed a compromise dock plan that accommodates Aquarius Harbor *and* your luxury marina and together—"

I don't hear the rest of what she says because the paddywagon is leaving the parking lot and its tires grind on the gravel. But I don't need to hear any more. I grab the blueprint from her and throw it towards the water.

"Why would I accommodate you when I can crush you?" And then I laugh while she chases the blueprint. She grabs it just before it rolls into the mud.

Hic nudges me from behind. "Sir, you may want to at least *look* at the compromise plan, so—"

"Why would I listen to you?" I say. "Besides, why would you care? I thought you quit."

"We can salvage this project if we compromise."

"Compromising is for losers," I say. "I know why you want to salvage this. Because you'd rather tolerate me than tell your wife how much you invested in our project. *Her* money."

"Not true," he says. "I have told her. She knows."

Then he hiccups, though he tries to stop it.

Which means he hasn't told her.

"I'll tell her," I say.

"You are as evil as you pretend to be," he says, and storms off. "Find yourself another flunky."

"You'll lose your stake."

No response. He's disappearing into the crowd.

"Wait," I say. "I'll up your percentage from twenty to thirty."

He stops, turns around. "Forty or nothing."

"Forty," I say. "But you have to dig up dirt on the chief, on Mayor Sally, on the pirate—"

"No, you listen to me." He's in my face now. "We're hemorrhaging money, paying for an office we can't afford, paying for a piledriver sitting idle on a barge. We'll break our office lease, and—"

He stops and his eyes widen, then this rapturous look appears on his face, like he's seen a vision. He's got the proverbial lightbulb above his head.

"I've got it," he says, hopping up and down like a silly kid. "We don't wait for the evictions. We bring in the piledriver *now*. Start building our dock *now*. Those suckers are so effing loud they'll drive the squatters away."

I start to argue with him out of habit but stop. That's not such a terrible idea. I rub my palms together. This could save our project.

"What are they gonna do?" I crow. "Whine to Chief Tin about the noise?" I rear back and laugh diabolically.

That always makes me feel better.

"What a brilliant idea," I say. "I'm so glad I thought of it."

9

Honest Pulls the Wagon
With the Keg and the Bong

When I arrive at the Aquarius Harbor Community Center, fifteen minutes early for the meeting, it's already buzzing with energy, buzzing with creativity. Mickey's in one corner, with Isaac, standing on a milk crate practicing his Fenton Felton skit.

The back floor is covered with a chalky blue tarp and nine artists are painting and dressing cardboard cutouts. The cutouts are life-size, five to six feet tall, with a fold at the bottom for the base, to weigh down with a sandbag, and a thin wooden dowel to prop it up. We're doing a "stand-in" the next time the police come, as opposed to a sit-in, and many of those standing are going to be cardboard cutouts, dolled up to look like houseboaters. Jude calls out instructions to the other artists while she staples a crazy-colorful tie-dye shirt on a leggy cutout. We're preparing for a two-pronged assault tomorrow, by sea *and* by land.

I circle around the perimeter of the large room to watch Mickey practice from various angles. His long hair is tucked into his black top hat, he's got the shiny black cape, and his imitation of Fenton's demonic laugh is funny. But he doesn't look like a villain. Maybe we can find him one of those curly, handlebar mustaches, waxed and pointed. That would do it.

"When I become Sausalypso dictator," he brays from atop his milk crate, "I mean city council member, I will use my power for good. My own good. To evict and crush those dirty hippies in Aquarius Harbor and build a luxurious harbor in its place, because Sausalypso is better bland and boring. We don't want to break the law. We just want to write it."

He raises his fist and steps off the crate.

"That is wicked," I tell him. "*Wicked.* If we can get five seconds of that on the TV, that's gold. Fenton Felton so deserves the ridicule."

"It's too easy," he says. "Like, it's not even satire. We're just mimicking him."

"It's not our fault," I say, "that he writes our material for us."

I still need to talk with Mickey about the firebomb this morning, but it's time to start the meeting and I don't know what to say that I haven't already said.

I walk up two steps onto a raised platform, detach my typewriter from its harness, and place it on the bar. I hit three keys. The typewriter bell dings. That gets everyone's attention. Pretty soon, everyone's sitting in a chair or they're standing or kneeling on the tarp with their brushes or staplers.

Honest bought this ramshackle old ferry six months

after our Mom and Dad's crash and moved us here to Aquarius Harbor. He stripped out the benches in the passenger lounge and we camped out here in sleeping bags on the hardwood floor. He built two cottages, one for me on the bow deck and one for him on the stern. Mine with a view of Angel Island, his of the Sausalito hills.

He did almost all the work himself, borrowing tools and learning from library books. But he did not believe in the eight-hour workday, and if I hadn't been project manager and deadline setter, it would have taken him forever.

Back when the Tiburon Ferry ran in and out of Richardson Bay every day, the passenger lounge accommodated a hundred people, sitting on benches made from oak slats, and buying coffee, beer, snacks, and cigarettes at the bar I'm standing behind.

Our original plan had been to turn the passenger lounge into another residence, but when we moved into our respective digs, we hosted a rollicking party in the lounge and where we camped became a spacious dance floor. Someone said that this would be a cool community center, and that's what it's become.

At first, I loved living at the center of everything, because of the late-night parties. I was a teenager with no curfew and Honest didn't even *try* to parent me even though he was my legal guardian. If anything, I parented him. But after failing my morning classes at Tam High, I established a regular bedtime during the school week and more than a few times I had to tell the partiers to quiet down or go somewhere else.

We haven't had a party in far too long, because we've been trying to save our homes. No, I mean, we *are* going to save our homes, because we are warriors for justice. I know that sounds like something Honest would say, in fact he has said it, but I'm not against adopting his good ideas. The problem is he thinks *all* his ideas are good.

I check my index cards. Take a deep breath. My whole life has led me to now. To seize this moment.

I can and I will.

"We're going to start now," I say, my fingers on the space bar of the typewriter. "Thank you all for coming tonight to plan for our continued resistance." There are nineteen people sitting in folding chairs and another nine in the back painting and dressing the cutouts. I type those numbers under today's date. Our last meeting, we had seventeen. Honest isn't here yet, but that's for the best.

"As many of you know, nine people were arrested today," I say, "all of whom have been released, though the police warned us they won't be if they're arrested again. We were on three TV news stations, and we're almost certainly going to be in the *Chronicle* tomorrow morning. We got amazing coverage *because* of the visuals, like the protesters pushing away the police boats with oars. Only four houseboats were towed, and we found a place to crash for everyone who lost their home. Tomorrow will be even more colorful because we'll be ready with our cardboard protesters. Thank you so much to Jude and all you other amazing and talented artists."

I praise as many people as I can by name and ask for a round of applause for our community.

"It's not fair to equate ourselves with the young black men who sat at the whites-only lunch counter in Nashville and endured being spit on by the hostile locals. Those young men, and others like them, changed the world, partly *because* the world saw them resist on their

TV screens. But we looked scrappy and we used similar nonviolent tactics. We're fighting for affordable housing and to keep our community intact."

I hold up my rolled-up blueprint. "This morning, after the sword fight, I presented a blueprint of a compromise plan that I drafted to Fenton Felton. He would not even look at it. I'm still furious about that. I'm not a licensed architect, but I've learned enough to draw a plan for Aquarius Harbor where *he* can build his luxury dock *without* evicting us."

"You can see on the easel here a simplified version of the plan—the two wide "W" shaped docks connected by a bridge that little boats can go under. Lots of corner berths." Jude passes out copies of the sketch.

"We need to make the compromise plan part of the community conversation. We need to get it on TV, in the newspapers. I'm sending it to Johnny Dash, and if you know someone who might have some sway, please share this sketch. It's got an info sheet on the back. We want to get the plan out there in the world. We also want the candidates to discuss it at the city council candidate debate tomorrow and—"

A clanging sound comes from the door. *No!* It's Honest pulling a red wagon with a keg and a bong on it. Trailing him are Larry, one of his disciples, and another one whose name escapes me. Harry? Honest stops the wagon in front of the stage, blocking me, and pumps the keg. "Pumping for the party," he sings.

No! No! No!

"To today," Honest says, raising an empty plastic red cup. "We showed those greedy, capitalist, bloodsuckers this morning." Cheers and whoops echo through the room. Harry and Larry pass out cups and people flock to the keg, *including Jude and Mickey.* I thought they were on *my* side.

Honest loves to be the fun-loving court jester and has no problem leaving the thankless grunt work to me. He hates that I'm taking charge, that I'm stealing his thunder, that I'm coming into my own. I have to take back control of this meeting, and I can't let him goad me into losing my temper.

"It's true we have a lot to celebrate," I say, as loud as I can above the chatter. I bang random keys on my typewriter as if I'm typing notes. "And it's been some time since we've had a party, but—"

Honest interrupts. "Hey, how about a big hand for my amazing sister Fate? We wouldn't be celebrating without her. All those dinghies pushing away the police boat—*her* idea."

The applause is loud and I blush. I was not expecting this from Honest, but it's all part of his ruse. As soon as the clapping dies down, Honest lifts the bong. "Time to party. The keg is flowing and now I'm going to fire up this sucker!"

More cheers.

I hit the carriage return on my typewriter and type until the right margin bell dings.

No one hears it. No one's listening. Honest struggles with the bong, his lighter flickering, but I smell the weed already. The room stinks of skunk.

Now Honest lights the weed and it's glowing in the bowl. I see where this moment is going and I have to stop the trajectory.

Honest will hijack the meeting, turn it into a party, and I will lose my temper and storm off and tomorrow the police will be back with more firepower, and we will all be evicted. Our community will disappear, and I'll end up living by myself in a crappy apartment in Daly City and bookkeeping for hair salons and yogurt shops.

I hated Honest for bringing me here after our Mom and Dad's crash, but now that our community is being threatened, I want to keep it more than anything.

Mickey offers me a beer. I want it, but I shake my head no. Then I reach out and take it. My mouth is dry. I'm thirsty. I'm on edge. But I will *not* let Honest sabotage this meeting.

He wheels the bong around the room in the wagon. Almost everyone partakes, but I don't. Even with my meticulously organized index cards and typewritten notes, I'm always afraid I'll lose track of where I am, and getting high will only make that worse.

I sip the beer. This morning was intense and our community came together like never before. We've long talked about ourselves as a community, but now, now that we're under siege, it feels real.

I step back on the stage, and ring the typewriter bell again. "Attention, please. We have to plan for the next raid, and we need to be sure that—"

"We need to be sure we're wasted, man." That's Larry, or is it Harry? They are almost indistinguishable, with their dark ropey brown hair, bushy beards, and pirate garb.

"Our success this morning happened because we *planned* as a community and we *acted* as a community," I say. "We were ready. We're here tonight so we'll be ready tomorrow. Because we want to protect our homes, our families, and our community, and we understand that requires planning and coordination. Do I have that right?"

"Right, right," says Jude. Others murmur in assent.

"I don't know about you," I say, "but I don't plan and coordinate so well when I'm drunk and high."

Harry whoops. "Party hearty!" Or is that Larry?

"So please, Honest, for the good of the community you profess to love, take your party outside. It's a balmy night. You can hang out on the deck and those of us who appreciate the value of planning can proceed."

"Fate's right," says Mickey. "We're, like, partying prematurely."

Mickey. I was surprised the other morning at the Dare Not when he supported me as spokesperson for the collective, and here in front of everyone, I'm even more surprised.

"Mickey," I say. "Can you come up here and perform your Fenton Felton monologue, while Honest wheels the keg out to the deck?"

Mickey does his skit and gets whistles and applause, but Honest makes no move to leave with his wagon.

I look down at my index card with the agenda and start again, but Honest interrupts immediately. "If it isn't Miss Forgetful, with her index cards to help her remember."

"Don't," I say. He's trying to make me lose my temper. "As if you don't forget all sorts of things, like how to speak respectfully, like how not to be a selfish prick."

I hear "oohs' from the audience. It's suddenly quiet. Jude freezes with a paintbrush in front of her face.

"My sister Fate," Honest says, "wants to be our spokesperson, wants to be on TV, but she's *boring.* They gave the sword fight and my boxers four times more air-time than her bland platitudes about affordable housing."

"Did you use a stopwatch to time it?" I ask. "Did you *plan* the sword fight?"

"We were *prepared*," he says. He is so frigging smug.

"The point is that this is a meeting," I say, "not a party, and you have to decide where you want to be."

Honest nods his head. "I get it. You feel the need to be responsible. You won't allow yourself to have fun. Because of what happened to Mom and Dad. As if you can ever make up for that."

How dare he!

I throw my cup at Honest, who ducks, but a splash of beer hits his face.

He laughs, wipes his face with his sleeve, then laughs again, this time like Fenton Felton, or rather like Mickey's send-up of Fenton Felton. "You want to be in charge, you can't lose your shit."

I know what he's doing and I know I have to chill, but I can't. He is so maddening.

My body is shaking. My blood is boiling.

I shove the typewriter off the bar onto the wagon and the bong shatters into pieces.

I hear boos and hisses. I've spoiled their fun. *Fuck them.*

Honest laughs. "This is the best party *ever*. I'll get a broom."

I run to my cabin and lock the door.

BRENDA DIAMOND

[Lonely waitress, houseboat resident, former mistress of Fenton]

10

Should I Stay or Should I Go?

The sky is dark but not black when I leave the Dare Not to walk home. It's still warm. Indian Summer is hanging on and the fog is on vacation. This is the first afternoon shift I've worked in months and I'm not used to getting off this early. I switched because I promised Fate I would go to the community meeting tonight. But my shift was super-busy because there was a World Series game on and now I'm tired and I want to go home and lie down.

I'm not nauseous like my first trimester, but my sleep is ragged and I'm afraid someone will pressure me into volunteering. No, thank you.

But I can't afford to lose my rental. When I received my eviction notice, I felt like I'd been assaulted. I knew it was coming, but then it did. Where will I go when the baby comes and my community is gone?

When I cross Quicksand Road, I'm leaving the commercial strip and heading into the Industrial District, which is quiet at night, until I get to Aquarius Harbor, which is usually *not* quiet this time of night.

Before this morning, I only told one person at Aquarius Harbor about my pregnancy. Jude, the artist, who has four-year-old twins, and she was excited for me. "Great. Wonderful. The more kids here, the merrier." Of course, she has a husband who seems solid. She promised she would help with the baby—if we don't all get evicted, that is, and scattered to the winds.

When I called my friend Grace from high school, she said I'm making a mistake keeping the baby and she offered to accompany me to get an abortion. I told her I didn't want one.

Now everyone in the world knows, which is crazy, but also a relief, because I don't have to hide.

As I walk down the dock to the community center, I hear shouts, and they get louder as I get closer. Now there's a crash and the clatter of breaking glass, and Fate stomps out the doorway, tears streaming down her face.

I start to follow her to her cabin, but she looks like she wants to lock herself in a closet. I stay put.

When Fate recruited me to be here this morning for the raid, she said she wanted me to be in front, close to the TV cameras. "So it's not just us white kids," she said. When my mom moved us to Concord, I was the only black girl in my class, and sometimes I felt like that was the only interesting thing about me.

I wish I could be more trusting, but I was blind about Fenton Felton, and the man before him too. The *men* before him.

I walk down the gangplank to the deck of the ferry.

The yelling inside has stopped, and Honest is speaking. I can't tell what he's saying. I hide behind the staircase to the roof level.

I hear Jude. She's loud, with a low, distinctive voice and a New York accent. "*You* broke it, Honest, *you* fix it. You hounded your sister out of here and now we have a meeting with no facilitator, a community with no leader, and we're going to be raided again tomorrow, and who's going to stand up here and organize people who don't want to be organized. It's not going to be me."

"How about Brenda?"

I flinch. Who said that? I duck further behind the staircase.

"She's not here." That's Mickey. He speaks like he's grinding gravel in his throat. Interesting that he notices my absence.

Now's my chance to make a run for it, but instead I stand up straight, and stride into the community center. As if I just arrived. "Sorry I'm late. I just got off work."

Honest is sweeping up shards of glass from the floor, in slow motion. He does not look handsome and dashing tonight—he's bleary-eyed, studying the broom, his mouth hanging open, like a lost little boy who needs a haircut and a bath.

There are thirty or forty people in the room, many holding red plastic cups, and the smell of beer and pot is intense, but it *looks* more like a meeting than a party. The chairs are in a half-circle facing the stage and a few people have notepads in their laps. Jude tugs a wagon with a silver keg on it toward the door, then stops.

"We're having a discussion," Jude says, "about who might be a good leader, a good ambassador for our community, and someone suggested you."

"Because I'm black," I say. I don't mean to be so blunt, but why else are they interested in me?

"No, no," says Jude. "I mean, yes, but also because you're a waitress and you know everyone in town and you're a serious person and not a hippie or a pirate and you would also be good at it."

That last part, about me being good at it, she raises her voice like it's a question. I'm tempted to ask how she knows.

"And because I'm pregnant?" I say.

"That's not the reason," says Jude, "but it doesn't hurt." Jude and I are talking like it's a private conversation, but everyone here is listening.

"I can't. *Because* I'm pregnant. *Because* I work nights. *Because* I don't know how to run meetings. Especially with you guys, who don't follow rules, like not drinking beer and getting high during a meeting. The thing is, I think that would be a good rule."

I feel like I stepped in dog poop. But so what. I don't want them to want me anyway.

Jude speaks up immediately. "I, for one, would welcome a rule like that."

There are boos, from Honest and the two bearded guys hovering around the keg.

"Why not you?" I ask Jude. "Everyone respects you."

She sighs. "We've been over this already. I'm an artist, a space cadet, right brain to the max, hopelessly disorganized. Plus I've got my kidlings and my hubby."

"Why not Fate?" I say, though I know why not because she ran out in tears. "She wants to do it and she *is* good at it."

"But she buckles under pressure," says Honest, "and—"

"The pressure *you* created," counters Jude. "*You* drove her out."

"Her cabin is thirty seconds from here," I say. "Let's get her back."

Everyone looks at me, as if they expect me to ask her. I sit down. It's good to be off my feet. I can't keep up what I'm doing now, so how can I do more? It's already hard to be on my feet so long and I'm only getting bigger. I lock in on Honest, who's finished sweeping, and is sitting in a chair holding the broom.

I stand. "Honest, go to your sister, apologize, and bring her back here."

I'm surprised by the authority in my voice. Honest looks like he wants to respond, but his mouth opens and nothing comes out.

"You're a strong enough man to apologize," I add. "We'll wait here."

HONEST ABERNATHY

[Pretend pirate, houseboat resident, brother of Fate, boyfriend of Dawn]

11

I Came to Apologize

If I move, I'll throw up, so I stay where I am, on my ass in a chair. I take deep breaths.

At least I swept up the broken glass and wiped up the watery mess. I don't know how I managed that.

I refinished this floor five years ago and it's scuffed and scratched, and it was dumb to open it up to this community because they don't respect hardwood floors like I do.

Jude pulls the wagon out the door and the wheels squeak. When I look up, the room spins, so I close my eyes.

I hear my name. It's Brenda. She wants me to apologize to Fate.

I'm too wasted to refuse. My stomach is churning like a washing machine. I don't even know if I can stand up.

At least I'm not kneeling in front of a toilet. Not yet.

I overindulged, but for good reason. After such an intense and stressful day, I needed to decompress. I mean, Fenton Felton stabbed me in the heart. Well, actually it was above the heart, a superficial wound, and the sword fight was top-of-the-line TV, possibly the highlight of my life.

I recorded Johnny Dash's newscast and watched the sword fight three times before coming to the community center. I don't know what the hell I was doing, baiting Fate like that?

Now Brenda says I'm a strong enough man to apologize.

But I'm not.

She stares at me and I push myself up with my hands and set off for Fate's cabin with a purposeful stride, hanging onto the railing so I don't fall over.

I stagger out to the deck, and collapse onto the bench outside Fate's cabin, by the garden bed where gold cherry tomatoes are still growing. I cannot do this. I'm a pretender, a loser, a pathetic coward full of bluster with nothing to back it up.

Fate sees through me. Dawn sees through me. Just because I've managed to hoodwink plenty of people doesn't mean I should believe my press clippings. My head is so heavy I have to hold it in my hands.

Fate is not my enemy. She's family, my only family. Not to mention she saved my life. She did.

I mean, after our parents' accident, I was a basket case, as reckless as could be. Plastered every night. Worse than tonight. But Fate was my baby sister and I had to provide for her.

If it weren't for her, I would have kept going down the tubes. I did a lame job as her guardian, but I bought our groceries and cooked every night, almost every night, even if it was rice, beans, and cheese half the time.

But man, she was hurting so much, so locked into her loss, *our loss,* and I didn't know how to help. I was legally an adult, but emotionally a child.

I push off the bench and stand. Only a few steps to Fate's door.

I knock. "It's me."

No answer.

I built this cabin for her, with my bare hands. I made mistakes, but I did a damn good job for my first time. The door, for example. It swells up and sticks in the frame when the air is moist. I've been meaning to fix it, but with the evictions hanging over us, it hasn't been a priority.

I knock louder. "I'm sorry," I say. "I came to apologize."

Maybe I am strong enough after all.

She opens the door, scowls at me with her fierce eyes.

"We need you back in the community center," I say. "You're the only person who can lead the meeting."

She's not crying, but her eyes are red. It hurts me to see her in pain like this. But I'm not doing so great either. My body is stiff from the sword fight and the soles of my feet feel raw. The ferry sways in the water. The moon is full. Bells clang in the distance.

Fate grips the door as if she's going to slam it in my face.

"Jude says she'll help," I say, "but she's not organized like you and she doesn't have an agenda. I'll stay out of the way."

"I'm pooped," Fate says. "I don't have the energy to deal with the rowdies. I need sleep. Tin will be back early tomorrow with more firepower. We'll do the best we can and if we lose everything, that's the way the world works."

She sniffles and rubs her nose.

"I'm sorry not just for tonight," I say, "but for everything. For letting you down. For not being there for you. For getting in your way. For whatever else I've forgotten."

She laughs. It's more of a snort. As different from Fenton Felton's laugh as can be.

"You think it's that easy?" she says. "You repent and your sins are wiped away? Those priests sure did a number on you. You have no idea how much you have to apologize for."

"I do," I say. "You'd be surprised. But don't act like a blameless victim. You question and judge *everything* I do. *Everything*. You—" No, no, this is not where I want to go.

"*We* need you. *I* need you. To go back to the center and run the meeting and help us save our homes. You're our leader."

I want to sit down, but she's blocking the doorway. I hold myself up with both my hands, one on each side of the door jamb.

"Look," I say, "all I'm saying is that I respect all the work you do, but it's hard to express my appreciation when you're always dismissing me as lazy, as an underachiever. But would Johnny Dash be coming around with his camera guy if there weren't clowns and pirates to film? You know the answer. What you do works because of what I do. And vice versa even more."

I'm surprised I'm able to make such a coherent argument.

"I'm sorry for sabotaging the meeting. That was childish. *Please,* go to the community center. Save our harbor. You're so capable it scares me. I'll apologize for the rest of my misdeeds later."

"You're capable too, and if you gave your *all* to beating Fenton Felton, you'd be unstoppable."

"I *do*."

"You *don't*. Look at you."

She's about to say I'm a disgrace, but she doesn't.

"I have to lie down," I say. "I feel like shit."

She walks to her kitchen sink, splashes cold water on her face, and wipes it with the sleeve of her shirt. I sit on the plywood box by the front door where she keeps her shoes. I built this box. It's sturdy and it has slots for four pairs of shoes.

"Look," she says, "I know Johnny Dash might not be coming around so often with his camera guy if you didn't put on a show. But why do you keep playing the clown when there are no cameras around?"

"I don't know," I say.

"Also, you could do more of the grunt work."

"I could," I say. "I will."

She heads for the door, but stops and turns to me before she leaves.

"After the meeting," she says, "I will knock on your door with instructions for tomorrow. Set your alarm for six."

[Greedy developer, father of Dawn, ex-husband of Alice]

12

I Hated You Before I Met You

I sit against the back wall of the Dare Not, the rough brick grazing my elbows. My seat is in the center of the wall, behind a tile table with two phones, and a bulging briefcase underneath. It's Wednesday, my first morning here and I'm going to make the best of this.

I'm on the phone with Hic, and he keeps asking dumb questions.

Since we're behind on our rent, Hic's suggestion that we abandon our office makes sense, but I'll be damned if I'm going to set up shop in the trailer, like he's doing. I'm more at home here at The Dare Not. This is where I met Brenda.

I wish I hadn't promised her I would never show up here while she was working, but she usually works nights, and anyway, I made the promise when my fortunes were not as dire.

"Why do we have a past due for the pile driver?" I ask. "Didn't we pay in advance?"

We learned yesterday that Chief Tin needs another day to line up reinforcements for the next eviction raid, which gives us more time to get our ducks in a row. Besides, the city council candidate debate is tonight and it will be contentious enough without more evictions. Too many people think I'm heartless and cruel, which is totally unfair, but I'm not stupid. The evictions are 100 percent legal, but even some reasonable, albeit misguided, people cheer for the underdogs, so we must tread carefully. Driving them out with the pile driver is a much better strategy than waiting until we evict them.

I finish the last bite of my bagel with red onions and lick my lips. *Uh-oh.* Here comes Alice, waltzing through the front door.

"Excuse me, Hic," I say into the phone, "I have a visitor, but remember, we let the protesters do their street theater and play their horns as long as they want. We want the arrests to go as slowly as possible."

I replace the receiver and slurp the last dreg of my espresso.

"If it's not *Hurricane Alice,*" I say, "the most wretched woman ever to grace the streets of this burg. Have I told you lately how much I *despise* you?"

She slides a chair from an adjoining table and stands behind it.

She's wearing a flattering knee-length black dress that looks expensive with a big red leather purse over her shoulder. Also expensive. Paid for with *my* money. She doesn't look half-bad for a middle-aged woman.

"I miss you too, Fenton. I went to your office and

it's closed." Now she sits. "Also, you're behind in your alimony."

"Cash flow problems," I say. "A temporary hiccup."

She leans back in her chair. "You know, I am so enjoying all the *spacious* space in my heavenly house up in the hills," she says. "*My house.* I love the sound of those words."

"What do you want?" I bark. "I'm busy."

"Why do you think I *want* something?" she says. "I'm here to reminisce with you about all the fun times we had together. Oh, that's right. We never had any."

She's in fine form today. Probably practiced in front of a mirror.

"Admit it," I say. "You were glad I hooked up with that waitress. Gave you an excuse to do what you always wanted to."

"Didn't I thank you for that? Oh, that's right. I took you to the cleaners. You know, I hate the way you *breathe.* It reminds me that you're not *dead* yet."

Oh, she wants to brawl, does she? My pulse races and my fingers twitch.

"I loathe you so much," I say, "I would walk on my hands through wet horse manure before I would touch you again."

"Multiply that by infinity," she counters, "and that's how much I hate you. I hated you before I met you."

"I hated you before you were born," I say.

"I hated your grandmother," she says.

I draw a blank. "Your grandmother wears Army boots."

She laughs at me. "That's your best shot?" She shakes her head and looks at me like I'm a pathetic child. I do hate her. I have never hated anyone more than I hate *her.*

But I miss this. Not *her*, but the adrenalin of the fight.

She's such a formidable opponent, and she's sharpened her game. But then, she has nothing to do except to torture me.

I would never have strayed if she satisfied me at home. Since she threw me out, she's hidden behind her lawyer, her silences, and her long, angry, handwritten tirades. I'm almost giddy she's back in my face.

Once upon a time, Alice was beautiful and I wanted her. I did what I had to do to win her over and we were happy for years.

She stands again and grips the back of the chair as if she's going to lift it over her head and whack me. But then she goes into this high-pitched squirrelly voice.

"I know you're headed for a disaster with your luxury marina, but in the *remote* possibility that you make a killing on your leases, well, I had an *illuminating* talk this morning with my lawyer, who says I can make a *claim* on your *future* earnings."

She pulls out a large envelope from her purse, unfolds it, and hands it to me. "You've been served."

And then she mimics my laugh. It's not a good imitation, but it's loud and everyone in the bar turns to look at us.

I speak quietly so she has to lean in to hear me.

"You don't understand. Every dime I make on the harbor is spoken for. I've got more debts than I can ever repay."

"I so miss taunting you." She is not quiet. Passersby on the street can hear her. "It gives my life meaning. Do you miss me?"

"I think it's time," I say, "that I apologize for all the nasty, awful, and *accurate* things I've said about you."

She winces, but then comes the hint of a smile.

"We should stop before we say a lot of things we mean." Then she turns serious. "I understand you have a *new* financial obligation."

"What?"

"I also had an *illuminating* conversation with a *waitress* at Aquarius Harbor. A *pregnant* waitress."

So much for secrets. I want to wipe that smirk off her face. It's a good thing we're in public. If we weren't, I would have no reason to restrain myself.

"She tricked me," I say.

Now she whispers. "You know, if you had some *documentation* of your financial woes, I could call off my lawyer."

"Documentation?" What is she getting at?

"Like your bankruptcy papers."

"You'd withdraw your suit?"

"Why waste my time?"

Why would I give her a weapon she could use against me? I don't trust her for a second. But then, why *would* she waste her time if there's no money to be had? The last thing I need is one more lawyer squeezing me for money.

I reach into my briefcase, pull out a manila folder.

ALICE FELTON

[Vengeful ex-wife of Fenton, mother of Dawn]

13

The Voice of Reason

I arrive at the Dare Not Wednesday evening an hour before the candidate debate, order a chef's salad, and sit at the square table in the bay window that juts out onto the sidewalk.

I see everyone walking by and coming in the front door. I'm not the only one here early. We're going to have a full house. Good, I think.

Where is Dawn? She said she would be here. Well, it's still early. I need to work on my patience.

I'm worried Fenton will slam me during the debate for receiving alimony and not working, but he might be less likely to do that in front of Dawn. I'm entitled to that alimony after fifteen years as a housewife, and I will go back to work again, as soon as I figure out my new calling. I want to avoid the construction business if I can, even though that's where all my experience has been.

Dawn keeps reminding me that I can't keep devoting my life to vengeance, that I need to make something of myself. That's why I'm here, running for city council. If Fenton does mention alimony, I will accuse him of being a deadbeat and being months behind on his payments. What's he going to say to that? He'd be a fool to bring it up.

I won't mention his affair, or if I do, I won't mention Brenda. I have an envelope for her, but I haven't seen her yet.

When I filed to run for the council, maybe it was to spite Fenton, poor wounded me lashing out, but now I'm here to make Sausalito better.

There's no reason for me to be nervous. I'm not debating Einstein. This morning Fenton couldn't keep up with me. I was on fire.

I look up from my salad. Honest's sister, Fate, is standing at my shoulder. I'm disappointed it's not Dawn and I don't hide my disappointment.

She backs away. "Do you have a minute?" She looks down at her feet. "I'm Fate Abernathy, from Aquarius Harbor."

"I know who you are," I say. "Fenton considers you dangerous. Please, sit."

I saw a photo of her the other day in the paper, and she wore a typewriter in a harness around her neck. Another houseboater gimmick to get attention, I'm sure, but I also hear that she's troubled and has memory issues. She has no typewriter today.

She pulls a white cardboard tube from her shoulder bag and slides a blueprint out of it. "I'm an architect," she says, "and I've designed a plan for Aquarius Harbor that accommodates those of us who live there now, *and* still allows Fenton Felton to build his luxury marina."

"You're an architect?"

"Well, I'm no Julia Morgan, I'm not licensed or anything, but I know how to draw plans."

I gesture to the empty chair across from me. "Order yourself dinner," I say, "or a drink. It's on me. How old are you?"

"Twenty-one. Almost twenty-two. Old enough to vote and to drink, and I *will* need a drink before I watch my brother embarrass himself and the houseboaters in this debate."

"It's a secret ballot at the polling place," I say. "You can always vote for me." Almost twenty-two. She's only a year or two younger than Dawn, but she looks like a girl, maybe because of her pigtails and how petite she is. Her skin is smooth and youthful, but her face is plain and her clothes are drab.

She unrolls the blueprint, which is bigger than the table. I put my plate on my lap, my wine glass on the floor. She slips a paper from her notebook. "Here's a simple sketch," she says. "This is easier to read."

"Thank you," I say, "but I can read blueprints." I'm sure she has no idea I worked alongside Fenton for years until I couldn't stand it any longer.

A waitress I don't recognize—not Brenda—comes to take Fate's order. She gets the eggplant parmesan and a glass of house red.

I study the blueprint—I see at a glance what she's proposing, a series of W-shaped docks nestled inside each other—but I can't concentrate.

Twenty-two years old. That's how old I was when Fenton proposed to me. That was, until it wasn't, the best day of my life. I remember it so vividly—he came to my apartment and asked me to help him perform a magic trick.

He gave me a quarter and told me to place it in the palm of his hand. He'd been a magician as a teenager and performed at birthday parties and talent shows. He closed his fingers over the quarter, waved a handkerchief, mumbled some magic words, and there was a puff of smoke. When he opened his hand, a diamond engagement ring rested in his palm. He got down on one knee. I said yes.

I knew what I was doing. I was no different than other girls from my sorority, who latched on to men with promising prospects despite significant reservations. I made my deal with the devil.

"What do you think?" asks Fate. I focus on the blueprint.

"You don't understand my relationship with Fenton," I say. "If I propose this, he'll be more adamant about rejecting it."

"I know the feeling," she says. "My brother is like that. But I was thinking that you could bring it up tonight during the debate as an idea worth exploring. Get the conversation going about a compromise." She unwraps the rubber band from the index cards. She's got paper clips and colored dots on the cards. I can't read them upside down, but the writing is block printing, all capital letters.

I'm feeling anxious again. Not about Fate, but about not being as ready for the debate as I need to be. I'm nowhere near as organized as Fate is. What if I forget my most important points?

"Excuse me," I say. "I don't mean to be rude, but I got here early so I could go over my notes." I point to her index cards. "I'm sure you understand the importance of preparation. You might want to get a good seat close to the stage before it fills up."

"I read your campaign literature," she says, "and you claim to be the voice of reason, and certainly your two opponents are anything but. Proposing a compromise for this standoff is a voice-of-reason kind of thing, don't you think?"

She's reading from one of her cards. Not that there's anything wrong with that.

"Can I keep this sketch?" I ask. "To study more closely."

She unfolds another paper from her notebook. "Here are the budget numbers. They add up. This is totally feasible."

I study the design, which is unusual in its angles, but also elegant in its simplicity. The numbers *might* add up, but I can't tell without comps and there's no chance in hell I'm going to bring up this plan tonight, let alone endorse it. Fenton will crucify me for even *caring* about the plight of the houseboaters. I need to own the center.

The waitress comes with the eggplant, but Fate has moved to a table of hippies near the stage. I give directions to Fate's table and study my notes again, but rehearsing makes me *more* nervous.

At five before seven, I take my seat on the stage. The bar is packed. There are dozens of people standing in the back and leaning against the bay window, where I was just eating. Three TV camera crews are here, squeezed between tables. Perspiration trickles down my left arm.

City council elections rarely attract much attention, but Johnny Dash's breathless reports from Aquarius Harbor have changed that, and other reporters and camera crews are rolling in like the fog.

Everyone in town is here too. Chief Tin is sitting with my friend Wendy from high school. I didn't know they knew each other. Fenton's partner Huck is here with his wife and teenage daughters.

But *my* daughter is not here.

Last week there were coin flips to determine the order and Fenton is going first. Then Honest, then me. After we each deliver our introductory remarks, Mayor Sally, the proprietress of the Dare Not, will moderate the Q and A.

Fenton starts. "I've built houses, apartments, office buildings, shopping centers, and marinas all over Marin County and the Bay Area. I've been a city leader for decades, a Chamber of Commerce officer. I've contributed to making this county a desirable place, where quality people want to live.

"My opponents are not serious people. Let's start with Alice, my ex-wife. She claims to be a feminist who believes in women's rights, but she lives in luxury off alimony I pay her. She sleeps till noon, doesn't work, has no drive or ambition, and has never contributed anything to this city."

A few catcalls come from the people standing in the back. I can't tell at first if they're for Fenton or not, but then I hear a hiss. I want to blurt out "the alimony you're behind on?" but Sally will reprimand me, so I bite my tongue. I can wait for my turn. Besides, I've decided the hiss was aimed at him, not me.

"She only entered this city council race to spite me," he says. "And then there's her voodoo doll, of me, that she pokes with knitting needles. This is not a woman you want making decisions about your city.

"As for Honest Abernathy, don't be fooled by his working-class rhetoric. He went to law school. Dropped out. He's not poor. He inherited money from his parents and blew it on drugs and boats—"

Honest interrupts. "That's a lie. That inheritance, the insurance from my parents' fatal hit-and-run accident was—"

Sally stops him, tells him to wait his turn. I was right to restrain myself. But Honest is not embarrassed. That's one of his strengths. No shame.

"Honest Abernathy is making a mockery of our city, running for office when he has no chance of winning, no intention of winning," Fenton continues. "He and his accomplices at Aquarius Harbor are not only taking drugs, they're selling them. The harbor is an open-air drug market. This picturesque town of ours is being sabotaged by criminals from the Haight-Ashbury and from Oakland, with their stealing and their parties and their loud music and their naked women. I am the candidate of law and order, peace, and prosperity. My luxury harbor will attract affluent people who will pay taxes and patronize our restaurants and bars. If it also makes me richer, isn't that what we all want?"

He finishes with his maniacal laugh.

I marvel at how Fenton embraces his villainy, how, with his laugh and the way he rubs his hands together in glee as if he were a cartoon character, he makes you *think* he's joking.

But he's not. No, that man is dead serious.

Honest, who's dressed like a pirate at a dinner party, his white shirt ironed, his black boots shined, hangs his head when it's his turn.

"It's true I don't intend to win," he says, turning to Fenton, "you got me there. I mean, can you imagine *me* sitting patiently through a city council meeting? Not a chance. I'm using this debate to highlight the outrageous *seizure* of our homes in Aquarius Harbor, and to provoke a discussion of the future of Sausalito and who gets to live here. This used to be a factory town, a working town, a place with affordable housing where carpenters and shipbuilders and waitresses could afford to live. Not just rich people.

"If you don't want to vote for me, don't vote for me. I've got nothing to be ashamed about." He stops. "Well, there are a few things, but now's not the time. For the record, that inheritance was the insurance payout my sister and I received because our Mom and Dad died in a car crash. A drunk driver. A hit and run. Thirty-seven thousand dollars. For the two of us. But there were debts. We were fortunate to find a berth here at Aquarius Harbor and a decommissioned ferry to build our cabins on. Now we have a community.

"There are eighty-three houseboats threatened with eviction by Fenton Felton, one hundred and fifty-eight people, including twenty-seven children. We demand a halt to the evictions and the right to keep our homes. And, one last thing, Fenton Felton is not a successful businessman. He's broke. He's a fraud. I have evidence."

Honest gets more applause than I expect. When he sits, I stand. Fate is eating her eggplant a few feet in front of me. What she said to me earlier, that I'm the voice-of-reason candidate, that's exactly right. I prepared my remarks with that in mind. But I was not expecting Fenton to launch into his "colorful" attacks right out of the gate. My voice-of-reason policy pronouncements are going to end up on the cutting room floor. If I want to be on TV, I can't be boring.

I look at the crowd, the TV cameras, and raise my water glass in a toast. The ice cubes clink against the glass. I'm scrapping my speech.

"Good evening, Sausalito. My name is Alice Fenton, soon to be Alice Almaden, my maiden name, and yes, I used to be married to that man over there, Fenton Felton, and since we are now divorced, I'd like to start with a story I heard, from a bitter ex-wife—*not me*—who sold all her husband's *crap* at a 'Divorce Yard Sale.'"

My friend in the second row of tables smiles. She told me this story.

"She put up signs around the neighborhood.

"'Caught husband cheating. It's all got to go, just like him.'

"'Come early, like he did.'"

That gets titters and one deep, reassuring *"ooh."*

Not as boring as you expected, huh?

"This bitter ex-wife—*again, not me*—priced everything low. Sold his golf clubs for five dollars, his beloved grill for half that. When everything was gone, she gave her ex the proceeds in pennies. In a jar. Soaked in curdled milk."

I sigh.

"As I said, I did not do that, though sometimes I wish I had. I didn't because I'm a reasonable person, and if you elect me to the city council, I will be a voice of reason. *The* voice of reason.

"I am the one and only woman candidate in this city council race, and sadly, that means I have to be twice as good as either of these men to be elected.

"I am twice as good. Though, if you pardon my bluntness, it's not a high bar."

The crowd whoops and claps. A woman calls out from the back. "You tell them, sister!"

"Now," I continue, "let me tell you about my vision for Sausalito."

BRENDA DIAMOND

[Lonely waitress, houseboat resident, former mistress of Fenton]

14

Full House

The fog is rolling in when I leave for work, and the only blue sky left is across the bay in Richmond, where I lived before I moved here. Wednesday is usually my night off, the night I take the bus and streetcar to SF State for my Econ class. Except I quit. I couldn't stay awake.

Sally called me in to work because she expects a full house tonight, on account of her hosting a city council candidate debate. I hear TV news crews will be there, too. Until tonight, Fenton has honored his promise not to show up at the bar during my shift, but he's one of the candidates, so I'll have to avoid him as best I can. He's called me three times in the past week and sent me two letters, even though I told him to leave me alone.

I step off the wobbly dock and crunch my way through the gravel parking lot to the sidewalk. The breeze smells of salt and fish. My humble little houseboat looks almost pretty in the light of dusk. I don't know what I'll do if the police tow it away.

I would have never considered living and working in Sausalito except that my father did, during the war, and one day, when I was sixteen, he took me here.

We sat in his red truck eating egg-salad sandwiches and humming along with "I Heard It Through the Grapevine" on the radio. The boats were more dilapidated then, if you can believe that. It was the first time I'd seen my father in a year. He pointed to an owl-shaped, brown shingle barn on a moss-covered barge.

"That's where our line was, right there. The boringest work ever, building ships, as sorry as picking cotton in Mississippi. But we had a sense of purpose. Sometimes I thought, oh, this is just their B.S. to keep us in line, but no, we *were* part of something important.

"God, I was proud of myself. Got myself out of Mississippi into the Army and then here to build ships. Nothing like having money in my pocket. My mama couldn't stand for me to leave home, but she understood. Damn if I haven't made some shit-for-brains mistakes, but I'm not back in Mississippi."

But he did go back. His mama was sick.

That day with my father in Sausalito was sunny and enchanting and it's the only time I remember him speaking to me from his heart. He never did that. He didn't know how.

He had told me before that he had lived on a houseboat, though it was, he said, "barely a house and barely a boat, more like a shipping crate plopped on a raft."

But he had never talked about his stint in the Army, or how he got wounded at Guadalcanal. I knew only what my mother told me. But that afternoon I asked him, and he opened up. Not that I learned much, but some. Like that he was a "grunt."

"You know what grunt stands for," he said, "general replacement unit, not trained. We were disposable. We ran into enemy fire."

"What was that like?" I asked. "Being in the war. Running into enemy fire?"

"Not something I want to talk about. I don't know what came over me."

I got the waitress job through my friend Jenna, but I got tired of driving across the bridge from Richmond and then I saw an ad for a cheap one-bedroom houseboat at Aquarius Harbor, walking distance from the bar. When I went to see it, I realized this was where my dad had worked. The owl barn is practically next door.

I cleaned myself up by the time I got here, and it's a good thing I work nights because there's so much partying at the harbor. It's pretty much weed and wine and it's encouraging that I can face temptation and say no, and mostly I do. When I get home, my desire to sleep is stronger than my desire to get high. Especially now.

Minutes after I clock in, and I leave the kitchen for the dining room, I feel Fenton's eyes on me. *Before* I see him. He's sitting in the stage area, the only one up there, though it's not a stage, just a corner of the floor. I refuse to meet his eyes.

When I get a free minute, I walk to the table where Alice sits, by the bay window, and hand her a menu. "I understand you have something for me," I whisper.

She opens the menu and studies it. "No dessert for me tonight," she says, slipping an envelope inside the menu before closing it. She stands and heads to the stage.

A few minutes later, as Sally welcomes everyone and

introduces the candidates, I hand the same menu to Fate and she slides the envelope into her pack. I'm relieved to get that over with. Tonight is stressful enough without this cloak-and-dagger stuff.

The Dare Not is hopping tonight, and carrying plates through the crowd is an obstacle course. I step over cables from the TV cameras, push past people standing between tables, and hold the plates above my head to get back to the kitchen. The smells are intense—sweat, garlic, grease, beer.

The kitchen is as noisy as the front of the house, but it's a different flavor of noise—the sizzle of the deep fryer, the click of the toaster, the scrape of the spatula, the bark of the cook as he slides plates onto the sideboard. It's a respite from Fenton's eyes and I take a ten-second breather before loading up for my next trip.

I'm making excellent money tonight, and I prefer being busy because I don't dwell on my worries, and for minutes at a stretch, I forget Fenton is watching me. I did not want to work tonight, but Sally promised a bonus, and I could make two or three nights' pay tonight, maybe more. I need to feather my nest.

I will not move back with my mother, I tell myself, even if I've exhausted every other option. But I cringe at how much work those other options entail. Finding a new rental, commuting to work, and how am I going to manage when the baby comes? I sold my car because I didn't need it, but now I'll need to find another one. It will be hard wherever I am, even if Jude and the other mothers at Aquarius Harbor who've offered their help come through. I would rather stay where I am, impossible as that might seem.

There are many new customers here tonight, but also

some of my regulars too, like Rachel, a housewife who drops by with a friend for wine every Thursday. She's sweet—always says she's happy to see me, always tips nicely. Tonight, she's here with—*oh my goodness*, I know this man, through Fenton. It's Cotton Booth. I didn't know he was Rachel's husband. He seems to have no memory of me, or he doesn't notice me. Fine either way.

We ran into him at this fancy restaurant in Napa and Fenton introduced us, like he wanted to show me off, and then later he bemoaned that Booth was the richest businessman in town and he wished he were him.

When I return from the kitchen with her dinner order, Rachel clutches my elbow.

"Brenda, I've heard about your, uh, situation, your breakup, your pregnancy. If there's any way I can help, tell me."

She's so direct, not qualifying her offer, which is generous of her, though I am bothered that so many people know my business.

"I know about, you know, the father, too, because..." and here she nods to her husband, who is concentrating on the debate.

"Rachel," I say, "you've lifted my spirits and I thank you for that, but I can't talk now."

"Of course, you're busy," she says. "I'm so sorry. Will I see you tomorrow?"

"Yes," I say, turning to leave. But I stop and whisper to her. "Does everyone here know I was, you know—?"

"It's Sausalito," she shrugs. "Small town, big mouths." She finishes her wine and points to the glass. Another one. "Not *my* big mouth," she adds. "I'm not a gossip."

"You can help," I say, "by making sure they don't

evict us." Then I'm off to my next table.

I don't know what I expect her to do, but she offered to help. Maybe she can bend her husband in the right direction, get him to lean on Fenton. I should get her a copy of Fate's dock plan. She knows influential people.

The next time I come out of the kitchen, carrying three Caesar salads, I hear Alice blasting Fenton for being behind on his alimony payments, and I gird myself, afraid she's going to mention he's also not paying the child support to me that he promised.

Alice might think she's helping, calling attention to my situation, but the last thing I want is attention. I sigh in relief when Fenton interrupts her.

I thought Sally was the moderator, but Johnny Dash seemed to have stepped in. He reads a question from an index card. For Honest. "How do you expect to win when your platform is essentially anarchy?'"

"Who said anything about winning?" Honest grins. "Does anyone here think I'll win? Show of hands?" He pauses, scans the room. "It's unanimous," he says, "except for my man Mickey and he's messing with me."

Then he talks about how Sausalito used to be a factory town, a place carpenters and waitresses could afford to live. "Like Brenda, the best waitress ever." He points to me. "She lives in our houseboat community. If she gets evicted, where will she live?"

I balance a tray of dirty dishes and Jenna nudges me from behind with a plate because I'm in her way. The audience is applauding me, Fenton louder than anyone. I rush back toward the kitchen, embarrassed, but also encouraged. Seemed like a lot of people applauding. Isn't that a good sign?

"Don't forget to give her a generous tip," Honest

adds as I nudge open the kitchen door.

It's true I was attracted to Honest and I guess I still sort of am. Tonight he shined his boots, pressed his shirt, and washed his hair, and he looks dashing. Which is why he gets away with his goofball bullshitting. If he breaks up with Dawn, which he seems to think is inevitable, and asks me out again, I *might* say yes. Though I would be foolish to expect him to stick around once my baby shows up.

In the kitchen, I drink half a glass of wine in one gulp, and when I return to the front of the house, while Alice is talking about stoplights, I decide not to cower, not to give Fenton power. As I weave my way to my next table, I look directly at him, though I focus on the wall behind him, where the framed Tour de France posters hang high.

I look *through* him, as if he's not even here. And then I meet his eyes and hold them.

He looks down first.

Somehow, I make it through the rest of the night, and I head home with ninety dollars in tips, starving for sleep. A block from the bar, someone bursts out of the darkness and blocks the sidewalk. I jump back and stiffen.

I immediately see it's Fenton, and my fear fades. Before it roars back.

"I want to be with you," he says. "I want to marry you."

I am so tired I feel like I've been beat up. I hardly have enough energy to be angry, but I muster all I can. "If you do not leave me alone," I say, standing tall, lifting my chin, and looking down at him, "I'm going to scream to bloody heaven and wake the whole neighborhood."

The streets are empty. Most of the crowd from the Dare Not is back home already. I might have to scream really loud for anyone to hear.

"I'm not going to hurt you," he says. "I've changed. I want to be with you. I want to take care of you, and *our* child."

"Go away," I say.

He steps back but doesn't leave.

As I open my mouth to tell him to leave, one more time before I scream, I feel my daughter jostling in my belly. Like she's swimming, somersaulting. Was that a kick? I haven't felt a kick before. I don't know what one feels like.

"Are you OK?" he says.

"I feel my baby moving." I almost said daughter. I know she's going to be a girl, I know it, but I don't want to jinx it, so I keep it to myself.

I'm getting all teary now and I can't let him see me soft like this. I take another step back and he stays where he is. It's dark. I don't think he can see the tears welling in my eyes. The nearest streetlamp is behind me, so my face is in shadow.

My sister in Stockton says I shouldn't freak out if pregnancy makes me crazy, that it's normal to be at the mercy of my hormones. Maybe my hormones are why I feel this tug, like Fenton's hand is inside my chest, reaching for my heart, reaching for my womb.

"I mean it about screaming," I say.

He gets down on one knee, then both of them, on the concrete sidewalk. *Oh God, he's going to propose.* "May I touch your belly, where our baby lives?" He gives me this wide-eyed pleading little-boy look. The streetlight illuminates his eyes and forehead. "For a few seconds. *Please!*"

My stomach flutters again. For a second, I can't breathe, but then I can.

I saw so little of my father growing up, but those times we connected were special and I want that for my daughter. "You promised me you would pay child support starting this month," I say, "so I could cut back on my hours. And if you're serious about taking care of me, you could start by not evicting me."

"That's a business decision, it's not personal. Everything I have is tied up in the harbor project. I haven't been myself. All this stress is driving me to distraction. I wasn't like this when we were together. I was sweet to you. Tell me you remember that."

I do, but that was when he was trying to get into my pants. He didn't stay sweet.

"When I scream," I say, "someone will call the police. That's not going to help you win your council race or build your fancy marina."

"Five seconds is all I ask. To touch your belly. To touch our baby."

I shiver, zip my jacket to my neck.

I want my daughter to have a father more than I want anything for myself. Even if Fenton evicts me, and rubs his hands in glee, I want her to have a father.

"I suppose you'd like to feel a kick in those five seconds," I say. Oh God, those hormones my sister warned me about are doing a number on me. I'm getting all emotional again and I have to fight back my tears.

He gets up from his knees. "Just the *chance* of a kick is enough."

HONEST ABERNATHY

[Pretend pirate, houseboat resident, brother of Fate, boyfriend of Dawn]

15

The Whole World is Watching, Part 1

On Thursday, I wake up five minutes before my alarm, determined not to be a slave to my hedonistic, narcissistic impulses. At least today. I am not as clueless about my flaws as Dawn claims. As Fate claims. As seemingly everyone claims.

But everyone knows who I am, and that's not nothing. It's not the same as being effective, or influential, or significant, or even decent. I know that. But it's not nothing.

After I do my business in my composting toilet, which I continue to be thrilled with, I pull on my pirate threads, including sturdy pants and boots. Today I'm going to act chastened and humble. I can do that, I tell myself, as I grab my trusty spyglass and head out. It's dark, but with enough dawn to see the mountain on Angel Island. It's a three-minute walk to the parking lot.

No police boats on the bay. Not yet. We expected

them yesterday, but they didn't show. Good thing, because we're more prepared today. A pod of pelicans skims the water. The brown pelicans are endangered, but they're coming back now that DDT has been banned. I've learned more than a few useful things from Dawn. The tide is lower than yesterday morning, the sulfur smell strong.

Playing the jester is a longstanding and honorable tradition, and I was a class clown in school so it's no mystery I'm on this path. I don't pretend to be Abbie Hoffman, but I follow in his footsteps. As long as I remember that I can only be a clown because Fate handles the details. I'm part of a community, not a one-man show.

I was out of line Tuesday night and if I want to be a leader of our houseboat community, I can't act like that. I have to control myself.

Through my spyglass, I see a police cruiser on Bridgeway slowing down to turn onto Gate 9 Road. Chief Tin is behind the wheel, and behind her is a bulldozer, a tow truck, and a paddywagon. So they're coming by land today. What are they going to do, bulldoze our docks?

I turn back home and start the phone tree—first Mickey, then Jude, then the others. Fate is outside her cabin, zipping her jacket, heading down the dock to shore. I bet she barely slept.

As I hurry back down the dock, a siren blares out, then a foghorn, whistles, and bells. That's Mickey's department. Wakes up the whole damn town. No sneaking up on us, Chief Tin.

Our parking lot is the size of two tennis courts, side-by-side, and we've parked half the cars to block the dock, the others across the entrance from Bridgeway. The piggies drive over the sidewalk into our lot, and moving slowly and deliberately. They know they haven't surprised us.

In the gauzy light of dawn, Fate and Jude are propping up the life-size cardboard cutouts in front of the dock. They are quiet and industrious amidst the discordant alarms and sirens. My job is to carry the sandbags to weigh down the cutouts. I like to do what men are best at, you know, lifting heavy things, drinking beer, making decisions. The sandbags are upwards of thirty pounds and I carry two at a time from the storage shed to the parking lot.

The cutouts were my idea, but Jude carved the shapes out of cardboard and painted and dressed them. Many have crazy colorful tie-dye t-shirts pulled over the top and a dress or patched jeans stapled to the front. There's even one that looks like a pirate, with a purple cape and a tricorne hat with a skull and crossbones.

I bid good morning to Fate as I plop a sandbag on the base of one of the cutouts. She's carrying a quiver bag over her shoulder, full of thin wooden dowels that look like arrows, and she pulls one out, jabs the pointed bottom into the sandbag and staples the top of the stick to the cardboard. In the center of the cutout's eyes. If it were the pirate, I might take it personally.

"Nice of you to join us this morning," she says. She wants to say more. I can tell by the way she squeezes the stapler.

We set up eleven cutouts within two minutes and I'm all warm now and the fifteen of us humans spread out among the cutouts. Close up, they look like cardboard props, but from a distance, we look like a crowd of people standing up for our rights, a *big* crowd.

Tin confers with Barney and a few other officers. We planned for an eviction raid, not a demolition, but either way, we've created formidable obstacles, and Tin and Barney are going to have to bulldoze us to get anywhere near the dock or the boats.

By now, Johnny Dash is on the scene, running as usual, his colleague with the bulky camera on his shoulder huffing and puffing to keep up. Two other TV news chasers mill around, waiting for something to happen.

I don't know what the police are waiting for, but they give us the time we need to set up our resistance.

Tin steps in front of her cruiser and barks into a megaphone. "We are here to enforce eviction warrants. If you do not disperse, you will be arrested for obstructing police action."

Like she thinks we're standing down after all this work? I stand tall behind one of the cutouts and shout. "We do not recognize your authority. We are in the autonomous zone of *Sausalypso,* connected to the international waters of the Pacific Ocean."

I promised Fate I wouldn't grandstand, but my home is being threatened.

"That the best you can do?" Tin retorts. But with a smile and without the megaphone. She's not a *real* pig.

Mickey, his ponytail tucked under a black top hat, stands on a blue milk crate and launches into his Fenton Felton impression. Above his upper lip is a curly black, handlebar mustache, waxed and pointed, and around his shoulders, a shiny black cape flaps in the breeze. Isaac stands on a smaller crate next to Mickey, hunched over, like Quasimodo, hiccupping one minute, sniffling the next.

"When I become Sausalypso dictator," says Mickey, "I mean city council member, I will use my power for good. My own good." I hear him for a second because the sirens and alarms have gone silent, but then the bulldozer revs its engine and drowns out the rest. Johnny Dash's camera guy kneels in front of Mickey for a closeup.

When Mickey steps off the milk crate, Isaac hands him his trombone and then wiggles his way into his tuba. The brass band marches toward the bulldozer, playing "When the Saints Come Marching In." There's not much room to march, so they pace back and forth and when they turn, two of the tuba bells bang into each other. Between the bulldozer engine and the chanting and squawking of the gulls, I'm not sure I'd recognize the tune, except they've been practicing for the past few days.

Fate said last night that the visuals are more important than the words, as if she thought of it herself, when I've been banging that drum since forever. Mickey stood on that crate and waved his arms wildly and foamed at the mouth more theatrically and confidently than I ever expected, and the band is an inspired gang of wild men with wild hair, and also, you know, trumpets and saxes and tubas. Pretending they can play.

Tin is back with her megaphone. "Attention, you are in violation of City Statute 307A, obstructing the police from carrying out eviction warrants."

Out of the corner of my eye, I see a police boat and a tug coming around the south spur of the dock, and four or five dinghies race into the bay to push them away with their oars. They're coming by land *and* by sea, but we're ready for them.

Johnny Dash's camera guy is capturing all of this. This is inspired theater and we've got more in our bag of tricks. The sun is coming up above the hills now and the sky is crisp and achingly blue. A fourth camera crew arrives and there appear to be a bunch of newspaper reporters as well, scribbling in their notepads. There's also a big crowd of onlookers over by the bulldozer, dozens of people. More than on Tuesday, many clutching rust-colored paper cups of coffee from the Dare Not. The brass band marches up and down Bridgeway calling attention to the raid. As if Mickey's sirens haven't already knocked all the leaves off the trees.

I unroll the Twister mat a few feet in front of Tin and remove my boots. Fate, wearing overalls and rainbow socks, puts one foot on the yellow circle and the other on the blue. This part of the lot is packed dirt instead of gravel so it's easier on our feet.

Brenda stands on the edge of the mat and flicks the spinner. "Right hand on green," she says. Fate and I manage our first moves, but on the second, Fate falls on her knee. No matter. We're playing for the cameras, not to win.

Mickey joins us after the band finishes the only song it knows and on his first turn of the game, he bends over in slow motion. I don't get why he's going so slow, and then I notice the soundtrack.

I hadn't been paying attention the other night when they were talking about this crazy idea, but now I understand.

After we set up the cardboard cutouts, Jude set up a record player and amplifier in the corner of the parking lot and now she's playing John Lennon's "Imagine." When Mickey bent over, she turned the speed of the record from 45 rpm to 33 and now she turns it to 16 and I extend my leg toward the red circle in super slow-motion. Gives the whole scene a surreal edge. Like I'm tripping.

Tin plays right into our hands. "You will be arrested if you do not get out of the road."

Mickey twists around me to put his hand on the yellow circle. "Remember, Honest, I can't get arrested today, so I'll be bowing out of this game any minute now."

Now Jude plays Bob Marley's "Get Up, Stand Up" at 78 rpm, and he sounds like the Chipmunks, but then she slows it down. This is all too good to be true.

Mickey is on probation, or so he told me, and Tin warned us after Tuesday's arrests that second offenders would *not* be released on their own recognizance. We've mapped out our civil disobedience strategy so no one arrested on Tuesday will be arrested again.

"Your Fenton Felton is so good," I whisper in Mickey's ear, "I wonder how much of Mickey is an act."

No one but Mickey can hear me, what with the cacophony of noises in the harbor—chanting protesters, dinghies splashing in the bay, halyards clanking against masts, foghorns from the Golden Gate Bridge, the psychedelic record player.

"That's like, a heavy, like, existential question," he says.

"I've heard that there's a mole in our houseboat collective," I say, "someone infiltrating us because we want to change the world, and I never once thought it could be you. Until this morning. Because you're such a good actor."

"Thank you for the compliment. Now if you'll excuse me, I'm grabbing my trombone and we're firing up the band again."

Barney and another piggie approach me as I contort myself on the Twister mat. "This is our last warning," says Barney.

I was not arrested on Tuesday so today it's my turn. I stand, raise my fist, and shout, *"The whole world is watching. The whole world is watching."* Then I go limp and drop to the ground.

I want my fall to be dramatic, but I also don't want to hurt myself, so it's a deliberate, slow sink, more like a yoga sequence than a collapse. I continue to chant as the piglets grab my arms and start dragging me.

The gravel is sharp, but my pants are thick and they pull me slowly. I don't get why they're going so slow. It's not because of the record player.

Now everyone is chanting, *"The whole world is watching, the whole world is watching,"* and it feels like we're making history and the cameras are capturing it all. I barely notice the jagged gravel.

Johnny Dash stands in front of me now, the back of his boots in my face. "This is Johnny Dash," he says, "*News on the Run,* reporting live from Aquarius Harbor in *Sausa-leeto,* where houseboaters are protesting evictions by lying down in the road and playing Twister. The police are making their first round of arrests, dragging protesters to the paddywagon."

The police lift me to my feet, but then they put me down. I'm dead weight. They're dragging Fate across the gravel too and she's gritting her teeth. I shout toward the camera.

"The revolution is being televised. Join us. Stop the greedy developers, capitalist warmongers, and—"

But Fate interrupts me—reading from an index card. "The Aquarius Houseboat Collective vows to fight these evictions through legal means and peaceful civil disobedience. We seek a resolution through mediation and compromise and good-faith communication."

God, she's so earnest and boring the cameras are going to fall asleep.

"Compromise?" I say. "You mean capitulation."

As a third officer pulls me away from the camera, I see a big crane-like structure on a barge, floating in by the northernmost dock at Aquarius Harbor, and Fenton Felton is on deck rubbing his hands with glee, just like Mickey was a few minutes ago on his milk crate. It's a pile driver. They're bringing a pile driver into Aquarius Harbor. *Shit, shit, shit!*

"*Mayday! Mayday!*" I shout. "They're moving in a pile driver. We have to stop them." But the police handcuff me and shove me into the paddywagon and no one hears me.

The back door of the paddywagon is ajar and I hear Johnny Dash's loud voice above all the horns and sirens. "We're here live with an update from Aquarius Harbor in *Sausa-leeto*. While houseboaters protesting eviction are being dragged away and arrested, developer Fenton Felton has steered in a barge carrying a pile driver, to start construction on a new pier."

A minute later, Johnny is interviewing Fenton Felton, who loves the camera more than I do. I can't hear Johnny's question, but Fenton responds in his usual booming blowhard voice and I catch every word.

"We are driving piles," he says, "for the soon-to-be-completed Heavenly Houseboat Harbor. Victory is mine." And then he unleashes his maniacal laugh.

This time I hear Johnny's question. "But what about the houseboaters who propose a compromise, one that includes affordable housing for the displaced residents of Aquarius Harbor?"

"*Affordable housing?*" Fenton Felton says. "We *are* building affordable housing—affordable for the people we want to live in Sausalito, successful people with money. Not deadbeats on drugs." Another laugh.

All of a sudden, there's a loud boom and the paddy-wagon shakes and at first, I think it's an earthquake, but then it happens again ten seconds later, and the boom is louder and the shaking is worse and my head strikes the wall of the van. I don't understand how they got the pile driver set up so fast.

"We'll be back with another live report at noon," says Johnny Dash. "Now stay tuned for a word from our sponsor—" and here he pauses as if reading from a card—"Heavenly Houseboat Harbor?"

16

The Whole World is Watching, Part 2

I'm on Castro Street in the City, surrounded by a throng of agitated protesters, itching to march down Market Street to City Hall to vent our outrage over the Dan White manslaughter verdict. When I get jostled from behind, I clench my fists and spin around, but it's a smiling pixie man in a pink ballerina outfit and he raises his hands sheepishly. He winks. "Sorry," he mouths.

"Aren't you cold?" I ask.

"My blood is boiling, so no," he says. "My friend has a backpack with a jacket, if I need it, but it doesn't go with my outfit."

He's sweet, but *so* flamboyant. That is *not* who I am.

I'm jumpy as all get out from a punishing day, *in uniform*, arresting protesters in Sausalito, so it's unsettling to be *out of uniform*, a protester myself, in San Francisco, where I once lived and worked. I don't know what I'm doing here except that Justine called me and demanded I come and now I can't find her.

"The Castro is on edge," she said. "You have to be here. Also, I would love to see you."

When she called, two hours ago, I was gritting my way through the paperwork from the evictions and arrests at Aquarius Harbor, and, as dinnertime approached, finally eating the tuna sandwich I packed for lunch. I was exhausted and looking forward to some mindless TV and an early bedtime, but Justine would not take no for an answer.

I wish I'd eaten more. My stomach is growling as I scan the crowd for her. She said to be here at six, and I got here early, but now it's ten after.

Behind me, the chanting grows more impassioned. *"The whole world is watching. The whole world is watching."* Like the houseboaters this morning chanted. Except it feels totally different.

I'm surrounded by gay people, noisy and angry gay people, who are chanting, singing, shouting, crying, and I'm one of them, one of *us,* and I've never been one of us before.

How many people are here? I'm better at counting crowds than I used to be, and this morning at the Aquarius Harbor protest, I counted three hundred, between the houseboaters and the police and the journalists and the onlookers. A huge crowd for a small sliver of land between Bridgeway and the bay, and the cardboard protesters made the crowd seem larger, even though we knew they were cardboard.

Tonight, there are four, five times as many people as this morning, way more than a thousand, maybe twice that, and more protesters stream in from 17th Street, from Upper Market.

Finally, I see Justine, with the pink ballerina man and a pair of heavy, butch-looking women in leather jackets. She wraps me in a hug. "So wonderful to see you, no matter the rage of the moment."

I met Justine thirty years ago when I worked at Sally Cal's cathouse on Nob Hill, and she was a rookie cop, the first black woman hired by the San Francisco Police Department. She wasn't out of the closet then, except as a defiant black woman. Now she works as a lieutenant for BART, the new transbay railroad that links the City and the East Bay, and she's very much out.

We're huddled at the top of the hill, in front of the Twin Peaks Tavern, which Justine explains is owned by a lesbian couple, and is significant because it has floor-to-ceiling windows. "You can see us," she says, "we can see you. No hiding in the closet here. Not the first gay bar, but the first with clear glass windows."

"This is the corner," she says, "where Harvey Milk used to shout, 'Come out, come out, wherever you are.' Before he was murdered."

I'm not out. Not with my foster family. Not in Sausalito, other than with Sally. Not with my police colleagues. Only with a few friends like Justine, who I haven't seen in ages, though I always send her a card on her birthday. But then my sexual orientation is a private matter and I don't have a sex life anyway, so where's the problem?

I catch a whiff of barbecued meat, then it's gone. Also, garbage, car exhaust, pot, and sweat. Lights start flickering on in the windows climbing Twin Peaks.

Dan White's trial has been on the front page of the

Chronicle for the past week and I knew a verdict was imminent, but the confrontations at Aquarius Harbor have been dominating my attention. And draining me. I forgot about the trial until Justine called.

Six months ago, White, a former San Francisco police officer, resigned his county supervisor seat and when he wanted it back, Mayor George Moscone said no. So White climbed through a window at City Hall, shot the mayor, and then shot Supervisor Harvey Milk, the first openly gay elected official in the country.

He faced a double premeditated first-degree murder charge, an open-and-shut case. But the defense brought in psychiatrists contending that he was hopped up on junk food and could not have premeditated anything. Apparently, after the mayor denied his request, the night before the murders, he binged on Twinkies and watched TV.

I never expected a jury would buy that.

We're still trapped by the crowds around us, but protesters ahead of us start marching down Market. "It was never about the Twinkies," Justine says. "The jurors were Dan White's peers and they feared, as he did, that the old guard, the San Francisco they grew up in, run by the Italians, the Irish, and most of all by the sanctimonious Catholic Church, was being replaced by hippies and gays and liberals. Damn right it is! They *had* to convict him— he confessed, after all—but they went for manslaughter, because they understood, maybe sympathized. They used the Twinkies as an excuse. Have I told you how wonderful it is to see you? It's been too long. I was afraid you wouldn't make it."

"There is nowhere I'd rather be," I say, "and no one I'd rather be here with." I surprise myself with the forthrightness of my statement, but the righteousness of being here, protesting a grave injustice, is visceral. Even though it's cold and foggy and the wind cuts through my three layers. When was the last time *anyone* told me how wonderful it is to see me?

Darkness hovers, and we finally ease into the march, filling Market Street curb to curb, for five, six blocks, down to the Safeway sign. There are so many of us, we move at the pace of snails. It's a traffic jam of people. Lots of starting and stopping. A phalanx of police officers stand erect at the next intersection, their faces tight and tense. I'm grateful I'm not one of them. The street vibrates under our stomping feet.

A police officer's job is to keep their distance from all these intense emotions. That was my job this morning. But not tonight. Squelching my feelings is no way to live. Not now. I don't know anyone here but Justine, but I feel engaged, enraged, part of a movement, part of a community.

Above the crowd are rainbow flags and hand-scrawled signs. "Avenge Harvey Milk." "A travesty of justice." "Twinkies my ass."

I've never taken part in a demonstration, not ever. I've only been on the other side. Even when I was an outlaw, working for Sally Cal on Nob Hill, I was a sheriff of sorts—a peacekeeper, at the least.

I'm tired and wired, and the cacophony is overwhelming, yet I'm caught up in my own thoughts. About my past in the city, about my hesitance accepting my sexuality, about my unlikely escape to the relative quiet of Sausalito. Here, it's too noisy for conversation, almost too noisy for thinking.

When I lived at Sally's, such a long time ago, I rarely

passed through the Castro, which back then was a sleepy working-class neighborhood full of Scandinavians and Irish and wasn't even called the Castro. This was long before it became a gay enclave, long before I became a police officer, long before I realized men didn't interest me.

I keep chanting as we march, but I'm operating on two channels, one sharing the pain and fury of my community, which feels clean and sharp, the other percolating on who I am, how I got here, and what a long, strange trip it's been. That feels uncomfortable.

Again, we chant, *"The whole world is watching, the whole world is watching."* Then, *"No justice, no peace."* There's more anger, more fist shaking, more out-of-control emotions than this morning. Two men climb on the roof of a bus and pull down the pole that connects it to the overhead electric wires. We walk around the marooned bus. The passengers exit. Several join the march.

We're riding the rapids of a swollen river, and every block another stream of protesters swells the surge.

Above the chants I hear honking horns. We're blocking traffic. On Dolores, a driver climbs out of his car and wags his middle fingers at us, his face contorted in rage.

My shoulders clench, because I don't want people to hate me. But the man is a hundred feet away and he doesn't see me or know me.

And he may not hate us for being gay. We're in his way and maybe he's picking up his kid from daycare. Someone he loves is expecting him.

We cross Van Ness, turn left on Polk, connect with another river of protesters flowing in from South of Market. The wind whips through the canyon of tall towers and I pull my jacket tighter. Our chants echo off the buildings.

We veer right on Fell, at the corner of City Hall, and I follow a pack of men who grab hold of the hood of an empty police car and rock it up and down.

The man in the pink ballerina outfit, who winked at me on Castro Street, climbs onto the hood of the car. He reaches out his arm, pulls me up on the hood with him. Then the roof. "Avenge Harvey Milk," he chants. "Avenge Harvey Milk," I chant.

Below us, a man in a hooded sweatshirt, his face covered by a mask, pulls a brick from his pack and smashes the side window of the car. It shatters, doesn't break. He whacks the window again. Now it breaks.

I should leave. This is not me. I'm not the kind of person who gets caught up in the craziness of the moment.

I climb down from the roof of the car to the hood, but the whooping men rock the car again and I lose my balance and fall. Into the arms of a surprised young man with bright red hair. He sets me on the ground, and immediately a police officer yanks me away, and hand-cuffs me to a lamppost.

I explain I'm a police officer in Sausalito, the chief of police, that I've never been arrested before, that I've never even marched in a demonstration before, that I don't condone vandalism, but he shoulders his way back into the crowd and arrests the ballerina and I'm left talking to myself. Now there's a whoosh of flame and the police car is burning.

First, I'm afraid the car will blow up and engulf us in flames and I try, in vain, to free myself from the cuffs. Another officer sprays the car with a fire extinguisher, and the flames die down, and I realize I'm not going to die from a car explosion, only from humiliation and shame. And I'm going to lose my job, and no one will ever hire me again.

Then it starts raining, and I am soaked until I can't possibly get any wetter.

17

The First Storm of the Season

My raincoat is waterproof, or so the tag says, as are the rubber boots that reach to my knees, but I'm wet and cold within minutes of climbing from the tugboat to the barge.

I wish I were still warm and toasty in the tug's dry cabin instead of on this suicide mission with my lunatic brother.

The first rainstorm of the season is a doozy, and the wind whips rain into my face, into the sleeves of my raincoat, into my boots. I feel drips of water roll down my chest and under my shirt, even though I zipped the raincoat up to my chin.

Honest hands me a long paddle and I plant my feet far apart to stand steady in the choppy surf. He's steering and I'm supposed to be the lookout, plus push us away from any boats we get too close to.

"This is a frigging disaster," I shout. We're steering a barge larger than the ferry we live on, and it's a dark and stormy night, just like in the movies, and we've never done anything like this before, so this is only the most nerve-racking night of my life.

I'm at the bow on the port side and Honest is starboard at the stern. I pivot my right foot and turn towards him. My headlamp is bright, but all it illuminates are blurry raindrops. I can barely make out Honest's silhouette and the reflection of his yellow rain slicker. He plants his feet farther apart than mine, like he's holding a yoga pose.

"If we don't drown in this frigging rain, we'll get arrested again," I add, though I don't think he hears me. "They'll throw the book at us for committing a crime while out on bail. We'll be in jail for years. We are committed to *nonviolence*. This is vandalism—"

He interrupts. "We're not *vandalizing* the pile driver, Fate, we're *getting in its way.*" I guess he *can* hear. "There's a difference. They've driven in ten piles already. And vandalism is not violence. Fenton Felton outwitted us this morning, but this is going to be as huge as the Boston Tea Party. Come on, I need more help steering."

"*The Boston Tea Party?* Give me a break. We're going to lose all the sympathy and support we've worked so hard for."

Honest taps my shoulder with his paddle. "But you said, and I quote: 'Fenton Felton is kicking us out of our homes, and we must oppose him with every fiber of our being.'"

"And therefore," I say, "I'm happy to join you on this dangerous misadventure? Even if we don't get caught, they'll be in no mood to compromise."

"Fenton Felton outfoxed us today, with all those distractions to sneak in his pile driver. He's a crafty bugger and we underestimate him at our peril. We have to strike back, retake the momentum. We cannot let him build his new dock."

I don't disagree. But that doesn't justify what we're doing.

"If you're so upset about this," he adds, "why are you here?"

"Because I sweat the details. Because you'd be more reckless if I weren't here. Because who else could you get to help? Mickey?" I spit out a mirthless laugh. Beyond all logic, I believe that if I do this for Honest that he'll support me on my dock plan. It's one delusion after another. "How many times have I bailed you out?"

"It's good to have a purpose in life," he says.

It's so maddening how he brushes off everything I say. The slightest criticism and I get defensive and I'm up all night replaying it from a thousand angles, every one of them more damning than the one that came before. I try so hard and he doesn't try at all. It's like he's walking through an orchard and he doesn't even have to pick the fruits. They fall into his hands.

The riggings of the sailboats at Gate 10 clatter in the wind. Lights flicker in the hills. We're weaving slowly between the straight line of sailboats on our right and the tangled knot of houseboats on our left, spread out like a spider web at Aquarius Harbor. Keeping our course in a straight line is next to impossible.

Mickey, piloting the tug, pushes the barge from behind, ever so slowly, so all we need to do is steer, but the rain pelts me in the face and my arms ache from holding the heavy paddle steady.

At least our landmark, Jude's colorful A-frame with the bright red light in the window, is easy to see from a distance. The passage widens now.

It's not good for me to get so angry with Honest. He's never going to change because of anything I say.

After Mom and Dad died, I had it rougher, no doubt about that, but those first few years, he was hurting too. He was smart enough to sail through College of Marin, but when he got to Berkeley, he was surrounded by kids who came from well-off families and had good study habits. Not to mention parents who were still alive. Somehow, he graduated, and got into law school, and by then, I'd started college and he was no longer my legal guardian. He had no excuse for flunking out other than his lack of discipline. Of course, I dropped out too, so who am I to talk?

He doesn't believe in therapy, so he's never gotten any help, and the little I got didn't make a dent. He should have made me keep going, but I was stubborn and wouldn't have listened no matter how much he nagged.

We enter another narrow passage, barely wider than our barge, and we're about to run right into our own ferryboat, but I lean forward with my paddle and push us away. Close call.

When we pass Jude's place, I hear snatches of classical music above the storm. She must have the volume way up or a window open. The passage gets wider and Honest steers us toward the pile driver. I see its murky outline. I exhale, not realizing I've been holding my breath. We threaded the needle and didn't ram any houseboats. A miracle.

Now we veer left and I stop our slow float with the paddle. "We're here." I slip a loose rolling hitch over the post at the end of the G dock.

The rain has quieted to a drizzle. Everything's quieter now that we're about to make a racket. I'm still wet and cold and miserable, but my arm is no longer aching.

"Look," I say, "you convinced me to help you with this *illegal* undertaking. I want *you* to help *me*, not *undermine* me. For once. *Can* you do that?"

He doesn't answer. This is nuts, attempting a serious conversation with an unserious person, with the wind and rain and roar of waves rocking boats. I shout at the top of my lungs.

"I need you to support me on this compromise plan, on the dock design I drafted."

"No, no, no," he says. "We can't give ground unless our backs are against the wall."

"Our backs *are* against the wall," I scream.

Honest removes his pack and takes out the chain saw. "You're the best," he says. "You put up with me. You keep me out of trouble. Now I'm going to fire up this sucker."

There's a burst of static as he turns on his walkie-talkie. "Back out, Mickey. Thank you kindly." The sound of the tug engine recedes as it backs out the channel. "I wish I could see their faces in the morning," he says.

"You'll be sleeping off a bender," I say. "I'm sure you remember *that* part of the plan. You're going to the Dare Not after this to get plastered and make a scene so everyone remembers you."

"I can already taste the beer."

He powers up the chainsaw and it's louder than the storm. Everyone will hear it.

I hear a voice from the darkness. "What are you doing?" It's a man's voice. "Who are you?"

Is it a guard? I can't see him. Where is he? He's on Honest's side of the barge, but near the front.

"Doing emergency repairs," I say, turning toward the voice. My headlamp catches him full in the face. He approaches me with a flashlight in one hand and a gun in the other. *Oh my God.* Now we're getting arrested or shot.

The guard is private security, not police. I don't recognize him. His boots are fluorescent orange.

"At night?" he says. "In a storm? A woman?"

"Women are perfectly capable of emergency repairs," I answer.

He turns his flashlight and gun on Honest. *Oh shit!* I tighten my grip on my paddle and shove the guard off the barge into the bay. He yelps before he splashes.

Oh my God, what did I do? Honest turns off the saw. "What if he can't swim?" I say.

"It's three feet deep," Honest says. "He won't drown. One more hole." He fires up the chainsaw again. "Hey, you did good."

Water sploshes through Honest's holes and the barge starts tilting, and I slide backward and flail my arms. There's nothing to hold onto, but Honest grabs me.

"Let's blow this joint," he says. "This baby is sinking fast."

"Wait, wait," I say. "Put your socks on. Over your boots. So the tread won't show in the mud. Here, I brought an extra pair." I put mine on in the tug.

The guard climbs back onto the barge. "No time," Honest says, hurling his paddle at the guard and knocking him back into the bay.

At least no one will find *my* footprints.

MICKEY MACGILLICUDDY
[Flaky burnout, houseboat resident]

18

Tune In, Turn On, Drop Out

When I get home from piloting the tugboat through the storm, I change into dry clothes, slip on my comfy slippers, and grab my trombone. I'm a mediocre musician, and the trombone is an impossible instrument, but I feel so jittery and blowing into the cup and moving the slide back and forth soothes me.

Honest assured me that if I could drive a car, I could drive a tugboat, but that was a lie. He had to take the wheel several times when I was going off course, and it's a miracle I steered that barge through that narrow passageway in the storm and got the tug back to its berth.

My feet are bouncing up and down like I've been main-lining coffee. I'm tempted to take a walk, but the storm has picked up again. The raindrops on my tin roof sound like gunfire. The choppy water makes my stomach churn.

I pour another slug of scotch into my metal cup. My

third. I better slow down. At least I'm not drinking from the bottle. There's a knock on my door.

"It's Fate. Can I come in?"

I open the door. "Welcome." I pull her inside and slam the door behind her. She's got her boots and slicker on.

I'm glad to see her. She's got to be as wired as I am.

"I heard you playing," she says. "I thought you were going to get drunk with Honest."

"You're like, sopping wet," I say. "You know, like, Honest does not need my help to get drunk."

"Only my jacket is wet," she says. "I changed when I got home. You know you don't have to put on your space case act for me. I know you're not the flaky burnout you pretend to be."

I panic for a second, but she can't possibly know anything about me. I hang her wet slicker on a peg.

"Like, man, I dig what you're saying."

"Exactly," she says.

I offer her my chair, my only chair, and give her a blanket. I sit on a pillow on the floor, with my back against my pantry cabinet.

"A drink?" She told me she's not much of a drinker anymore, but still.

"Please."

I pour one for her and another for myself. A small one.

"I thought you were more into weed," she says.

"There's nothing like distilled spirits to take off the edge." Rain shakes the roof. "How did it go?"

"We did it," she says. "We'll see better in the day-light, but the barge is sunk, sticking out of the water at like a 20-degree angle."

"Yeah, I took a peek with my headlamp. Fenton Felton is not going to be happy."

"It will not be easy to unsink," she says. "We had to run away from a guard who tried to stop us, and I pushed him in the water. Fenton Felton is going to lose a few days, maybe longer, but I'm sure he'll be on Chief Tin's ass about arresting whoever did this, and…"

She trails off and then gulps down the rest of her drink.

"And?" I ask.

"I want to kill my brother."

"What a surprise."

I finish my drink, reach for the bottle, then stop. The scotch is harsh, not smooth. When I was undercover with the drug gang, I drank expensive scotch enough times that now I notice the difference.

I get up and fill my cup with water. "I never drove a tugboat before tonight," I say. "It's harder than it appears. And I was in the fucking Navy."

Fate holds out her glass for more. There's not much left in the bottle, so I pour it all in her glass. "While you were nudging us through that channel," she says, "and we were using our paddles to keep us from bumping into anything, I had this heart-to-heart with Honest about how I needed him to help me because of how much *I've* helped *him*. I asked him to help with the compromise plan, the one I showed you.

"He acted like he didn't hear me, and it *was* windy and raining, and then it turns out he did hear me, and he said 'no, not until our backs are up against the wall,' and I said they are, and then he distracted me by praising me for putting up with him."

She takes a deep breath and talks rapidly until she has to breathe again.

"He drives me batty. He acts like my patience has no

limit, that he can take me for granted forever."

I nod my head and say "uh huh" every so often and she's prattling away double-time, from her troubles with Honest to her memory issues to her fear of getting caught for sinking the barge to where she'll live if she gets evicted. She speaks in long run-on sentences with no pauses.

Tomorrow, I report to Davis, my case officer, and he'll be happy to hear about the barge-sinking operation, especially if the houseboaters are blamed. He would have loved the molly explosion in the police sedan a lot more, but there's no need for him to know that was even a consideration. This morning, there was no opportunity to instigate violence, what with the cardboard cutouts and playing Twister and standing on a milk crate performing my Fenton Felton imitation. Besides, Fate has been watching me closely because of almost throwing the molly. She doesn't trust me.

There will certainly be an investigation of the barge sinking, and if the police look into me, they'll find out soon enough that Mickey Macgillicuddy does not really exist.

"This isn't just about me," Fate says. "What about you? Where will you go? Where will Brenda go? She's going to have a baby and I know she doesn't want to move back with her mother and—"

She stops. "I've been blathering since I got here and it's time for me to stop talking and to listen." She holds up her empty glass.

I finish my drink of water. "You're sure you want more? You're not used to drinking, are you?"

"I drank plenty when I was a teenager," she says. "Just a wee bit more. It's calming me down."

I stand on my toes and reach the top shelf for a fifth

of vodka. It's close to empty. I pour her one finger.

"You keep asking about me," she says, "but I don't know anything about you. You're a man of mystery."

"I'm not big on talking about myself," I say. "You know, Honest said to me that you *exaggerate* your forgetfulness. And he's got this other theory that you forget when you're angry."

"That's ridiculous," she says. "I was angrier than I ever was with my mother the day of the crash. And I remember that as if it were yesterday. And you're changing the subject. I would have never guessed you were an actor or a musician, or that you have a serious side."

"It's better that way," I say. "No one expects anything from me. That simplifies my life."

"I don't need your life story," she says. "Just a little bit, like where were you before here?"

The rain has let up. I stand and open the window wider.

"Where were you born?" she says. "Where did you come from?"

"Born in Rockford, Illinois, and you know the mantra—tune in, turn on, drop out. I came out west, ended up in the Haight, had some mishaps, escaped here. The end, by Mickey Macgillicuddy. Don't know my next chapter."

"You don't have a job. How do you survive?"

"SSI. Savings from when I had a job."

"What kind of job did you have? And where did you learn how to make a Molotov cocktail?"

"Enough with the questions," I say. "I'm a private man. I live in the present. I told you I was in the Navy. Long ago. That's where I learned acting. We had Mess Night, where we performed silly skits about the brass, about our ridiculous rules. All in fun. We got laughs, but

I don't know if we had any talent. We were hams. We were a break from the routine, and occasionally, we were provocative."

That satisfies her. She gets up and grabs the vodka and empties it in her glass. Barely a sip left. No more bottles on my shelf. "You know, earlier, on the barge, before Honest fired up the chain saw," she says, "I stood up for myself and asked for what I wanted, for Honest to back my compromise plan, even though I didn't think he could hear me. I've been replaying that conversation ever since and I don't know if it was all in my head or I said it out loud."

She looks up at me and waits until we make eye contact. Then she looks down.

"Anyway," she says. "I think it's good for me to ask for what I want."

I swallow the water I've been holding in my mouth.

"What I mean is," she says, "what if what I want is to be more *friendly* with you?"

I open the kitchen window a few inches. The air that rushes in is fresh and clean. The rain has turned to a drizzle.

"I'm flattered," I say.

"But?" she says. "There's a but coming, I can tell."

My legs aren't bouncing anymore, and I'm no longer obsessing about driving the tugboat, but now I'm afraid I'm going to hurt Fate and I don't know how to avoid it. I certainly can't tell her the truth.

Despite her veneer of toughness, she's too innocent, too young, too troubled. I like her and admire her, and she's attractive in a quiet and unshowy way.

Two assignments ago, in Sacramento, I briefly got involved with an amazing woman, and she never knew who I was or what I was doing, and then I disappeared. I'm not going to do that again. Even though it's *allowed,* if it serves a good purpose, like keeping my cover.

She's waiting for me to say more, but I know that if I wait long enough, she'll fill the silence.

I don't have to wait long. "It doesn't have to be meaningful," she says. "I mean, I don't expect any commitment. You're kind, and that's not something you can fake."

"Oh, I think it is," I say.

19

A Punishment That Fits the Crime

After my night in jail, I take a cab home and arrive as the sun rises. I have visions of a shower and a nap, but the phone rings as soon as I open my front door. My head hurts. My back is sore. I'm tempted not to answer it, but I do. Of course, I do.

I slept an hour in the cell, maybe two. I alternated between berating myself for my dreadful judgment and giving myself pep talks about how today I'm going to stand up unflinchingly and take responsibility for my actions. With humility and honesty.

Maypole, the city manager's assistant, is on the line, and he's all riled up.

I chide him for calling me at home, but he's already saying how sorry he is. I cut him off, mid-apology, not hiding my irritation. "What is it?"

I fill my coffee carafe with water, but I can't reach

the coffeemaker, even with my long curly phone cord stretched tight.

"It's Fenton Felton," he says. "Mad as a hornet. As a swarm of hornets."

I feel a wave of relief wash over me. Familiar territory. Fenton Felton is furious. What else is new? I happen to be furious with him, too, for using me to run interference for his pile driver. "Call the station. Tell him to wait until business hours. I'm not an all-night diner. Hold on one second."

I set down the phone, empty the carafe of water into the coffeemaker, and scoop six tablespoons of ground coffee into the filter. It takes fifteen seconds, not one, but close enough.

I get back on the phone. "Mayor Sally told me to call you," Maypole says. "Fenton Felton claims the house-boaters sank a barge last night, disabling his pile driver and—"

"Claims?" I hear Fenton Felton's scream through the phone as if he's in my kitchen. "I have witnesses." I smell my coffee brewing, and inhale deeply.

"Two of your officers are at the scene investigating," Maypole says. "But it's important that you—"

"That I get my ass to the station and bear the wrath of Fenton Felton."

"Yes, ma'am. That's right. And—"

"And he's calling for my resignation if I don't."

"You're a mind reader. Sally says to come to her office first, please—"

"I'll be there. After I shower."

As I walk the four blocks downhill to City Hall, in my crisp olive dress uniform, I drink the scalding coffee from my thermos, spiked with more sugar than usual.

My hair is still damp, and I hold my hat in my hand and the warm sun does its work. The sky is pink and the air smells clean and earthy after the first rain of the season. I adjust my gait to avoid stepping on a worm. I lust for sleep, but that will have to wait.

Sausalito City Hall sits on a steep hillside above a park, across the street from the police station. The mayor's office is on the top floor of five, but from the parking lot at the top of the hill, it looks like a one-story building. The brick pathway leading to the front door, which is in the shade, is slippery with damp moss.

I take a deep breath. Fenton Felton is going to be breathing fire when I arrive and demanding immediate attention.

He's not there when I enter Sally's office, and the tightness in my neck eases. Her TV is on and there's Johnny Dash on the screen, standing in front of the march down Market Street last night. I had no idea he was there.

Sally sits behind her desk rubbing her forehead. "There's something I have to tell you," I say, pointing at the TV screen. "I was there last night, in the City, protesting the Dan White manslaughter verdict, and I was arrested for malicious mischief to a police vehicle and spent the night in a cell. Also, I'm a lesbian."

Sally looks me up and down and gives me a half smile. "What you do in your bedroom is not my concern," she says. "As for your arrest, that—"

And then there I am, on the screen. I turn up the volume. The camera zooms in on me handcuffed to the light post.

"Among those protesters arrested tonight is Sausalito Police Chief Tin Holland," says Johnny Dash. "Earlier in the day, she was arresting protesters at Aquarius Harbor in Sausalito, as they attempted to thwart the police from carrying out eviction orders."

A commercial for Bufferin comes on. I turn off the TV. "I will resign if you need me to," I say. I take another sip from my thermos. Too much sugar.

Sally shakes her head. "You are one lucky woman. You can't *possibly* resign because I have a job for you, the perfect 'punishment' for your, um, alleged crime. Johnny Dash and plenty of other reporters are headed to Sausalito as we speak to report on the sinking of the barge last night—Fenton Felton's flunky has been working the phones since daybreak—and they'll be coming *here* at nine for a press conference where *you* will announce our *peace plan* to address the civil war that has broken out here in our not-so-sleepy small town."

"Peace plan?"

"You asked for this," Sally says. "Community justice, mediation, alternative policing, remember? Now's your chance."

"Throwing me to the wolves, are you?"

"Your words," she says.

I obsessed all last night about whether I need—or want—to come out publicly as a lesbian. Taking part in a protest with thousands of gays doesn't *necessarily* mean I'm gay, though for some people it does and besides it's something I should do even if I don't have to. Especially after last night.

But now I have more urgent matters to attend to—coming up with a peace plan in an hour.

When I open the door to leave, Fenton Felton barges in, wearing his usual penguin outfit, top hat and all. "Can't talk now," I say, passing him, "but we'll be hosting a press conference in an hour about your pile driver."

He follows me, but I duck into the assessor's office, hide behind a wall of file cabinets, then escape via a back door, grabbing a pad of paper and a pen from an empty desk on the way out.

Instead of heading across the street to my office, I head down the stairs all the way to the City Hall basement and set up shop in the boiler room. There's no one here. I grab a folding chair and set up an impromptu office behind a tall metal storage locker.

At ten before nine, I sneak over to my office at the station to retrieve some important documents, then make my way back to City Hall without being spotted.

I wait inside the stairwell and peek out a window. I count four camera crews out front, hovering around the podium that Maypole set up on the plaza above the park. There are also dozens of spectators—sitting on the steps, on benches, spreading out blankets on the front lawn, as if they're attending a concert. There's Honest Abernathy sitting on a swing in the playground, his curly red hair under a black bandana. He holds a cup of coffee with both hands. I push open the exit door and shield my eyes from the bright sun.

Johnny Dash jogs across the plaza and stops in front of the podium.

"This is Johnny Dash, *News on the Run,* live at Sausalito City Hall, where the mayor and chief of police are about to address the twin scandals that have *rocked* this bucolic bayside enclave. This morning, at Aquarius Harbor, where houseboat protesters have been resisting eviction orders with street theater and civil disobedience, pile driver operators arrived at work to find a wooden barge had been towed into the cove overnight and sunk, blocking the construction crew from building piers for developer Fenton Felton's controversial Heavenly Houseboat Harbor. Also, we learned that Police Chief Tin Holland, the woman responsible for enforcing the eviction orders and arresting protesters at Aquarius Harbor, was herself arrested last night in San Francisco for vandalizing a police car. Now here's Mayor Sally Cal stepping to the podium."

When I get to Mayor Sally's side, she grips my arm tightly and adjusts the microphone. She whispers in my ear. "I *am* throwing you to the wolves. Work your magic."

She introduces me with one short sentence, steps back, and nudges me forward. I'm prepared to take charge, but I was expecting a more supportive introduction. Maybe this is part of my punishment.

"Good morning," I say. "I'm Police Chief Tin Holland and we are heartened to see so many of you taking an interest in city affairs."

I glance at Fenton Felton, who's right in front, and meet his eyes. There's no warmth in them. I stare him down until he averts his gaze.

"Tomorrow, Saturday," I say, "at nine in the morning, in the Edgewater Room at City Hall, we will convene a community justice meeting to address this ongoing dispute at Aquarius Harbor. We will work *together* to come to a peaceful resolution."

I've written another page of notes about the sunken barge, but it's gobbledygook, and the Saturday meeting is news enough. I say I have five minutes for questions. I would rather not answer questions, but I don't want to appear afraid.

"What about the vandals who sank the barge?" Johnny Dash asks.

"The police are investigating at Aquarius Harbor at this very moment."

Another newscaster asks about my arrest. I'm relieved. Over the past hour, my top priority was supposed to be this community justice meeting tomorrow, but I haven't been able to stop thinking about the questions I know are coming—about me.

Before I answer, I scan the crowd. I recognize a bunch of people from yesterday morning at Aquarius Harbor, others from the city council debate at the Dare Not on Wednesday. What a wild week—it seems like the TV cameras have been following me wherever I go. There's a gaggle of houseboaters by the pillar at the edge of the playground. Fate and Brenda are sitting at a picnic table eating sandwiches, and that short artist woman who painted the cardboard characters is by the swings with her hubby and children. I forget her name, but I remember she told me she could not get arrested because of her kids.

"As you know if you follow the news," I say, "yesterday, a former San Francisco police officer who killed two well-loved politicians was sentenced to manslaughter instead of first-degree murder, even though he climbed through a window at City Hall, with a gun, to avoid the metal detector. There comes a time when even a mild-mannered, law-abiding police chief has to take to the streets.

"I joined the protest march in the Castro last night, a march organized by the gay community in San Francisco. I am a gay person. I have been private about my sexual orientation because I don't believe it's relevant to my role as a police chief. Now you all know and there's part of me that is relieved that now I am out publicly.

"I was arrested last night for standing on the hood of a police car. I got intoxicated by the righteousness of the cause. This morning, I was released on my own recognizance.

"If I am convicted of a crime, it will most likely be a misdemeanor. I did not hurt anyone or cause any damage.

"A misdemeanor is a less serious charge than, say, drunk driving, and I mention drunk driving *because,* on March 17, 1976, a police chief in a nearby town was pulled over for drunk driving, and no charges were filed. And a year later, on August 2, 1977, the same offense, a different chief. Again, no charges. You can look this up in the I-J archives at the library.

"This morning is still young, and I have already heard multiple calls for my resignation, whether because I was arrested at the protest, or because I'm a homosexual, I don't know and it doesn't matter. I have offered my resignation to the mayor and she has rejected it. Instead, she has assigned me to host this community justice meeting tomorrow morning at nine, here at City Hall. You, the community, are invited.

"We will share details later today. Thank you for your attention."

Back inside, Sally elbows me in the ribs. "If I were a reporter," she says, "I'd be out of here like a bat out of hell, chasing down those drunk-driving police chiefs. Have you been holding that dirt in your back pocket, waiting for the right moment?"

"My file cabinet," I say, "not my pocket. I learned a few things watching *you* operate, back in the day. But what if everyone who needs to be here tomorrow isn't here?"

"What worries me more," Sally says, "is that everyone shows. Primed for battle."

FENTON FELTON

[Greedy developer, father of Dawn, ex-husband of Alice]

20

One Humiliation After Another

I step into the phone booth across from the entrance to the yacht dock, one pocket with my few remaining dimes, the other with a pint of scotch. All afternoon I've been calling the local movers and shakers, eighteen of them, to make sure they show up at City Hall tomorrow and support my Heavenly Houseboat project. If we can't stop the meeting, we have to dominate it.

Way too many of them are hesitant. They're not moving or shaking for me, they're cowering. *The spineless bastards.*

I'm still fuming about the sunken barge. Everyone I call to unsink it wants cash up front, which I don't have, and says it could take days or even weeks, which I also don't have.

I don't know who I'm more furious with—the depraved hippies who sank the barge or Chief Tin, who, instead of throwing the perpetrators in jail, is planning this stupid-ass community meeting, which will be a waste of my precious time.

I'm also pissed at Hic—it was his lame-brain idea to bring in the pile driver *before* completing the evictions. He needs to fix this. But he won't answer his damn phone or open his front door. *What a coward!*

It's warm tonight, and the sky over Richardson Bay is red and orange, as if that matters.

I fortify myself with a few slugs of scotch and resume my calls. All day, I've been trying to reach Cotton Booth, the chamber of commerce president and my most important ally, but the phone just rings and rings.

Finally, I get through, but he's as weaselly as everyone else. "Wait til this blows over," he says. "Throwing these poor kids out of their homes is not great PR."

"Poor kids?" I snarl. "They're drug dealers, criminals, and spoiled, lazy shits, a cancer on our community. We're doing the citizens of Sausalito a favor by evicting them."

The last time I talked with him, Booth had my back, and I've been counting on his continued support.

"I'll be there," he says, his tone softer, but still cool. "I'll listen to what everyone has to say. Mind you, I'll make fewer enemies if I stay out of the fray."

Goddamn him. The richest man in town and he's afraid to make enemies.

"You want to get rid of the houseboaters," he says, "give them something they want."

I take another gulp from my bottle. Better slow down. I've drunk half the pint already.

I start to say, "I don't have anything to give," but I don't want Booth to know that. For the same reason I'm not telling him I'm sleeping on my yacht. Sure, it's seventy feet long and my marina is the opposite of the shantytown at Aquarius Harbor, but still, it doesn't look good. Better that everyone thinks I'm still bunking at that luxury hotel in Tiburon.

I'd sell the damn yacht if it weren't already hocked to the gills. If I had somewhere else to sleep. When did everything start going down the tubes?

It's been a roller-coaster week, what with two half-ass eviction raids by our hapless police chief and fleeing my office *and* my hotel because of cash flow issues. I can't even buy a cup of coffee without cold hard cash. Not to mention that I humiliated myself in front of Brenda and she threatened to scream bloody murder if I didn't leave her alone. She could save me, allow me to provide for her, if she didn't have so much damn pride. If only she hadn't gotten herself mixed up with those damn squatters. Like my own daughter, she's been conned by that hippie cult.

The only bright spot of the week was Wednesday when Alice and I had a knock-down, drag-out battle of wits and bantered like the good old days. Sneaking in the pile driver was exhilarating too, until the damn hippies sunk that barge, but arguing with Alice was better.

I miss her. I wish I didn't, but I do.

When I have no more dimes and no more scotch, I climb in my car to see Alice.

Once I start the engine, however, I head in the opposite direction, into the City to see Dawn. My daughter, who called me an asshole in front of everyone on the waterfront Tuesday morning. In front of the TV cameras, too, though, as far as I know, that didn't make it on the air.

I'll give her a chance to apologize, and if she won't, I'll warn her, again, about consorting with a criminal, a criminal who's destroying *my* livelihood. Her pirate sank that barge and I won't rest until he's behind bars.

Yesterday, she called to tell me she moved to an apartment in the Outer Sunset. She wouldn't give me her phone number—she claimed she didn't have one yet—but she shared her address. Presumably so I know where to send the checks, though there aren't going to be any more of those until my fortunes change. She's not that different than when she was fifteen. "You treat me like a baby," she used to say. "I'm a grownup. I can make my own decisions. I need twenty dollars."

Her apartment is an in-law unit, above a garage, in a canary-yellow stucco row house on Quintara Street, a mile from Ocean Beach. I knock three times. I see lights inside. She's home.

Finally, she answers.

"What do you want?" she says. Not a great start. She hides behind the door.

"I want to see you. Isn't that reason enough?"

"You're drunk," she says.

"Maybe you can make me coffee," I say.

She opens the door and points me to an overstuffed sofa with a blue sheet over it. "Sit there," she says, and then returns with a glass of water. "Do you want sugar or milk in your coffee?"

"Tonight, both."

Her apartment smells of salsa and beer, though she doesn't offer me any food. She hasn't kicked me out, and maybe that's because she doesn't want me to drive, and that's a fine enough reason, but I'm hoping, just maybe, she'll listen to me for once.

I'm going to forget the apology—she's got her defiance cranked up high tonight, so instead, I'm going to ask for her help getting the new harbor built.

Outside her living room window is a streetlight that looks like it's growing out of a bay tree. Cardboard boxes are neatly stacked against the wall, and she's tacked up posters on either side of the window—"Save Mono Lake" and "Women Hold Up Half the Sky." I'm paying for her to live in this apartment, and I can't even afford one for myself.

My father didn't need to beg *me* to help the family business. I wanted in before I was out of diapers. He struck it rich building homes in the North Bay and drove Cadillacs and Jaguars. But he gambled more than he could afford to lose and ended up bankrupt. He took out the biggest loan possible on his properties, and poured it all into Marincello, a proposed city of thirty thousand in the Marin Headlands over the ridge from Sausalito.

But the tree-huggers and the not-in-my-backyarders prevailed. The developers never developed. I lost my stake too, but it wasn't that much and I recovered. My father did not, and he drank himself to an early grave.

I will *never* be a failure like he was, I promise that to myself. Which is why I should lay off the scotch.

Dawn returns to the living room with two mugs of coffee, and hands one to me.

I blow on the coffee and take a small, scalding sip.

"I came here," I say, "to ask *you*, on bended knee, to help *me* run my business. This is a great opportunity for you. You love a challenge."

She does not seem surprised, though I am. I don't actually kneel, because I'm sitting deep in the couch, both hands clutching a hot, sweet coffee.

But I bow my head.

For years, I've asked her to join the family business, but then I stopped asking because she kept saying no and

I didn't want to give her that power anymore. The power to humiliate me.

I'm giving it to her now.

She hasn't said no yet.

"I am awed by your smarts and competence," I say. "I need you. I'll be different. I will seek your council. I need you, *need*, do you hear that? To fix what's broken?"

"What about Hic? I thought—"

"Hic is part of what's broken."

"You don't care that you're evicting Brenda," she says, "you, the father of her baby-to-be? Because I care a great deal about that, and you're evicting Honest too. No matter that my relationship with him is complicated."

"You moved here to get farther away from him."

"It's closer to school."

She doesn't say farther from me, and that makes me feel better. I take another sip, but the coffee is still too hot. I clutch the mug with both hands as if it's my salvation.

"If I was fixing what's broken," she says, "I would build the harbor to include the Aquarius tenants, not evict them. You want to put me in charge? I'll make that happen. I haven't seen the plan Fate designed, but I've heard about it."

She's baiting me. She knows I hate compromise.

"I have homework," she says. "You need to go. Take the coffee with you. I have plenty of mugs."

"It's Friday night," I say, but she shoos me to the door. I stop in her dim hallway and face her.

"Your mother has poisoned our relationship. I'm not the man your mother claims I am."

"Go." She folds her arms and tilts her chin. Her uppity look.

I put my hand on my heart. The bulb hanging by a

chain from the ceiling flickers. "I'm going to be better, I promise," I say. "But I am being destroyed. By the deadbeat squatters in my marina, by the do-nothing police, by stingy bankers, by do-gooders barking for affordable housing.

"And every day, your mother cuts into my veins and feeds on my blood. That's what it feels like."

"You don't believe in her stupid voodoo, do you?" Dawn says. "I hear you've stopped paying her alimony."

"I'm sorry," I say. "For all the things I have to be sorry about."

She looks directly at me, then her eyes dart to the floor and to the door behind me.

She exhales. "Apologizing means a lot to me. If it's real."

I can't remember the last time she's spoken to me without anger.

"It's real."

"You'd better go. And one last thing, and I say this with love. You really need to tone it down with that cologne, whatever you're wearing. I could smell you through the front door."

On my way back to Marin, I stop at a bar in the Richmond that's been around since before Dawn was born. I need more liquid courage before I see Alice.

DAWN FELTON

[Defiant daughter of Fenton and Alice, girlfriend of Honest]

21

Fenton Felton Is a Failure, Part 1

My mother has not stopped talking since we left the house, complaining wall-to-wall about how ungrateful I am, and how, if I cared, I would have been there for her at the city council candidate debate on Wednesday.

It's Saturday morning and we're headed to City Hall for some kind of community meeting about the Aquarius Harbor houseboats. We clomp down the steep narrow concrete steps of Live Oak Lane toward Bridgeway. The steps are mossy and scattered with leaves, and when I grab the metal railing, flakes of rust come off in my hands. There's a pink stucco house on our left and two skinny redwoods on our right. The jasmine vines climbing the house are so perfumy, it's too much. We have two more blocks of steep stairs to go after this next landing.

"I was expecting you," she says again, as if I can rewind my life back to Wednesday. "I kept peering into the audience thinking maybe you came late."

"I told you," I say, "I was moving to the Sunset. I was studying for my oceanography midterm. I don't even *live* in Sausalito."

"You promised. And you're still registered here in Marin."

I did promise. I promised my mother. I promised Honest. But I couldn't. The midterm was the least of my problems. Tuesday, I called my father an asshole in front of everyone, including the TV cameras, and then Honest hit on Brenda, and then I found out Brenda was pregnant. *By my father.* Not to mention I was moving, a hassle under any circumstances, but especially because Honest was too busy leading the revolution to help carry a few boxes.

"If you weren't so self-absorbed," she says, "you would understand—"

"Self-absorbed? *Jesus!*" I groan, too theatrically I'm sure, but then this is my mother. "You *begged* me to come back home when you divorced Dad, and I came, even though I wanted to stay in Rhode Island. I stayed with you in the house for *four* months and I rebuilt my life, which is something *you* need to do, *yesterday*. I mean, when are you going to throw away your voodoo needles?"

She stops, lifts her chin and gives a little princessy sniff.

"Don't you understand the position you put me in?" I add. "You can't just *demand* I take your side."

"Do you know how humiliated I was when I found out about your father's affair," she says, "from one of my friends? From Rachel, Cotton Booth's wife.

"Your father flaunted his affair in front of Booth, knowing it would get back to me. Everyone knew before me, it was—"

"Mom, how could I possibly know all this except that you've told me a dozen times. You can't keep playing the victim. You divorced him. You got the house. You got your alimony. You hated him anyway, and now you're free."

"I'm not young and beautiful like you are."

"Come on, Mom. You were *gorgeous* when you were younger. The photos of you when you were my age, you were adorable. You still are. But that's not a ticket to happiness. Especially if you want men to treat you with respect. You have to move on. You can't make a new life for yourself when all you care about is vengeance."

"I am moving on," she says. "I guess I am a little stuck. I'm trying."

But she's not. She stuck with my father despite years of domineering and abuse, and when she talked about leaving, when I was in high school, I supported her. I remember well, because I was applying for colleges and she begged me not to go away or at least not to go so far. "You can't leave me here alone with your father," she said.

"If it's as bad as you say, Mom," I said, "and I don't doubt you, *leave* him. This is a community property state. You're entitled to half his wealth. You can support yourself. You're resourceful."

"Your father is hiding his money," she said, "and he will leave me with nothing."

She finally left when she found out about his affair. And she was left with a lot more than nothing.

"Try harder," I say.

She throws up her hands. "Why are you so hard on me? I am all about moving on and trying harder. Why else would I be running for city council? That's why I wanted you to be there Wednesday, to see the new and better me."

"Oh," I say, "OK. Point taken."

"You saw through your father before I did," she says, "and you punish me for that. But I grew up in a different world. Men were powerful. Women knew their place. I was late to the women's lib party."

She cocks her head. "Did I tell you I'm writing an erotic romance? It's titled, *Wet When We Met.*"

"*Mom!?!*"

"Dawn the prude," she says, in a sing-songy voice. "You're so easy to shock. All I've written is the title. I understand you know about Brenda and her baby, who will be—"

"My sibling," I say. "Half-sibling. But how do *you* know?"

"Brenda told me."

"*You* talked to Brenda?"

"I knocked on her door at Aquarius Harbor."

"What?" I say. "When? I thought—"

"Earlier this week," she says. "I wanted to see the woman your father cheated on. That's when I found out she was pregnant."

It's hard to be surprised by my mother after all these years, but I didn't see this coming.

"What did she see in Dad?"

"She said she forgot," she says, "same as me. So we bonded over that."

The morning quiet is interrupted by a cacophony of horns and drums echoing off the walls.

"What's that racket down there?" she asks.

At the bottom of the steps are two drummers, banging on snares. "Must be the houseboaters marching band," I say. "Honest told me something about it." We have one more set of stairs before we get to Bridgeway. The sky is blue and the sun is bright, but it's chilly in the shade.

More people are descending the stairs now, some slower, some faster, so we walk single file, my mother in front. Now I hear a bunch of loud horns marching on the sidewalk below.

"Actually, that's not true what I said about your father," she says. "I do remember what I saw in him. He was extremely charming, while he was wooing me, even once we were married. It's just that he has this bottomless need to have everything his way. He spoiled *you*. You got more attention from him than I did. I was jealous. There, I said it."

My mother is always telling me things like it's the first time when it's usually like the hundredth, but this she hasn't shared before, not these words anyway. *Extremely charming.* I would remember if she told me that.

"Dad keeps asking me to join the family business," I say, "no matter how many times I—"

"I thought you weren't talking to your father. You promised."

"I did not promise," I say. "You *wanted* me to promise." No way am I telling her about his visit last night. She would go ballistic. I'm still not sure what to think about it. His regret was new. I had not seen that before. I'd like to believe he *is* different, but all the voices in my head tell me otherwise. What's that saying, the best predictor of the future is the past?

I never *wanted* to be estranged from my father, but between my self-respect and my feminism, I had to set boundaries.

"I gave you my new address and phone number."

I shout into my mother's ear. Can she hear me above the braying horns? "He doesn't even know I've moved. How's that for taking sides? I'm floundering, Mom. You think I have the world eating out of my hands. I don't."

"Your father wanted another son, and when he found out you were a girl, he stomped out of the hospital room and snarled at me. 'Bring me a boy next time.'"

"He didn't do any better with the son he had," I say. "Where is Junior anyway? He used to write, but he stopped." My mother has told me that hospital story enough times, it's become part of my identity, something I've told friends.

As we approach the street, there's a gaggle of hippies strutting like peacocks with their horns and drums. I don't see Honest, but he must be around. He wanted me to join in with the band and sit with him today, and he gave me grief when I told him I was coming with my mother.

"Mom," I say, "when we talked on the phone, and I agreed to come here with you, I specifically said I could use some mothering, which was not easy for me to ask for, and here you are continuing to hold it against me that I missed the debate."

My mother stops as we approach the bottom of the stairs until I'm a step ahead of her. "I appreciate that you are going to this, whatever it is, community mediation, with me." She places her hand on my cheek. "I'm sorry if I implied that it's easy for you. I'm doing a fair amount of floundering myself."

"The thing is, Mom, I can't even talk to my friends. I told Wendy about maybe breaking up with Honest and she asked me for his number because she thinks he's hot. But he doesn't respect me as a woman. And the way he treats his sister is even worse. Though he did build a composting toilet on his ferry, for me, which is sort of the best birthday present *ever.*"

Now it's too noisy to talk. When we reach the bottom of the stairs, we're in the middle of the marching band. My mom hesitates.

"Come on, Mom," I holler in her ear, "we can march with them. They're headed to City Hall too."

"I can't be seen with them," she says. "That would destroy my credibility."

"OK, let's go around them," I say. "They're staggering along."

Everyone in the band is dressed colorfully, as if they're headed to the circus and not a community meeting. There's Fate, wearing a typewriter on a harness around her neck as if it were a musical instrument. She's tapping away on the keys. I haven't seen her in pigtails before. They're cute on her, but she is one weird girl.

I see Mickey wagging his head side to side as he wails on his trombone and I yank my mom out of the way so he doesn't hit her in the head with his slide as we pass. Some marchers carry picket signs instead of instruments. "Save our homes." "Housing is a human right." "We shall not be moved." The band takes up most of the sidewalk and the street is clogged with traffic, so it's slow going.

There must be three dozen people with instruments, and almost that many with signs. I see Honest now, at the front of the pack, of course, pounding a big bass drum with "Aquarius Harbor Pirate Marching Band" stenciled on the skin. I slap him on the butt as we pass and he pokes me in the back with one of his mallets.

Once we're ahead of the band, the music sounds decent. They're playing "When the Saints Go Marching

In." Without realizing it, I'm bobbing my head to the beat.

City Hall is straight ahead, and there's a poster on a telephone pole with a picture of my father.

"Look," I say, "it's Dad."

Above an unflattering photo is a big headline in blocky type that says, "Fenton Felton Is a Failure."

"Oh God, he's going to freak," I say. I read it out loud. "Fenton Felton is a sniveling, cowardly failure on the verge of bankruptcy, his personal failures more dis-graceful—" I grab my mother by the arm. "Mom, did you know about this?"

"No," she says, putting on her glasses to read the poster. Under the headline and type is a red rubber stamp that says "BANKRUPT" over what looks like a financial statement.

"Well, maybe. I mean, no, not *directly*." She points up the street where there are two more telephone poles with the same poster. "Look, there's your dear old dad again. Is he on every telephone pole on Bridgeway?"

FATE ABERNATHY

[Forgetful architect, houseboat resident, sister of Honest]

22

Fenton Felton Is a Failure, Part 2

Saturday morning, we assemble early, with our instruments and protest signs, to march to City Hall. We're in a loose circle around Honest's big black bass drum, on which he stenciled, in rainbow colors, "Aquarius Harbor Pirate Marching Band." Where is he anyway? His drum is on time, but he isn't.

I argued against including the word "pirate" in the band name because why should Honest always get his way? It's not that he doesn't have good ideas, it's that he thinks protests come together organically. He ridicules my lists, because he keeps everything in his head.

Jude painted the band name on an old sail that she cut and stretched between two spars. She and Brenda are going to carry the banner. Behind the bass drum, because, of course, Honest wants to be in front.

Last night, instead of sleeping, I kept replaying my

conversation with Mickey Thursday night, rehearsing my speech, and obsessing about all the things that could go wrong today. I also decided to join the marching band. Why not? Who's going to tell me I can't be here?

I'm wearing my most colorful outfit, my orange batik granny dress. My hair is in pigtails, and I've laced up my still-new-looking magenta high-top sneakers. I'm excited to be part of this wild scene. Good thing, because I'm exhausted from not sleeping.

Since musical ability is clearly not a requirement, I'm playing the typewriter, which is strapped to the harness around my shoulders. Honest helped me reinforce the harness with wire and tape—he is good for some things. The clickety-clack of the keys and the ding of the carriage return will barely be heard under all the horns, so it won't matter that I can't keep a beat.

Still, I feel self-conscious joining in with the others, afraid someone will ask me what I'm doing here. Mickey, resplendent in head-to-toe tie-dye, heavy on the purple and blue, is practicing his trombone. He seems to have some talent, or at least comfort with playing music. "Hey, glad you could join us," he says. "Do you need sheet music?"

I shake my head. He's being nice because he feels sorry for me. I was so shaken Thursday night when I visited him after our barge-sinking mission and all I did was talk and talk and talk and then came onto him in the clumsiest way imaginable. He must think I'm a nut case.

Now here's Honest, in full pirate regalia, including a jet-black headscarf, and on top of that a red and blue Tam High drum major hat. He straps the big bass drum over his shoulders. I would keel over forward with all that weight. He wiggles a drum mallet in one hand and a baton in the other and he's as hyper as a squirrel scoring a bucket of acorns.

We start marching and the band sounds like screeching cats, but between the fun and the visibility and the boost to our morale, well, what does it matter that we don't know how to play?

Once we've marched a block or two, I no longer feel like an imposter. I hit the carriage return every count of eight and I try to type along with the beat of the drum. The sheet of paper I've rolled into the typewriter is full of gibberish.

ddffkkj
mmwerrr
rreesjjj

Maybe I'll turn that into a poem.

The sun is out. The sky is blue. We pass the Dare Not where Brenda works and I smell coffee and bacon. Pot, too, though that's from the band. Geez, it's not even nine in the morning—I don't like to be a scold, and I've consumed my share of drugs, but now, with our future at stake, does not seem like the ideal time to be getting stoned.

As we get closer to City Hall, we pick up more marchers and there are more bystanders. Some drivers on Bridgeway honk in support, but others flip us off. The funkier the car, the more likely they are to honk in support, and when I see this old, bearded guy in a Porsche convertible veering toward the band and revving his engine, I tense up, scared that he's going to plow into the horn section, but he straightens out and then raises his fist in solidarity.

The band launches into "When the Saints Go Marching In." I'm not sure if it's because the band is playing better or because I know this song, but it's easier to play along. Some bystanders are singing or clapping.

There's Dawn and her mother up ahead, arriving at the bottom of the stairwell by the shoe store, right into our band. They wind through the band to the street and pick up their pace and get ahead of us. Dawn slaps Honest on his butt, and he pokes her with his drum mallet and then he flips it into the air like a juggling pin. When he fumbles it on the way down, the drum falls off his shoulders and hits the sidewalk. We pause our march until he reattaches it.

The marching band to City Hall is going way better than I imagined. We're capturing the imagination of the Bay Area today, with our theatrics and our righteousness, and people of good will everywhere are going to rally around us. Bystanders are joining our march as we pass, swelling our ranks. One woman and her little girl bang tambourines.

What's even better about this parade is that I didn't organize it. Our movement is taking on a life of its own— it's not just me. Other people are stepping up. Like Jude building and dressing those cardboard cutouts for the civil disobedience in the parking lot on Thursday, and Isaac pulling the band together this morning.

Reporters and TV cameras follow us as we march. Johnny Dash runs alongside us talking into his microphone as his cameraman struggles to keep up. I wish we had more discussion about the signs. The "Save Our Homes" ones are fine, but "Fenton Felton Sucks" and "Smash Capitalism"—those messages aren't going to help us earn support from locals.

But other than that, it's all coming together. We're going to pull this out of our hat. Brenda is going to speak first, humanizing the houseboaters. She's the perfect opening act—being pregnant, being a waitress, being a college student, not to mention being black, *and* humble *and* nice, *and* the spurned mistress of Fenton Felton. I don't get why Brenda has struggled so much. She seems to have her act together so much more than I do, though she is older.

Huck Hennessee is slated to be the second speaker at City Hall, and he'll be all boring with his numbers, which will set the stage for me to present my plan, our plan. This is not about me, I remind myself, but about us.

I've got a hundred copies of Jude's sketch in my pack. It's not the full plan, but a simplified version that will make sense to people who can't read blueprints. I'll say my piece, then pass the sketches out. If I pass them out first, everyone will look at the drawings instead of listening to me.

I don't expect the plan will change Fenton Felton's mind, but I don't need to convince him as much as Mayor Sally and Chief Tin and the council members and business leaders. We've got a colorful history here in Sausalito, with the shipbuilding and the artists and the bohemians, and Aquarius Harbor is upholding that tradition.

Tonight, my brilliant berth plan is going to be the talk of the town. Important people are going to know who I am. The whole world may not be watching, but plenty of people are.

We're a block from City Hall when the band slows and stops. There are too many people trying to get into the meeting. I walk toward the front where I see Mickey, holding his trombone at his side, reading a big poster on a telephone pole.

It's got a nasty photo of Fenton Felton under a tabloid headline—"Fenton Felton Is a Failure."

Mickey reads it out loud. "Fenton Felton is a sniveling, cowardly failure on the verge of bankruptcy, his personal failures more disgraceful—"

I tear the poster off the pole. The top part is a newspaper story from the *Chronicle* and under it is a rubber stamp that says "BANKRUPT" in red over what looks like a financial statement.

Honest comes up behind me, unhooks the drum from its harness. "You took that off the pole," he says. "Put it back."

"This is *you?*" I am so furious I can hardly restrain myself. "You did this behind my back. We talked about this and—"

"You would have toned it down, made it all nice."

Mickey takes two steps back, as if he's giving us privacy to squabble among ourselves, but he's still close enough to hear my ragged breaths.

I turn towards him. He took my side earlier this week, twice, at the Dare Not with Lander, our new lawyer, and then Tuesday night when Honest crashed our meeting with his red wagon and keg and bong, but now he's staying out of it.

"Dude, you're a moron," I say to Honest. "You gave away our leverage. This was something we could *hold* over Fenton. Promise not to go public with his bankruptcy in exchange for concessions. Instead—"

"The truth will set us free. No concessions."

"Truth? You wouldn't know the truth if it bit you in the face. You even lie about your name. This financial statement was *so much more valuable* before you plastered it all over town."

I look to Mickey, but he won't meet my eyes.

"Aren't you going to compliment me on the stellular job I did on the layout?" Honest says, not reacting at all to my insult. He nudges Mickey. "Looks like a real newspaper, doesn't it? That high school editor gig turned out useful."

It takes all my willpower not to heave my typewriter at him.

"You've ruined everything. All our planning. All our colorful civil disobediences and cardboard cutouts and our exuberant band. That's why you were late this morning? *This?* All our deliberate work, down the toilet. You sabotaged us!"

I'm panting. I'm hyperventilating. I need to stop and breathe, but I can't let him interrupt me.

"These posters make us look like bullies and they turn Fenton Felton into a victim. Now everyone is going to hate *us* because we went on the attack, and such a mean-spirited attack, too, no matter that he deserves it. How could you be so *stupid?*"

Honest looks down at the poster in his hands and nods his head. "I wish you would tell me what—"

"No," I yell, and he drops the poster to the sidewalk. He holds his hands up, palms facing me—somewhere between stop and surrender. Mickey picks up the poster and hands it to me.

"You hate my poster," Honest says, a thousand times calmer than I am. "But you're giving an important speech this morning and you have a chance to win the day. You will knock them dead."

He's changing the subject. I can't tell if he's patronizing me or not.

"I know you're going to unveil the compromise plan,"

he says, "the plan you *know* I disagree with because it's *surrender.* Meanwhile, I will keep fighting, *in my own way,* to defeat Fenton Felton and his project."

"How do you propose to do that? We've lost nine houseboats and—"

"I heard," he says, "that someone sank a barge that's going to stop construction for weeks." He smirks and leans back on his heels. "You know, that kind of thing. That's what I propose to do."

He lifts his drum, snaps it in his harness, and pounds it four times.

HUCK ('HIC') HENNESSEE

[Sniveling sidekick to Fenton]

23

A High Tide Lifts all Houseboats

When I pick up Fenton Felton for the short drive to City Hall, he's quiet. Not his usual bombastic self. Something is off.

After a minute of silence, I ask, "So, are you still pissed you can't speak today because of Tin's *arbitrary* rule?"

He stares at the expensive leather satchel in his lap and doesn't say a word.

He's dressed in all black, in a tailored Italian suit, though his shirt is actually dark gray. He looks pale, like a vampire who hides from the sun. I've got my boring off-the-rack brown suit from Macy's. Nothing that will call attention to me.

Fenton thinks it's important to look affluent and that may be true when we're trying to convince a banker to extend a loan. But for today's meeting at City Hall, making our case for evicting a bunch of poor hippies in their rag-tag duds, the satchel and suit send the wrong message. Not that he listens to me.

"I'm going at everything the wrong way," he says. "My dastardly villain act is tired. I hate to ditch the laugh, but it's no longer serving me. I'm not just a builder, I'm a salesman and a showman, and if I'm misunderstood, which I am, it's my own damn fault."

I wait for the other shoe.

He clutches my arm. I've turned into the parking lot and I need my arm to shift into reverse. I shake him off, but he grabs me again. What is going on? He's never clingy like this.

"I went to see Alice last night," he says. "I told her I wanted us back together. She laughed at me. I need to change who I am."

He's said this before—he repented and declared he was reinventing himself as a man with integrity. That lasted a day.

"That sounds hard," I say. I've learned a few things listening to Cath talk with her friends.

"You're supposed to tell me I should never change," he says.

"You wouldn't respect me if I did."

I wait for him to say that he doesn't respect me and never will, but he just scowls, and shifts his satchel from one hand to the other.

As I climb out of the truck, I straighten my bunched-up suit jacket and tighten my tie, and, one more time, run through my speech for the meeting.

I have thirty seconds, so I have to pack a lot into five sentences.

One, the luxury houseboat marina we're building

will add to the Sausalito quality of life *and* its tax base. Two, we are a law-abiding business, and our new harbor will attract residents who will patronize Sausalito's restaurants and merchants. Three, the houseboaters have violated public health laws, with impunity, impacting us all. Four, they have known for a long time that evictions were coming. Five, they are engaged in drug use and drug dealing, not to mention parties till the wee hours of the morning that can be heard from miles away.

No, no, I forgot to mention naked women. At the parties. I'll end with that.

There's a parade coming down Bridgeway toward City Hall—the hippie squatters pretending to be a marching band. They are a riot of color and they sound like squawking crows, albeit with a beat. There are a lot of drums.

People are streaming in toward City Hall from every direction and the street is clogged with traffic.

We weave through the hippie band to the sidewalk. They stink of sweat and pot.

My financial arrangement with Fenton Felton is better than it was two days ago, when I *tried* to sever ties with him, but forty percent of nothing is still nothing. I should never have let him reel me back in. If only I weren't so afraid of fessing up to my wife.

I am *so* relieved she's not here today. I asked her if she wanted to come and she said she would, if *I* wanted her to.

"It will be a big, fat, ugly mess," I said. "You don't want to be there."

We never thought the hippies would fight back. Fenton called them deadbeats on drugs so many times I never imagined they could be so creative and resourceful.

Uh-oh, there's Brenda up ahead marching with the hippies. I stop, to block Fenton's view. He's calm now, but what if he sees her?

"I practiced my speech a dozen times last night," I tell him.

The hippie with the scraggly blond hair, the sidekick of Honest, is gyrating wildly as he plays his trombone, and he and his horn section, including two tubas, march past and Brenda is swallowed up by the band. Fenton didn't see her, and he doesn't seem to care how much I've practiced.

I've heard about this compromise dock plan being pitched by Honest's sister, but I haven't gotten my mitts on a copy. Supposedly it has the same number of berths as our Heavenly Houseboat Harbor, and grandfathers in the majority of the existing houseboats on the other side of the spit. Fenton, of course, is against *any* compromise, even if it saves our project.

I used to look at Fenton and think, he's not that smart, but he's confident, willing to take risks. I wanted to be more like that. I thought that was something I could learn from him. But too much confidence is more dangerous than too little.

I remind myself that Cath and I may be on the road to ruin, but there's a turnoff. We can sell our house, move to New Mexico. Cath's sister Celeste likes it there, in Los Alamos. We can start over. If we have to.

We're not facing financial failure because I was greedy, but because I wanted to *please* Cath—she wanted the bathroom remodel, the new deck, so we refinanced. A bad decision for an admirable reason.

I wanted to impress her, show her I could play with the big boys. Not be a second banana forever.

A hiccup erupts from my chest. OK, I'm lying to myself. Tomorrow, I quit for good, no more sucking up to Fenton Felton. I promise.

That is, unless Chief Tin's mediation somehow resolves the conflict, and we can build our long-delayed project. Not that that's likely, but I sure would like to avoid bankruptcy. That's an albatross that will be on my back for years.

As we approach City Hall, I see a row of posters with Fenton's mug on them, pasted on a sagging wooden fence.

Up closer, I read the headline above his head. "Fenton Felton Is a Failure." It's a newspaper clip, from the *Chronicle*.

The failure himself is coming up beside me, fussing with his tie. My shoulders tense. I anticipate his growl before he opens his mouth.

I read the headline and the first paragraph out loud—Fenton is too vain to wear his glasses in public. "Dashing local tycoon is really a criminal, a sniveling, cowardly failure on the verge of bankruptcy—"

"Quiet," he barks. "We don't need everyone in Sausalito to hear."

I continue reading: "'His personal failures are even more disgraceful than his business failures. His ex-wife and his daughter despise him.' Under the newspaper clip is a financial statement that says you're bankrupt. But that's from when you *pretended* to be broke so your ex—"

"Enough," he shouts. "Who did this? Why didn't you stop this? This is what I pay you for."

I squint on the type on the bottom of the poster. It's not a newspaper clip after all, but a well-rendered phony. "'Brought to you with peace and love," I read, "'by the Aquarius Houseboat Collective. A high tide lifts all houseboats.'"

He rips a poster from the fence and pulls it close to his face. "This is so unfair. This man is not me. I've changed. I've seen the error of my ways."

"So, you'll consider the compromise dock plan?"

"Don't be stupid." He tears the poster into pieces. "I will *kill* whoever is responsible for this with my bare hands. Well, no. I expect *you* to do it for me."

He keeps ripping posters from the fence and tearing them up. He's got spittle dripping from his lips. Like a rabid dog.

"The bankruptcy filing was for your divorce, right?" I say, "You told me you have money sheltered in your Tahoe condos. Right?" I should have known. We are in deeper shit than I imagined in my worst nightmares. He has nothing left.

But these posters might help us, because now the houseboaters are the aggressors. We're legally entitled to evict them, we have our permits in place, and we have the support of the business community. If Fenton wins his council race, we'll have the majority of the city council too.

"Don't interrogate me," Fenton says, pointing across the street to more posters on more telephone poles. "I don't know who I'm more furious at—Honest and his scumbag squatters, Alice and her sleazy lawyers, or you, who—"

"Me?" I say. My voice sounds high, like a little girl's. I hate that. I'm a grown man. "I'm your loyal partner. How can—?"

"The police won't sink the squatters' boats," he snarls, "so we'll have to do it. Then comes his laugh. I cringe. "*We* meaning *you*," he adds.

There's a sign outside City Hall that says the meeting has been moved from the Edgewater Room to the gym in the basement. The entrance is jammed with people.

"You have to rewrite your speech," Fenton says, "to protect my honor. I will not be disrespected like this."

When we get inside the gym, I spot two seats on the edge of the second row. He sees them too, the moment before I decide that it would be better *not* to sit next to him. He grabs me by the shoulder, his thumb digging into my collarbone. "Here's what you need to say."

BRENDA DIAMOND
[Lonely waitress, houseboat resident, former mistress of Fenton]

24

Community Justice

When I peek at the crowd from the wing of the stage, I don't see a single empty chair. In the bleachers, there are a few gaps, but mostly, everyone's shoulder to shoulder up there. Dozens of people stand against the back wall, under the basketball backboard. Camera crews set up in front of the stage, where workers are still scurrying around with their levels and wrenches and clamps. They've created a stage in a manner of minutes with a couple dozen four-foot by eight-foot plywood boxes bolted and clamped together.

We're in the windowless basement gym of City Hall, the biggest meeting room available. The meeting was scheduled in the Edgewater Room, but Tin told me it was full twenty minutes ago, so they moved to the gym. Now a man in a navy jumpsuit is walking around the stage and bouncing here and there. To test it, I guess.

I'm behind a stage flat made of pine and black muslin, next to a ladder and a coiled extension cord, and I see the audience through a slit where staples have come undone. Fate is standing in the second row, next to Honest, looking cuter than usual in her pigtails and wild orange and yellow hippie dress. She looks like a child, but with the tiredness of an adult. She struggles with sleep more than I do, but I have the excuse of being pregnant. She can't turn off the voices in her head, she says.

She detaches the typewriter harness she wore for the marching band and slides it under her seat, then sits and shuffles through her index cards.

Last night, Fate worked on my speech with me. She says I'm the perfect messenger—a pregnant, black waitress who just happens to be the ex-mistress of the man who's evicting everyone from their homes.

Fate acts like this is all about the community and not about her, but she's also determined to push aside her brother as the spokesperson for the houseboat collective, and I know that she's using me to make that happen.

But she said she'll help when the baby comes, and I have to believe she will. She's speaking third today, and she should get lots of attention when she unveils her dock plan.

Alice sits five rows back in her gold and black caftan. She's become a crunchy granola type with her yoga and her smoothies and her organic vegetables, but she's no penniless hippie, that's for sure. She *also* said she would help when the baby comes, but I'm not counting on that.

Sally steps to the lectern downstage. "Welcome to Sausalito City Hall," she says. "I'm your mayor, Sally Cal. We're here to find a peaceful resolution to the rancorous dispute at Aquarius Harbor."

She gestures toward Tin, who stands by a blackboard, where she's written the order of the preliminary speakers. After me comes Huck Hennessee and then Fate, then Cotton Booth, the Chamber of Commerce president.

"I'm sharing the facilitator duties tonight with our police chief Tin Holland," Sally says.

This promises to be a grueling day and Sally looks frail. She's coy about her age, but she must be in her eighties. Jenna asked her once, and she retorted, "Older than you." She has the voice of a lifelong smoker and her tinted gray hair is thinning.

"Some of you know, or *think* you know," she says, "about me and my house of ill repute in the City, but don't believe everything you hear. It is true, however, that I have a history of making people happy. Making men happy, that is. What you may not know is that Chief Tin worked for me for years." She pauses and there are a few twitters. "No, it's not what you think—she worked as a maid when she was a teenager, and later she ran security. Once she had to muzzle a dog for sticking his nose into someone's business."

I feel the anticipation and excitement in the crowd, but under that there's tension crackling like electricity. At least they bought in pastries and coffee from the Dare Not. They're gone already—I grabbed two, but then I'm eating for more than just me.

Tin joins Sally at the lectern. "I'm here today as the police chief, and as a mediator, certified by est and the Tamalpais Valley Self-Improvement Association."

"We have selected six community members to speak," says Sally. "Brenda Diamond is first, on behalf of Aquarius Harbor. To respect your time and keep this process moving, we are enforcing a strict 30-second rule."

She points up to the scoreboard clock at the back of the room, where it says "0:30", and points over her head to another clock that we can't see, but the audience can.

"Then I cut off the mic," Tin says.

Sally introduces me. I grip the microphone with both hands, my fingers interlaced. The last time I remember holding a mic, I was singing in a talent show in high school.

"I'm Brenda. I work nights as a waitress at the Dare Not and I live at Aquarius Harbor in a small houseboat walking distance from the bar. I pay my rent. I follow the rules. I have a baby coming, and I look forward to loving my baby with all my heart and soul. I will be a single mother whose survival depends on an affordable rent. Also, three members of the houseboat community have promised to help me."

I feel Fenton's eyes on me, but I know where he's sitting and I'm not looking anywhere in that direction. But I'm paying too much attention to *not* paying attention to him and I lose my place in my notes.

I'm not going to panic. I know what to say.

"I'm being evicted from this supportive community, by that man, Fenton Felton, the father of my child, a child I want to keep, but he does not—"

Tin makes the "cut" gesture across her throat as Fenton leaps to his feet.

"I do. I do," he shouts. "I want to keep our baby, and I want to marry you and—"

"No interruptions," Tin says sternly.

He ignores Tin. "I will love our baby with all my heart, with all—"

"You will sit and silently respect the speakers," she says, "or we can escort you across the street to a cold

178

cell that smells of ammonia."

She turns to me. "Brenda, please finish your statement. I'll turn the clock off."

I look at Fenton, and he looks at me. His eyes are different. They are imploring, not menacing. I stare back at him.

"If you build your luxury dock, we will resist. Nonviolently. In front of the TV cameras."

I'm surprised by how wild the applause is.

25

How Dare You?

The entrance to the gym is jammed and I can't slither through the crowd because I've got this ridiculous typewriter strapped to my shoulder harness. Honest is right about how hard it is on my shoulders, but I'm not going to give him the satisfaction of gloating.

When I finally squeeze inside, I don't see any seats, but Mickey is standing and waving. He's saved me a seat, in the front row. I hesitate, because I'm uncomfortable about my visit Thursday night, but all morning, he's acted like nothing happened.

He gently moves his trombone from the empty chair to the floor and helps me detach my harness and put the typewriter under my seat. We're three feet from the stage. Above our head is a basketball backboard and a net, tucked in and strapped to the ceiling, like legs on a folding table.

The room is windowless and there's a musty, sweaty gym socks smell, as if they've been playing basketball here all night long.

Mickey asks me if I'm nervous about speaking.

Of course, I am, I tell him, but I'm so livid about Honest and his poster stunt that I've almost forgotten I'm speaking. Honest is on the other side of Mickey, but he's talking animatedly with Harry and Larry, his stoner pirate sidekicks, so I vent to Mickey.

"Honest's posters make everything worse," I say. "How could he not know they're going to backfire?"

Mickey listens without comment. People continue to stream in and the only seats left are benches high in the bleachers. Workmen roam the stage with wrenches and levels getting it ready for the meeting.

"The inflammatory rhetoric on the poster *might* make my compromise plan sound more reasonable," I say, "but I can't see how our community will *ever* be reasonable as long as Honest has this pathological need for attention. He won't abide by our agreement that I'm the spokesperson. I feel like he'd rather we lose our homes than risk that I might get credit for saving them."

Mayor Sally Cal welcomes us, introduces Tin, reviews the ground rules. Thirty seconds or we'll be cut off, blah, blah, blah.

Dawn and Alice are several rows back, and Fenton is in the row behind us, in his black and gray suit, about eight seats to my right, next to his sidekick.

I had this nightmare last night and now it's coming back to me. I was lost in a department store, which is weird because I haven't been in one for ages, and Fenton Felton was there, in profile, doing his maniacal laugh, and when he turned, I saw the other side of his face and it was Honest, shouting, "Property is theft," with his fist high in the air.

That disturbed me so much I couldn't fall back asleep.

And now I'm trapped between them. The two most aggravating men in the world—Fenton Felton and my lunatic brother. Each makes me crazy in their own special way.

Finally, Brenda's speaking and she starts off fine, but she goes too slow and when she looks up to the seconds ticking down on the scoreboard clock, she panics. Her eyes get big, and she blinks again and again. She's lost her place. *Oh God, what a disaster!* We rehearsed for hours yesterday and she nailed it over and over. Now all the pressure is on me, and what if I get flustered too?

But she snaps back into herself, points her finger at Fenton Felton, and calls him the father of her child. *That's not in her script.* She was adamant about *not* saying that when we practiced.

When Fenton Felton interrupts, Tin scolds him. She gives Brenda as much time as she needs and Brenda ends with a bang, and the applause is loud and enthusiastic. She hit a home run. No disaster after all. I'm wound so tight, I fear the worst.

When Sally steps to the lectern to introduce the second speaker, Honest and Mickey jump up from their seats.

"The ocean is free," Honest shouts. "Rent is theft."

He waves a flag that says, "Save Our Homes."

"Long live Aquarius Harbor," says Mickey.

Tin blows her whistle. I'm sorting through the notecards in my hands and I can't cover my ears in time.

"That's enough," Tin says. "No interruptions. The next person who interrupts will be removed." Honest and Mickey sit down. The whistle was deafening. It's still vibrating in my eardrums. It sure is quiet all of a sudden.

"Our next speaker," Sally says, "is Huck Hennessee, speaking on behalf of Heavenly Houseboat Harbor."

He wears a brown suit with a tan tie, quite the contrast with all the tie-dye color in the room.

"I'm speaking on behalf of a special man," he says, "the lead partner of Heavenly Harbor, Fenton Felton—" He pauses as if he's about to hiccup, but it doesn't come. He clears his throat and continues.

"Who has been libeled, slandered, and besmirched by the ruthless and truthless Aquarius houseboaters, who escalated the conflict when wise city leaders called for calm."

Tin, her whistle in her mouth, holds up ten fingers. Huck picks up his pace. "Fenton Felton denounces the houseboaters for fabricating libelous stories and stapling them on the telephone poles in violation of no-solicitation rules. I yield my remaining—"

Tin blows her whistle, even louder than before, this time for about three seconds. Now it's my turn.

As I approach the lectern, Brenda wheels out the blackboard draped with a floral bed sheet. She unrolls one corner of the sheet, so there's only one bold red stroke from Jude's sketch of the proposed dock that's visible. I count to five, milking the tension. The scoreboard clock counts down to 0:25. We practiced this over and over again and it's going exactly as planned. The audience is leaning forward, waiting for me to speak.

"The Aquarius Collective is committed to resistance," I say, "*and* open to compromise.

I hold up the rolled blueprint. "I've been studying architecture and I've drawn plans that allow Heavenly Houseboat Harbor to build their marina *and* accommodate us. And it costs half as much to build."

Brenda pulls off the sheet, revealing Jude's full sketch. Bold red and black lines in marker outline the bones of the marina—two W-shaped docks nestled inside one another, then another pair of "W"s at a 30-degree angle from the first pair, and, on the other side of the spit, two more after that.

I hear a chorus of oohs and aahs, and not just from our people. I have twelve seconds left.

I use my rolled-up blueprint as a pointer and tap the first two pairs of W-shaped docks. "*Here* is the luxury marina, and *here*—I point to the third pair of "W"s—is Aquarius Harbor."

Jude passes out copies of the sketch to audience members. Everyone reaches for one. "More berths in less space. Simple, elegant design. Look at all those corners—who doesn't want a corner berth?"

I finish with one second left. Fenton Felton screeches, "That woman stole *my* plan. How dare she present this dock design as her own. She's a *thief*, a *plagiarist*."

What the fricking hell?

I'm livid but I keep my cool. The audience boos Fenton Felton, and I wait until the boos subside. "You're saying *your* plan accommodates us? Hallelujah, let's run a victory lap. You—"

Fenton won't let me finish. "No, no, no, typewriter girl, there's no place for Aquarius Harbor in *my* plan, only—"

"It's not *your* plan. It's *mine*." He's shouting, but I have the microphone. "How dare you accuse me of stealing?"

My voice is calm and measured, but I don't hide my fury.

FENTON FELTON

[Greedy developer, father of Dawn, ex-husband of Alice]

26

Cut

The crowd is booing me and that damn typewriter girl keeps talking, insisting that the plan is hers, not mine. The scoreboard clock reads 0:00. Her time is up.

"Chief Tin," I howl, "why are you letting her speak?"

Honest and his blondie accomplice interrupt again with their signs and chants. "Fenton Felton," Honest bellows at me, "You're jealous *her* plan is *better* than yours."

I look again at the sketch of Fate's plan. It *is* better than what my *lame* architect came up with, though it can't possibly work because my tenants won't stand for a shantytown in their midst.

Tin holds the whistle an inch from her mouth as if she's going to blow it again, but she doesn't. She waits until the room is silent. "Fate, please proceed," she says. "We will reset the clock. You get ten more seconds."

"Why are you giving her a second chance?" I shout. "Why are you giving Honest a second chance? You promised anyone who interrupted would be removed. He's still here. She's still here." I wave my arms above my head. "I call for the firing of Police Chief Tin Holland and Mayor Sally Cal. For being *too fair* to the houseboaters."

"*Too fair?*" Sally says, from a chair on the side of the stage.

"Too fair to *them*," I say. "Unfair to *me*. Why is everyone against me?"

Sally throws up her hands and glares at me. "Can't you all act like grownups, sensible people who listen to each other and solve problems together?"

I take my time sitting down. When I win my council seat, I will squeeze Sally out as mayor and take over the reins myself. My first day in office.

I still have a sticky piece of one of those libelous posters on my thumb. I've been picking at it since we got here and I can't get rid of it.

"We're going to start again with Fate Abernathy," Sally says, "and if I hear a peep, *this time* I am going to get angry, and you do *not* want to see that."

Honest pops up again, hops onto the stage. "Fenton Felton," he bellows at me, "your breath smells so bad, even people on the phone hang up."

That's it. I've had it. I squeeze past Hic's knees into the aisle, climb on the stage, my fists balled. Barney, Chief Tin's deputy, appears from the wing, his hand on his gun.

"You're so stupid," Honest continues, "it takes you *two hours* to watch *60 Minutes*."

He holds up the poster with my mug on it and waves it in my face, like a matador in a bullfight. He's baiting me.

I charge him and he backs off, raises his hands in surrender. "Hey," he says, "nonviolence, remember?" Barney hesitates, watching us face off.

I lower my fists.

Honest shoves me in the chest and I stumble backward. I regain my footing and attack. I feign for his waist, tackle his legs, like I used to in high school wrestling.

He goes down. I'm on top and I pummel his stomach with my fists. He squirms away and gets to his feet. I spring up and go for his neck, but all of a sudden, the stage is full of bodies, and someone wraps his arms around my chest from behind.

Dawn grabs my left wrist. Where did she come from? Someone is punching me in the back, by my shoulder blades. That must be Alice. I recognize her punches.

Honest is swinging wildly but he's got people climbing on him too. It's like the dugout emptying in a ball game for a brawl on the field. I go for Honest's throat.

The lights go out. Someone grabs my leg and pulls, and I fall, but I land on top of Honest, I think. He swears under his breath. On my other side, someone is panting in distress.

I roll off Honest and lie on my back. I'm so tired I want to lie here forever.

What a mess I've made. I was determined never to end up like my father, but here I am, divorced, drowning in debt, on the verge of a massive failure. My mistress thinks I'm stalking her, my son has disappeared on me, my daughter defies me, my ex-wife despises me, we haven't had a Heavenly Houseboat berth deposit since Tuesday, the next interest payment is due Monday, and I've already racked up four late penalties.

I see a glimmer of light from the exit sign and four

or five shadows hovering. I climb to my knees, push up off my left foot. Someone bumps my shoulder and I spin around. There's a blow to my chest and I stagger. I've been sucker punched. No, I've been *stabbed*, sliced open. Liquid dribbles down my stomach. My heart throbs.

I stumble over my foot. My knees buckle. I hit the floor with a thwack.

There's the exit sign again. All I need to do is slip away in the dark and disappear and all my problems will be solved.

I'll steal away in my yacht, sail somewhere no one knows me. Siphon gas when I need to. Catch fish for dinner. Perform magic for children's birthday parties. *Abracadabra*, watch me make Fenton Felton disappear. Poof, he's gone. My laugh will scare the children with delight.

I hear the click of a lighter, see the beam of a flashlight. I can barely breathe.

Wait, I need time to change.

I wrap my arms around my chest. My blood, sticky on my fingers, is warm and smells of rust and regret. The rest of me feels like ice.

[TV cameraman]

27

Behind the Camera

When the lights go out, my camera's battery kicks in, but my light bar is plugged into the City Hall electrical system, so I can't see a thing through my viewfinder. It's total darkness.

I hear the melee continue on the stage and I point the camera at the noise. They're tripping all over each other up there. Grunting and gasping.

Then comes a whimper, no, a cry. A groan. Followed by a thud.

My eyes adjust—the exit sign stage left is dim—but I set my camera down. There's not enough light to capture anything usable. I make out a shadowy blob of human bodies center stage, more limbs than an octopus. Behind me I hear the strike of a match. Over by the lectern comes a click and a flare from a lighter. It's Mayor Sally—I see her mouth and nose in the flickering flame.

A flashlight snaps on. It's Chief Tin, her face in shadow. She sweeps the beam of light across the floor of the stage, stops on a puddle of red liquid.

Oh my God! Fenton Felton lies on his back, a knife in his chest. It's *blood*. That puddle of red liquid is blood. Is he dead?

Her flashlight beam catches me in the eye. I duck behind my camera. I don't want *anyone* to notice me, so I pick the camera back up and zoom in on the splayed body as if I were the jaded cameraman I pretend to be.

But my hands shake.

That's *my father* in the pool of blood. The father I *ran* from, only to stalk from behind my camera.

"Fenton Felton has been stabbed," says Tin.

I hear shrieks as the murmur of the crowd grows louder. No one notices me. If I keep my cool, no one will.

"I know CPR," says Fate, and she rushes to the body. He's not moving. He's not breathing.

Tin speaks into her radio. "10-52. Body down." She holds the flashlight steady as Fate kneels next to my father, *my* father, pressing his chest and forcing breaths into his mouth. She has blood on her dress. On her hands. Honest crouches at Fate's side, blood on his nose. A siren gets louder.

The lights flicker back on. The speaker in front of the lectern hums.

There's blood everywhere. On Honest's white pirate frock, on Huck's wingtips, on my mother's gold caftan. There's even a splatter of red on the lectern, ten feet from my father's body.

Tin has taken over CPR from Fate, but it's no use. My father is dead. What do I do now?

Keep filming, for one. I'm a professional and this

will surely be the top story on tonight's newscast. Keep quiet, for two. I've kept my identity secret through six assignments here in Sausalito and I can't possibly unmask myself now.

Or can I? I disguised myself so I could film my father without him noticing me, but now he's gone. My sister and my mother must be even more stunned and shocked than I am. Why hide from them?

But Johnny will be furious. He's been digging under rocks for dirt on all the parties in this houseboat drama and I haven't told him a thing.

Another police officer has relieved Tin and continue to press my father's chest and blow into his mouth. Tin steps to the microphone with her bloody hands. "I want everyone on the stage to freeze where you are—your legs, your arms, your face." She gestures to me. "Can you take a still with that camera?"

My hands tremble and I grip my camera as if it will hold me up. I feel like she's seeing through me, into me, even with my dark glasses on. But she can't see my eyes. That's just me being paranoid.

"I packed a Polaroid in my case, which prints right away." I disguise my voice. As low in pitch as I can go. I don't want my mother or sister to recognize me. They have enough to be upset about already. Since my first assignment here, I have never spoken out loud in their presence.

I find the Polaroid in my bag, and raise it, waiting for Chief Tin to give me the signal. She does. I press the button.

Fate, on her knees, slithers away from my father's body. Brenda, standing behind Fate, inches back so Fate doesn't bump into her. Mickey, lying on the floor, rolls onto his side, his hands covering his face.

On the floor in front of the lectern, my mother and sister hug. Dawn buries her face in my mother's chest.

I pull the print out of the Polaroid. The photo darkens as I hand it to Tin.

28

Hundreds of Witnesses

The lights are bright in the gym, and the paramedics arrive to remove Fenton Felton's bloody body. They declare him dead and stand by while my deputy Barney and two other officers take more photos, swab more samples, and cordon off more of the stage with crime-scene tape. Sausalito does not have enough crime to justify a dedicated forensics officer, but my deputy Barney has enough training to handle this murder scene.

We don't have a homicide detective either because we have so few murders, but I'm on the scene and am the most experienced of our officers, so I'm taking charge.

My primary job as police chief is to *prevent* crime, which I failed to do this morning. My job now is to bring the murderer to justice.

I huddle with Sally behind the lectern and study the audience members. They look at their watches, jiggle change in their pockets, sneak furtive glances at the exits. I feel the uneasiness in my bones. There are clumps of visible defiance—audience members folding their arms across their chests and frowning. I've reminded the crowd twice that this is a crime scene and they need to stay in their seats and the second time I heard a smattering of boos. I'm hesitant to remind them again.

Even Johnny's cameraman is jumpy. Usually, he's as still as his camera, but now he switches it from one shoulder to another as if it's suddenly heavier than before. He's the opposite of Honest in that he's deliberate in *not* drawing attention to himself, but now he squirms like ants are marching up his back.

The seven people who were part of the melee and on the stage when the lights came back on sit in folding chairs at the back of the stage. They're impatient too, but not defiant. Four are splattered with blood. So am I.

The paramedics leave with Fenton Felton's body on a stretcher.

We have a problem. Barney, who thinks he knows more about murder investigations than he does, tells me we need to clear the stage.

"We run the risk of contaminating the crime scene," he says, "and destroying potential evidence. You know that."

"I do know that, and I respect your protocols," I say. "However, we have *hundreds* of witnesses who were *in this gym* when the murderer struck, and I want *them* to help us identify the killer. Find out what they heard, what they saw, what they know—while their memories are fresh."

"You hear them grumbling," Sally says. "They want to leave. We can't keep them here."

"We can and we will," I say, "Of course they're upset. They witnessed a murder. They saw a dead body lying in a pool of blood on the stage, something most people never see. But we will *never* have this opportunity again, hundreds of witnesses and the murderer, all here together. I'm going to *deputize* them, sort of, to *help* with this murder investigation. So they are as invested in finding out what happened as I am. I'm also going to question the seven persons of interest, in front of the crowd."

It sounds ridiculous when I hear my words out loud. But not impossible.

Barney is incredulous. "You want to lock the doors and conduct a homicide investigation in front of all these people?"

Sally rubs her temples with her gnarled fingers. "How long?"

"It is standard practice," I say, "to lock the door of the interrogation room in the station. I need an hour." As chief I can countermand Barney's decision, but he can be a hothead, and I need his cooperation. I can't imagine an hour will be enough.

"An hour and a half tops," I say. "Not that I expect to crack the case today, but we must seize the moment. I know it's risky, but so was bringing hundreds of people together to craft a peace plan."

"You see how that turned out," Sally says.

I ignore that and turn to Barney. "How about this? You collect as much forensic evidence as you can in the next twenty minutes, while we give the audience a break, and let's get the city workers who assembled this stage this morning to disassemble it, just part of it, so you can grab the plywood boxes closest to the spot of the murder and bring them to the station for further examination."

I point to the stage floor downstage from the lectern. "Those two with the puddles of blood and the eight or so around them. Take those. They'll have to reassemble the stage and it will be smaller, but we'll make it work."

Barney's not thrilled, but he's already instructing another officer to take apart the stage and procure the ten plywood boxes.

"Sally," I say, "we have to feed the crowd, and I need you to make that happen. Call the Dare Not, call wherever you need to—charge it to my budget. I also want you to tell the audience you have my back."

She stares at me like this is the last thing in the world she wants to do, but she nods, and steps to the microphone. "Thank you for your patience. We're taking a break, in a few minutes, but we've locked the doors and no one can leave City Hall. We're bringing in sandwiches, drinks, and dessert—lots of desserts—from *my* bar, on *my* dime, so I don't want to hear any complaining. Our dessert special today is cheesecake and that alone is reason to stay. Now please give Chief Tin your full attention and your full cooperation."

I take Sally's place at the lectern. "Fenton Felton's death is a tragedy," I say, "for his family, for this community. You all witnessed the murder. Yes, it was dark, but maybe you saw something, before the melee, during it, after it. Maybe you heard something. Maybe you know something."

The grumbles return, though not as loud, and not from all corners of the gym. I feel like at least *some* of the audience members are invested in solving this murder and if I can hold onto them, I can make this work.

When I explain we're passing out index cards, and collecting everyone's names, addresses, and phone numbers, the crowd gets agitated again.

"If I don't keep you here," I say, "then I'll have to call you into the police station, one at a time."

That quiets down the crowd.

"Once we break, in a few minutes, you're welcome to use the facilities, but you need to stay on this floor or the stairwell or the basement, which is mostly locked storage rooms for supplies and city archives. We've commandeered the corridor outside the women's locker room to set up the refreshments. We've locked the doors, and the stairwells going up, and we have officers posted at the exits. You came to the meeting with the expectation that we would go to 2 pm, and we aim to honor that expectation. When we return—"

A man with a booming voice in the back of the crowd interrupts. "Unlock the doors," he shouts. "Unlock the doors."

Dozens more join him, stomping their feet as well.

I hold up my arm and wait. I don't try to speak over the crowd. I count to thirty before the chants and stomps lose steam, but I know they can start up again in a second.

"As I said, the desserts and coffee will be here soon. If you have a pressing need to leave, you'll have to make your case to the officers at the exits. And those of you who interrupted me just now with your stomping and chanting, please pay attention: I'm letting you off with a warning, but any further disruptions will have consequences, like arrest for interfering with a police investigation."

More grumbles, but no chants. I've already assigned two officers to crowd control and I need more. I've reached out to Mill Valley and Tiburon for reinforcements, but they're at least ten minutes away.

"Before we break, I'd like each person of interest to

stand and say your name, your age, and your relationship to Fenton Felton. We'll go in the order you're seated,
starting with Fate."

Fate stands stiffly as if her knees no longer bend. She
has blood on her hands, her face, and her dress, a rusty
brown now that it's dried. Her pigtails are undone and
her hair is unruly.

"My name is Fate Abernathy," she says, "and I'm
twenty-one years old, younger sister to Honest, and an
Aquarius Harbor houseboat resident for seven years and
Fenton Felton is attempting to evict me and my neighbors
from our homes and our community. You've seen that
I designed a berth plan that can accommodate Fenton's
project and Aquarius Harbor, but he refused to even look
at it, and when I presented it earlier, he falsely claimed
that I stole it from him. I did not."

She continues to stand. I signal her to sit.

"That's way more than enough. The rest of you, keep
it short. Name, age, and relationship to Fenton Felton.
That's it. Honest?"

"I'm Honest Abernathy, twenty-five years old, older
brother to Fate, and, like Fate, I am resisting Fenton
Felton's plan to evict us and destroy our community so
he can build a luxury houseboat harbor for people who
are going to use them as second homes as opposed to us,
for whom this is our only home. Oh, and my girlfriend,
last I checked, is Dawn, the daughter of Fenton Felton."

"Still too long," says Tin. "How about you, Brenda?
Be brief."

Honest sits as if sleepwalking.

"I'm Brenda and I've introduced myself already.
I'm an Aquarius Harbor houseboat resident, soon-to-be
single mother, and I *was* involved with Fenton Felton,

the deceased. He is the father of my baby-to-be. I'm twenty-eight."

Brenda's eyes twitch but she holds herself erect, her hands cradling her belly. She's wary, as if we're going to blame everything on her.

Honest, Fate, and Brenda all have powerful motives, but they don't seem like the murdering type. But then, no one here does, yet one of them did the deed.

I used to think murderers were different from you and me, and some are, but often, they're regular people with everyday problems and they snap or stumble or succumb to some irresistible temptation when their guard is down. They would never condone murder, but something happens.

But how can you be impulsive and at the same time deliberate enough to blow the circuits *first* so you can do your dirty business in the dark? That is an even bigger mystery than whodunit.

I pride myself on how well I read people, but sometimes the most dangerous people give nothing away and the most innocent look like they're guilty of something. Honest, for example, whom I have to consider seriously, has a relaxed air about him and he lies with ease. While his sister seems sincere and yet not relaxed in the least.

"Mickey, you're next," I say.

"I'm Mickey Macgillacuddy, thirty-one, and, like, I don't have a relationship with Fenton Felton, except he served me an eviction warrant. Two, to be precise."

Mickey smiles, shrugs. He seems less rattled than the others.

"Alice?" I say.

"I'm Alice Felton, soon to be Alice Almaden, as soon as the paperwork goes through, and I'm the ex-wife of

Fenton Felton, who I divorced when I discovered he was having an affair with Brenda. I'm forty-eight."

She looks distraught, even in her striking caftan, and I wonder how much of that is for show. I have no idea if she feels elated or relieved, but if she is, she knows to hide it. She's Fenton Felton's ex-wife and I can only imagine the turbulent water under that bridge. She once told me she lived to punish him.

Dawn stands before I call on her.

"I'm Dawn Felton, daughter of Alice and Fenton, and I turned twenty-three a week ago."

She doesn't mention her relationship with Honest.

Last and certainly not least—he's the largest of the seven people on the stage—is Huck.

"I'm Huck Hennessee and I was Fenton Felton's business partner. I managed the financial aspects of the company. I'm forty-three."

Sally whispers in my ear. The van with the first of three deliveries of refreshments has arrived.

"Time for our break," I say. "When we return, I'm going to ask these seven persons of interest a few questions, and then I will call on *you*—to share what you saw or heard or know.

"See you back in your seats at 12:30. I recommend the cheesecake."

29

I Need a Favor

I don't know why I lug my camera with me to the bathroom when the doors to City Hall are locked, but I'm a creature of habit. Earlier this year, someone stole my camera outside Candlestick Park, in the thirty seconds I ran to our van for a replacement cord. I thought Johnny Dash was watching it.

As I exit the bathroom, my camera on my shoulder, Chief Tin walks toward me. "Excuse me, Mr. Camera Guy, do you—?"

"Me?"

"You."

I set my camera down on a chair in the corridor.

My father was already dead to me, but his actual death is hitting me like a mallet on my skull. I'm reeling.

But if he was dead to me, why did I work my

connections to sign on with Johnny Dash to cover the houseboat wars?

"I'm Tin Holland," she says, "chief of police. Can I ask you about that camera? What kind is it?"

"I know who you are. I've been shooting you for hours. For weeks, actually. I'm Jazz. The camera is a Stony Marconi Featherweight."

"Were you filming when the lights went out?" she asks. "Did you see anything? Did the camera see anything?"

"No, it was dark, but—"

"Listen, Jazz." She glances at her watch. "I need a favor."

30

What You Did in the Darkness

I step to the microphone. Not everyone is back in their seats, but I said 12:30 and I believe in starting on time.

I have a plan. The beginnings of a plan, anyway. During the break, I asked Jazz to show me the footage he shot before and after the lights went out. The janitor has wheeled in a white screen where I can project the footage.

But not yet.

I wait thirty seconds for the crowd to quiet down, enough so that I hear the air whooshing through the ventilation tubes on the ceiling. I wait ten seconds more, an excruciating ten seconds, and now it's even quieter. The crowd is wary, but also engaged. I think. I hope.

"I'd like to thank you, our community members, in advance, for your patience, and for helping us to solve this murder, together," I say.

The seven persons of interest sit in a semicircle at the back of the stage. I sweep my arm in their direction. "The people on stage now were on the stage when Fenton Felton was murdered—Honest, Fate, Brenda, Alice, Dawn, Mickey, and Huck. I'm going to ask you, the audience members, who witnessed this murder, what you saw, what you heard, and what you know, but first, I'm going to ask these seven people to get up and go back to where they were when the lights went out.

"During the break, Johnny Dash's cameraman, Jazz—thank you, Jazz—showed me his video footage and from that, I've mapped out where each of our seven persons of interest were *before* the lights went out and what they were doing." I hold up my notepad with my sketch. "On the stage floor, there are strips of blue tape with the names of these seven people." I turn back to the seven. "Please stand on the tape with your name. The blue tape. Deputy Barney is standing in for Fenton Felton."

When they are in their places, I approach Honest and Barney. "At the center of the melee were Honest and Fenton Felton and just seconds before we were plunged into darkness, Fenton Felton had his fingers around Honest's throat and Honest was grabbing Fenton Felton by his thigh. Honest, please reach down and place your hands around Barney's left leg. And hold that position."

He goes for the right leg first, then realizes his mistake. He holds up his hands and flashes a goofy grin. He's been serious since the murder, and this moment of levity is brief, but this is who he is. I've already instructed Barney where to place his hands.

"Jazz, our cameraman, is filming all this, at my request, and he will continue to record as we proceed with this reenactment. Meanwhile, I'm going to use

Jazz's Polaroid to take still photos of everyone up here as they freeze. These photographs will help us as we move forward. Honest, Barney, are you ready?"

They nod and once I've taken the photo, I instruct them to let go of each other, but continue to stand on the blue tape. It's tricky to handle the mic and the camera, so I call on another officer, Peter Glick, to take the photos.

"Honest, when Fenton Felton had his hands around your throat, did you feel like you were being choked?" I hold the mic by Honest's chin.

He presses his lips together with the hint of a frown and squints, as if he is straining to remember. "A little," he says, "but he didn't have a good grip. I didn't panic. I knew I could slip loose once I grabbed his leg."

I have more questions for Honest, but I want to get everyone set up in the tableau first. "Alice, you're behind Fenton Felton. Do you remember what you were doing?"

She looks down, a pained look on her face. I'm certain she remembers. I hold the mic in front of her for another couple seconds to see if she'll answer. She doesn't.

"You were pounding your ex-husband on his right shoulder with your fists," I say. "Can you do that now? Soft and slow so you don't hurt Barney."

She grits her teeth and punches Barney twice. "I couldn't stop myself," she says. "I raced up here because I followed Dawn, and I *was* going to pull him away from the fight, but once I was here, something came over me, I can't explain it, and I started hitting him with my fists. He probably didn't feel a thing."

"Dawn, you were yanking your father's left arm. Could you grab Barney just above the elbow and do that now? Pull, but not hard. What were you trying to accomplish?"

"Break up the fight before someone got hurt."

"Why did you pull *your father* away from the fight instead of Honest?"

"He was closer, I guess. It was chaotic. I acted without much thought."

"You acted without much thought?" I repeat. "Mickey, you're next. Dawn, you can let go."

Compared to Alice and Dawn, who were unhappy with the attention, Mickey seems to revel in it. He's standing between Alice and Dawn, behind Fenton Felton's back, his face animated, waiting for my instructions.

"You had your arms wrapped around Fenton Felton's chest. Can you do that now with Barney?"

He stretches his arms around Barney, under his armpits, clasps his hands together, and squeezes. Barney flinches. Mickey lets go before I tell him to.

"What were *you* trying to accomplish, Mickey?"

"Climb on his back, knock him to the ground, land him on his ass." He has a twinkle in his eyes like he's hoping for a laugh and there are a few giggles.

When I switch to the three standing on the other side of Honest and Barney—Fate, Huck, and Brenda—I get similar answers. They all say they went up to the stage to break up the fight, though Brenda says as soon as she grabbed Honest's belt, she was tugged forward and she let go because she didn't want to get hurt.

I ask everyone to go back to what they were doing in the reenactment for a photo. There are no *significant* revelations from this first part of my plan, but the crowd is with me, and I've set everything up for the second part.

"Thank you," I say. "You can relax, but stay where you are. I'm going to try an experiment."

I hold up a short piece of bent wire shaped like the

letter "U." It's got black insulation around it, but bare copper wire on both ends. "You may remember that the power went out and that after we replaced the blown fuse, we discovered this wire near the electric outlet in the stage floor.

"This is not the actual wire that Mayor Sally found. That's secured in our evidence bag. But it looks the same.

"One of these seven people up here blew the circuit by jamming a wire into the outlet. Most likely the same person who committed the murder, but not necessarily. Fate, you were behind Huck and close to the outlet. I'd like you to scoot over to the outlet, and mime jamming this wire into it."

I hand the wire to her. "You can run, crawl on your hands and knees, your choice. Tell me when you're ready and I'll time you. Don't stick the wire in the outlet. Just pretend. We don't want another blackout."

"I'm ready," she says. I hover my thumb over my stopwatch. "Three, two, one, go."

She's fast. On her hands and knees in a second, at the outlet two seconds later, then she swings her arm to the floor, an imaginary wire between her thumb and finger.

"3.77 seconds," I say. Faster than I expected.

Why would Fate be so quick? Reverse psychology? See, I can get there in a flash and I'm not afraid you'll be more likely to suspect me?

I ask Alice next.

"It couldn't have been me," she says, her voice rising in pitch. "I had no idea you could blow a fuse with a wire."

"You were as close as Fate to the outlet," I say.

She hesitates when I say go, and she doesn't hurry. She gets the task done in 5.67 seconds.

Dawn and Mickey are both faster than Alice, but

slower than Fate—4.72 seconds and 4.3 seconds respectively. Brenda and Huck are slower—6.12 and 7.34 seconds.

What the crowd does not know is that in the four seconds before the lights went out, Jazz zoomed in on the grimacing faces of Honest and Fenton as they wrestled each other. Until the lights went out. So Honest could not have blown the fuse *and* whoever did blow it was not captured on video. Since I'm keeping that to myself, I need to time Honest too.

He slips out of Barney's chokehold easily and throws himself at the outlet. He's the second fastest after Fate at 4.2 seconds. He looks pleased with himself.

There are two other important pieces of evidence I don't share—one is that the murder weapon was Honest's knife and two is that we found no fingerprints on the blade or the handle of the knife. It's *possible* that happened by accident, but I'm assuming the murderer wiped off any fingerprints.

"How many of you in the gym just saw Honest move to the outlet? Raise your hands." Most everyone does.

"How about Alice? Did you see her?" She was partly blocked by Huck and Honest. Again, almost everyone.

"Now, I'd like you to think back to this morning, before the lights went out. How many of you saw *anyone* slip away from the scrum toward the outlet?"

I hold my breath.

No one raises their hand.

The murderer was audacious, that's for sure, killing Fenton Felton in front of hundreds of witnesses, but that was in darkness. He or she, if the fuse-blower and the murderer were the same person, had to get to the outlet with the lights *on,* and risk being seen. I was here on stage, and I had an unobstructed view, and you'd think that I would have seen someone, at least a blur of motion out of the corner of my eye.

But I didn't. My eyes, like everyone else's, were on the melee.

"Now we're shifting to *after* the murder when the lights came back on. We were in the dark for less than two minutes, but a lot happened during that time. I've drawn another sketch based on Jazz's footage and now I want all of you on stage to stand on the red tape with your name on it. That's where you were when the lights came back on. If you were sitting or kneeling or lying on your back, please get in that position. I'll refresh your memory if you need me to."

When they're all in place, I walk over to Fate, who is on her back, furthest from the center of the melee. "Fate, you have blood on your dress, your face, and your hands, yet you ended up on the floor, further from Fenton Felton's body than anyone else. Tell me what you remember. From the moment you were pulling Honest's arm to your present position."

She sits up. "I lost my grip after the lights went out and stumbled over someone. The blood came from doing CPR."

"You didn't race over to the outlet, blow the circuit, and then run back to the melee, steal Honest's knife, and stab Fenton Felton?"

The crowd gasps. Fate gulps. I did not intend to accuse anyone during this reenactment—my plan was just-the-facts-ma'am, like Sergeant Joe Friday, but I felt like it was time to amp things up.

"No," she says. "I tripped, like I said."

"Fate did it," someone in the crowd shouts.

I hold up my arm until it's calm. "Let's not race to conclusions. We're gathering information. Honest, you were sitting on the floor, a foot from the body. What were you doing when it was dark?"

"Wrestling Fenton Felton, and then, I can't remember, it was so crazy. I got, like, pulled or grabbed in three directions and I fell. When I sat up, I heard this loud groan and a thunk on the floor."

"What about you, Huck?" I say, pointing to the blue tape with his name on it. "You were wrapping your arms around Honest just before the lights went out, and when the lights came back on, you were two feet away, still on your feet."

"I got pushed or pulled and lost my balance and stumbled, but I didn't fall. Once I was standing solidly on my feet, I didn't move."

"How long were you standing still?" I ask.

"Ten seconds, maybe twenty. Maybe longer. Long enough to wonder what happened, how long we'd be in the dark, whether I should do something more than stand here."

I cut short the rest of the reenactment. The before and after parts haven't been as informative as I'd hoped, but timing the race to the electrical outlet gives me a lot to mull over.

Those who were closest, like Fate and Alice, could have gotten there fast enough, and they could have hidden behind the scrum of bodies and not been noticed. Fate made it in less than four seconds and Alice *could* have. Dawn could have too.

I can't eliminate Brenda, but I would say it was unlikely she could have gotten there in time. I'm certainly not eliminating Mickey—he's more cunning than he appears. During the first eviction raid, he cut the rope that we attached to tow his houseboat and I didn't see him do that, and then shortly after that, he slipped into the water unnoticed.

I'm tempted to eliminate Huck. Unless he's wily enough to hide an explosive nimbleness behind his portly frame, I don't see how he could have made it to the outlet quickly enough and without being seen. And, poor guy, he's so tethered to Fenton Felton, I can't imagine anyone else on stage who could be his accomplice.

I can't rule anyone out entirely, except Honest, who was wrestling Fenton Felton. But he could have had an accomplice.

I'm trying to practice beginner's mind. It's a Zen thing that's easy to grasp, but extremely hard to do. I'm absorbing every piece of information, everything that could be a clue, without jumping to judgment. That's the idea, anyway, but I'm already failing. My concern is that if I lean too much toward any one of the seven as the murderer, I might close my eyes to something important.

I confer with Barney for a second, and he gives me his microphone and then drags a worn wooden bench from the wing onto the stage. I turn to the crowd.

"I promised that I'm going to ask *you*, the witnesses, what you saw, what you heard, what you know, but first, I'd like the wronged women in Fenton Felton's life—daughter Dawn, ex-wife Alice, pregnant ex-mistress Brenda—to sit on this bench."

ALICE FELTON

[Vengeful ex-wife of Fenton, mother of Dawn]

31

Who Has it Worse?

Chief Tin wants Dawn, Brenda, and me to sit on the bench. She calls us the "wronged women in Fenton Felton's life." She's got that right.

"Alice, I'll start with you," Tin says, "because we've *talked*, you and I, and you told me, *more than once*, that you hated Fenton and wished he would die. And yet, I can't imagine that you aren't experiencing *complicated* feelings now that he's dead."

Complicated? Tell me about it.

Of course, I'm *distraught* that Fenton is dead, and what's worse is that Tin thinks I did it. And what's worse than that is how she just forced me to act out punching Fenton in the back—in front of everyone in town. I have *never* been so humiliated in my life.

Even more pathetic is that while I held my pose, balling up my puny fists behind that deputy's back, I heard the click of cameras. There will be photographic evidence of me at my lowest. I will *never* live that down. This will not win me votes for city council.

I stand up from the bench. "I know I'm the vengeful ex-wife," I say, "but I *never* said I wished he would die. *Out loud.*"

I bury my face in my hands. "I am in shock. This morning I watched my husband of twenty-five years die in a puddle of blood."

I sigh. My shoulders slump. "I loved him once," I say. "But he did me wrong and making him miserable is the *only* thing that gives my life meaning. Why would I kill him?"

Tin turns to my daughter. "Dawn, what do you think?"

What the—? I expected Tin to ask questions, but I didn't think she would *sic* Dawn on me.

"You could move on, Mom," she says, "but no, revenge is too intoxicating."

Now she chooses to be honest?

"And be more like you?" I say. "So intent on defying your father you take up with a *pretend* pirate *because* your father hates him. *Hated* him."

Now I start crying. But why? I'm certainly not crying for Fenton.

I stop my tears and perk up. "Not that I'm blind to Honest's appeal," I say, running my fingers through my hair. "He was charming and *flirtatious* that time we met."

"Oh God, Mom, *please.*"

"You don't know what it's like to be going on fifty," I say. "I can't believe Fenton left me."

"*He* didn't leave you, Mom," she says. "*You* left him. And *someone* murdered him. You're the ex, so you're the prime suspect. And you've got blood on your lovely dress."

What is she *doing?* Doesn't she have any sympathy for my situation? How am I going to show my face in this town if everyone thinks I'm a murderer? How am I going to get these bloodstains off my caftan?

Chief Tin is just standing there not saying anything. It's like she's checked out or something. Her eyes are glazed over.

"You have as much motive as I do," I say. "You—"

"No. *No!* I wanted to reconcile," Dawn says. "All he had to do was apologize and stop being a prick, but now—"

She stops, takes a breath, starts again. "The only way he showed love, if you want to call it that, was with money, but I'm a liberated woman and I refused to take it, even for grad school tuition or rent—"

"Tell me if I have this right," says Tin, finally stepping in, "he was a *horrible* father, but a *worse* husband?"

"No," Dawn says, "he was *worse* as a father."

"*No,* I had it worse," I say. "And for far longer."

"*No,* you had a choice," Dawn says. "I didn't get to choose my father."

That's true, though when she was young, she *adored* her father.

I turn to Dawn. "You know your father's will leaves everything to *you,*" I say. "There may be nothing left but debt, but still—"

"Dad left *me* everything? But I don't want anything to do with the family business. I've got grad school. What will happen to Heavenly Harbor?"

"*That* is up to you," I say.

Dawn looks pensive but doesn't say anything. The

audience starts to grumble, and I look at Tin, whose eyes are wide open but seem to be staring into the distance.

That man in the back with the booming voice who interrupted earlier stands and shouts, "Unlock the doors. Unlock the doors."

Within seconds, the entire crowd has joined in the chants. They're also clapping their hands and stomping their feet.

32

Look Chief, No Hiccups

I wake up as if from a trance. The entire crowd is chanting, "Unlock the doors. Unlock the doors." The plywood stage shakes under my feet.

I hold up my arm and wait, like I did earlier. But the chants and the stomps get louder. A man in the aisle folds up his chair and bangs its legs on the gym floor. I've lost the crowd.

Because I lost myself.

I count to thirty before the chants and stomps lose steam, but I know they can start up again in a second.

I knew keeping everyone here would not be popular, but I did not anticipate that one person chanting would turn into a loud chorus so quickly. When audience members arrived this morning, they expected to be here until 2 pm. I can't believe anyone thought we would resolve the conflict in a couple hours.

The audience is loud, but I have the microphone. There's a one-second space between the chants, and I wait for the next one. "Give me ten minutes," I say.

But the stomping and chanting escalate.

Then, in the next space between chants, I hear a familiar, husky voice shouting from the back. "Give her ten minutes. We must find the killer *now*, while the blood is still warm."

It's Justine, my police friend from the City, riding to the rescue. My spirits leap. The chants don't stop, but fewer people are chanting.

I called her yesterday to tell her about my night in the San Francisco jail, and also how great it was to see her. I told her about today's meeting, though I did not invite her. I didn't think she'd be interested.

I squint into the bleachers where her voice came from, but I don't see her.

"I'm keeping you here," I say to the restless crowd, "because you witnessed the murder. We have to ask these questions. It's my job, the job you pay me to do. To keep you safe. Our only other option is that we talk at the police station, in the interrogation room."

That worked before the break, but now it only amplifies the grumbling.

"Ten minutes," I say. "Give me ten minutes and then we reassess."

The crowd picks up the chant again, until Justine's voice rings out. "Give the woman ten minutes, for Christ's sake."

Now I spot her. She's tall and her black face and afro stand out in this crowd. But she's so far away I barely make out her face.

I point at Justine. "Going once, going twice," my

voice double-time, like an auctioneer. "Ten minutes it is," and with a button under the lectern, I reset the score-board clock, up above the bleachers, to "10:00."

I wait until the audience quiets down. The timer's yellow numbers are down to 9:41.

"Alice," I say, "I have one *final* question for you, about the bankruptcy statement on the posters outside City Hall. You saw the poster?"

"I did."

"Might *you* have contributed in any way?

"No," she says. "I wondered the same thing—where the bankruptcy papers came from. Huck does the finances. Not that *he* would ever be *disloyal* to Fenton."

"Huck, will you join these lovely ladies on the bench?"

He hesitates. "I'd be happy to," he says, but he does not look happy as he trudges to the bench. Alice slides closer to her daughter.

"Huck, you prepared the bankruptcy statement on those posters?"

"For his *divorce*," he says. "He was not *actually*—" He pauses. I see the wheels turning. "I used numbers he gave me."

"My understanding is you were partners, yet you were angling to withdraw *your* investment from the project."

"I don't know what you're getting at," he says. He squeezes his throat with his fingers like he's trying to hold back a hiccup.

"When my officers were examining the crime scene," I say, "they found a letter that must have fallen from your pocket during the scuffle. A letter you wrote your wife."

Huck's hand twitches toward his pocket, but he stops it. The crowd is quiet. I should have started my questioning with him, but Alice is the ex and anyone else in my position would have gone after her first.

I unfold the letter. Huck is as rigid as a plywood board.

"Let's project the letter on our screen," I say. Barney rolls a cart with an overhead projector to the center of the stage, taking an exaggerated step over the orange extension cord.

I take a deep breath, as Barney lines the projector up with the screen.

I lost control there with Alice and Dawn. My night in jail caught up with me. I feel like I've been awake forever. I have all sorts of excuses, like that I'm only human, but I'm not going to lose focus again.

Justine is here, and I've recovered and maybe the heckler did me a favor by throwing cold water on my face. This is a once-in-a-lifetime opportunity and I am not going to bungle it.

Barney clicks on the projector. The letter is upside down on the screen. He turns it around and nudges it with his thumb till it's centered.

"For those of you who can't see this," I say, "I will read it out loud."

Huck looks at the screen, then down at his folded hands. He knows what's up there.

"'Dear Cath,'" I say. "That's Cath, Huck's lovely wife, for those who don't know.

"'I'm writing you this letter because I'm too ashamed to tell you this in person.

"'I invested more money than we can afford to lose in this houseboat harbor project, which is in jeopardy of failing, and my biggest mistake is that I did not consult you.

"'I know you want me to sever ties with Fenton Felton, but I did this because I want to please you. When you wanted the remodel, I said of course, but that cut our financial cushion to the bone and I thought I could build back our nest egg by investing more in this harbor project, and—'"

"That's enough, please," Huck says. "There's no need to humiliate my wife. She bears no blame for my mistakes."

I walk over to the projector and click off the light. "Tell me if I have this right," I say. "You told your wife you would sever ties with Fenton Felton, but you *couldn't* because you invested more than you could afford, and if you abandoned the project, you would lose your entire stake."

Huck squeezes his eyes shut, clenches his fist. "This is going to be like ripping tape off my arm," he says. To himself, under his breath, but I hear him.

"It's worse than that," he says. "Cath entrusted our finances to *me* and I invested *her* money *without* telling her. Unless we build the harbor, *we* go bankrupt—Cath and me—so I stuck with Fenton because I had no choice.

"Look Chief, no hiccups. That's how you know I'm not lying. I mean, if ever there was a man who deserved to be murdered, it was Fenton Felton—he was a horrible man who took pleasure in hurting others."

He's acting like he's on Valium or something. His arms and legs are rubbery and wobbly. He widens his stance so he doesn't fall over. There's a woman in the front row whose mouth is open in disbelief.

"I speak the truth," he says. "And please, no lectures about why I stuck by Fenton Felton for so long. But there's no reason I would *kill* him. His death will stall the project. It's a win for the houseboaters. At least tempo-rarily. Money down the drain for me."

After the reenactment, I pretty much ruled out Huck. I still can't see how he could have made it to the electrical outlet in time to blow the fuse.

But he has so many reasons to kill Fenton Felton and he's so desperate and desperate people do desperate things.

BRENDA DIAMOND

[Lonely waitress, houseboat resident, former mistress of Fenton]

33

Honest's Flimsy Alibi

I sit on the bench next to Dawn, quiet and still, while she and her mother squabble over who has it worse. I'm surprised they are opening up like that. I'm not going to.

I'm trying to blend into the background, but it's not so easy in my sunshiny yellow dress. I wanted to look bright because I was giving the first speech and now I wish I'd gone with my gray jumper.

Alice says Dawn is inheriting her father's business, which *could* be good news for us houseboaters. Though not necessarily.

I feel a flutter in my stomach and I wonder if that's my daughter, reminding me she's there. If it's a kick, it's a small one, but what I felt the other night, when Fenton accosted me outside the Dare Not, that *was* a kick. The first one. And then I felt one last night, while I was lying in bed trying to sleep.

I don't understand why I'm being treated like a suspect. I don't have any blood on me, like a bunch of the others do, and I can't imagine *why* I would want to kill Fenton. Well, other than that he was stalking me outside the Dare Not Wednesday night, and I threatened to scream and wake the whole town. But no one else knows about that, and besides, I'm not the kind of person who would kill another person, let alone my daughter's father.

Tin asks Huck to join us on the bench, and questions him about a letter he wrote to his wife. Maybe Tin will forget about me and I can go back to my chair. The bench has no back support.

The chief is crafty. She projects such decency and friendliness, but she goaded Dawn and Alice into accusing each other and now Huck is fumbling with his answers and changing his story and she's not accusing him of murder or anything, only asking about this letter, which apparently fell out of his pocket during the skirmish. That sounds fishy to me.

Huck is talking about what a horrible man Fenton was and though it's sort of true, it makes me feel sorry for him. Fenton, I mean, not Huck, though I suppose Huck deserves some sympathy as well. When people act like the way those two do, there's something broken inside them.

Tin sends Huck back to his chair and turns to me. "I'm sorry, Brenda, you must feel left out."

"Not at all."

"Yesterday," Tin says, "my deputy Barney interviewed you about Honest's alibi on Thursday night."

Uh-oh.

I promised Fate I would support Honest's alibi and I did, but that was before I knew why, before I knew how flimsy Honest's story would be.

I stand before I answer. "I said he was an obnoxious drunk. Honest, I mean. Not Barney." I'm taller than Tin, so now that I'm on my feet, she's no longer looking down on me. The room is stuffy, but my hands feel chilly and I pull the sleeves of my dress over my wrists.

"You told Barney Honest was in the bar from seven on," she says.

"That's right."

"That's right, as in that's what you told Barney, or that's right as in that's what really happened."

"Both."

"The thing is," Tin says, pressing her index fingers together into a steeple and resting them on the tip of her nose, "we have a bootprint that matches Honest's boot, and the only time that it could *possibly* have been made and not have been washed away by the tide would be at eight Thursday night, or later. We also have the testimony of a private security officer that a man matching Honest's height and build ran off that sinking barge at approximately that time. Honest is quite the magician, but I don't see how he could be in two places at once."

"Nor do I," I say, "but he makes a spectacle of himself wherever he goes."

Tin smiles, but then she gets this glum look, as if she's forgotten that someone just died and maybe it's not appropriate to smile.

She glances at Honest. She thinks *he* murdered Fenton Felton? Why else would she ask about the barge? To catch *me* in my lie? How does that help?

Unless she's trying to trip up Honest.

"I understand you're in a serious predicament," Tin says, "Where else are you going to find an affordable rental? A community of like-minded people. Where you can walk to work? The thing is, we interviewed customers at the Dare Not who say Honest arrived *after* nine, with wet hair."

"In my experience, drinkers are notoriously poor witnesses," I say. "And by the way, thanks to you and your police force, I *can* walk home late at night and feel safe." Honest's hair *was* wet. It was sopping and matted to his head, and I noted that because his hair is quite becoming when it's clean and dry and brushed. Thursday night, he looked like a drowned rat.

"Nice save there," Tin says. "But there *were* three witnesses."

It was easy lying to Barney, not so easy with Tin. She seems to know how uncomfortable I am.

"I know you feel loyal to the houseboat community," she continues, "and that it's important for you to stand by your tribe, but why are you protecting Honest? *Everyone* knows he sank the barge. Including you."

She stops, raises her eyebrows.

I look over to Honest, but he stares blankly into space.

Why am I lying when I'm not fooling anyone? Do I owe enough to my Aquarius community to go against my better self?

But I support what Honest and Fate did, blocking the pile driver. I wouldn't lie if I thought Honest were the murderer—Fenton is my daughter's father, and even if I don't mourn his loss, someday she will.

"One witness," Tin says, "told us Honest *bragged* about what he did. In the Dare Not that night with his wet hair. That sounds like Honest, doesn't it?"

"I waited too many tables Thursday night to listen to wild-goose stories. Honest says a lot of crazy stuff when he's drunk."

TIN HOLLAND

[Sausalito's first woman police chief]

34

Unlock the Doors

I ask Dawn, Alice, and Huck to return to their chairs. "Mickey, Honest, Fate," I say, "please join Brenda on the bench."

Brenda frowns as she watches the others walk to their chairs. "Why do I have to stay?"

I feel like I've regained control and the crowd has my back. But not everyone.

I see audience members glancing at their watches, whispering to each other. Worst of all, I see some yawning. Also, the gym is hot, stuffy, and rank. The scoreboard timer reads 4:42.

"You live at Aquarius Harbor," I tell Brenda, "and, like Mickey, Fate, and Honest, Fenton Felton was evicting you."

I look down at my notes, but I've hardly written any. I usually take notes when I am questioning suspects, but

I've let my fear that the audience will get impatient knock me off my game.

Starting now, I'm going to take a second, no, three seconds, even five seconds—*before* I ask a question, *after* I get an answer, *while I'm waiting for one*—and write down the name of the person I'm questioning, and whatever comes to mind, based on clues or hunches or whatever. I won't let the crowd pressure me to hurry.

I write "Brenda" on my notepad, then, in the right column, "pregnant."

Well, that's not helpful.

Honest, Fate, and Mickey are sitting on the bench now, and Brenda seems to have accepted that she has to stay.

"Mickey," I say, "you live in a *small* houseboat, is that right?"

He pops to his feet with an impish grin, like he's been waiting for this moment all morning. His tie-dye leisure suit is rumpled and his long blond hair disheveled. "Man, like, my houseboat is so small," he says, "if I order a large pizza, I have to eat it outside." He holds his thumb and forefinger, almost touching, under his chin. "It's, like, so small, the only pet I have room for is a termite. It's so small, my wall-to-wall carpeting is a welcome mat. Thank you, I'll be here all week." He bows.

I was not expecting that, but I suppose I should have. *Mickey Macgillicuddy!*

I write "Mickey" on my notepad, then "Not as flaky as he pretends to be."

When I look up, Lander Jarrett, the houseboaters' lawyer, is rushing onto the stage and approaching Fate and Honest on the bench.

How did she get in? Has she been here all morning?

"Lander, what are you doing here?" Honest asks.

"I called her," says Fate, "because you are in big trouble."

"Me?" he says.

I hold my tongue. When I let Dawn and Alice go after each other, I lost control. But the audience is quiet. They want to see what's going to happen between Honest and Fate. So do I.

"I hate it when you pretend to be dumb," Fate says. "You *are* the most likely suspect."

On my notepad, I write "Justine." Oops. Lost focus again. I cross out her name and write, "Fate."

I have to be vigilant. I will call Justine when I climb out from under all this, but now I have to put her out of my mind.

"Because Fenton Felton and I ripped into each other viciously?" Honest says. "That was theater. I didn't hate *him*. I hated the *system* he—"

"Excuse me," Fate says, "your knife was the murder weapon."

"How do they know it's mine?" he asks.

"Your name is on it. I saw it when I did CPR."

Fate wrinkles her forehead, but her eyes betray her. She's gloating. On my notepad, I write, "As angry at Honest as at Fenton."

"Someone *else* could have written my name," Honest says, "someone who always writes things down because *she* forgets."

"*She?*" Fate says, "Men are the violent ones."

Before Honest can answer, Lander claps her hand over his mouth and steps in front of him. "I have advised my client not to answer any more questions—even though keeping quiet makes him look guilty."

Honest pulls his chin to his chest and looks down. He's not looking for attention now. Why did Lander wait so long?

The crowd is still enough now I hear Fate shuffle her index cards.

My ten minutes are almost up. There's too much to juggle. I need to be three people. To manage the suspects *and* the antsy crowd, *and* ask questions, *and* listen to the answers, *and* pay attention to everyone's body language, *and* map out my strategy.

I promised I would give the audience members a chance to speak, but that could go off the rails fast.

I *might* learn something valuable. I *might* get away with taking another ten minutes.

"Now I want to hear from you," I say, sweeping my arms out wide to encompass the whole gymnasium. "You are witnesses. Did you see anything before or after we were plunged into darkness? Did you hear anything when the lights were out? Do you know anything that we don't know?"

I point to the microphone in the left aisle, which we set up during the break, and about a dozen people scurry to line up.

"Comments are limited to thirty seconds, because I respect your time. I'm going to reset the clock. We're going to take another ten minutes."

Jenna, a waitress from the Dare Not, is first in line. "My name is Jenna Worthmore, and I work as a waitress alongside Brenda at the Dare Not. I know Brenda is a suspect, but I want to speak about her soul and her heart. She is the sweetest and most evolved woman I know and it's impossible to imagine that she killed him."

"I appreciate your sentiments, Jenna," I say, "but I'm

not looking for character references. This is also directed to those behind you in line."

Next to the mic is Cotton Booth, the chamber of commerce president, as unctuous a man as can be. "I propose," he says, "renaming our berth project the 'Fenton Felton Memorial Harbor,' or, for short, 'Felton Harbor.' It's the best way to remember him."

I keep my groan to myself. A headache creeps up from the nape of my neck. Booth didn't even like Fenton Felton. "Mr. Booth, you obviously did not heed what I said to Jenna," I say. "And the best way to remember Fenton Felton is by apprehending his killer. Next."

He glares at me, but heads back to his seat.

There are now more than twenty people in line behind the mic. At the front is an older man I recognize, but don't know. His hair is white and his glasses are thick.

"I'm Peter Hawthorne, a long-time across-the-street neighbor to Alice and Fenton Felton, now only Alice. Last night, Fenton parked his car in front of my house, sat in the driver's seat while I brushed my teeth, and then knocked on Alice's door. She came out, but didn't let him in. I couldn't tell what they were saying, but then I heard Alice say, 'If you show up at my door again, I'll kill you.' Ten minutes later, a cab came and Fenton climbed in, his legs wobbly. His car was still parked in front of my house this morning."

"I thought you couldn't hear what we were saying," says Alice, who is calmer than I expect.

"You shouted that," he says.

"Alice," I say, and let my silence ask the question.

She stands, clasps her hands, purses her lips. "Fenton was lonely and he was drunk. He said he missed me. I was polite, patient. I'm proud of my restraint."

Dawn is watching her mother, her shoulders tight. She grips the seat of her chair so hard her fingers tremble. This late-night visit is news to her.

"You threatened him, but didn't kill him?" I ask.

"We say things late at night when we're tired. I've said far worse." Her voice turns dreamy, as if she's talking to herself. "When he was standing there on my porch, I pitied him. He has no one who will listen to him."

I keep my eyes on my notes, my fingers on my pen. I take ten seconds and ignore the impatience of the crowd. On the left side of the pad, I write "Alice," on the right, "why would she kill him?"

I take a few seconds more, and next to Honest's name, I add "combative," "craves attention," and "came to meeting with knife and sword."

Next in line is the woman who runs the flower stand near City Hall, who says she's offering half-off discounts on flowers to commemorate Fenton Felton. I cut her off before she finishes.

After her comes a man who argues that I have no right to keep him here against his will and that I should be fired because of my "participation in a gay riot" and my "arrest for vandalizing a police car."

I swallow, take a deep breath. "Next," I say.

But he stays at the mic. "Fenton Felton had many enemies who wished him harm," he says, "one of whom is you."

He pauses, to let everyone's eyes focus on me. I hold his gaze with a neutral expression. I don't welcome this distraction, but it's one more dollop of glue keeping people stuck to their seats, so after he milks the pause, I do the same.

"No one is beyond suspicion," I finally say, "not even me. Though I did not wish him harm and did not consider him my enemy."

"Unlock the doors," he shouts, and within seconds, he's joined by the man in the back, who started the earlier chants. Dozens more join them, stomping their feet as well.

I blow my whistle, which prompts a chorus of boos.

I have two rabbits to pull out of my hat. One is a trap I can only spring once, and I don't know yet who to spring it on. The other is a distraction, which I don't want to use until I have to.

Which might be now.

I lift my left arm and wait.

The chanting and the stomping of feet loses steam, and finally subsides enough so that I can speak.

"I have a question for Johnny Dash," I say, "about Jazz, his cameraman."

JAZZ

[TV cameraman]

35

Exposed

I'm as discombobulated as ten minutes ago, but my arms are steady now, and once again I'm the unflappable cameraman no one sees. I'm invisible behind my headphones and heavy equipment, and that's how I like it.

Chief Tin is giving audience members a chance to speak and Johnny yanks at the cable to get my attention, but I've already zoomed in on the woman at the front of the line, Jenna, a waitress I recognize from the Dare Not.

I study her through my viewfinder, willing myself to become one with the camera, to take in the world with its dispassionate gaze. No judgment. No thinking. No grieving.

When we filmed the city council debate on Wednesday, I remember noticing how pretty Jenna was, but only now does she remind me of Lisa. Lisa, as in what-an-idiot-I-was.

It's the way Jenna's bangs and her thick black hair frame her face. Lisa's hair was like that. Plus, Jenna has the same willowy grace and she holds her head high when she speaks.

I don't think of myself as someone who is easily shocked, but I will have to process what happened today, I know, and I suppose it would be healthy for me to grieve, if I can.

But not now, not here. Though there is part of me that aches to show myself to Dawn.

I abandoned her to our psycho parents, and she didn't run and hide like I did. Though she chose a college all the way across the country in Rhode Island, and now that she's back, she's defying our parents in her own way—by hooking up with her scoundrel pirate.

There will be a funeral and I can't go to the funeral without blowing my cover, but I can't *not* go. He was my father.

Johnny wants me to keep filming, but we already have more footage than we can possibly air. We can't devote our whole newscast to Sausalito. We already have the murder, and Fate's dock plan, and my father's accusation that she stole the plan, and there's the melee on stage before the lights went out. Possibly a clip of the reenactment, too. That was suspenseful.

After Jenna comes some smooth business guy who calls for the new dock to be named after my father. *Jesus Christ*. Chief Tin dismisses him politely. Too politely. She doesn't want to play the bad cop, but she should.

I'm trying not to think, but the harder I try, the more my brain races. I haven't thought of Lisa for weeks, but now here she is again, clamoring for attention.

Better her than my father, though. I've shoved

memories of him deep into a closet and locked the door. What I remember most vividly about him now is not *him,* but the intense and teary conversation I had with Lisa. *About* him.

Lisa asked me many times about my family, and I always said there wasn't much to tell. Which only made her more relentless. "I'm nosy," she said. "I want to know who you are and where you came from."

That was a year, maybe two years ago, when I was taking cinematography classes at L.A. City College. By then, I was going by Jazz.

One afternoon, Lisa and I were walking in Santa Monica with our cameras—we met at school—on a cliff above the beach, and she asked me *again* about my father. She gave me this piercing look with her big brown eyes and her tongue between her lips, and I spilled.

We weren't "dating" because neither of us believed in that, but I had kissed her hello when she picked me up in her car, and when she kissed me back, she held my face with both hands. She looked super cute that day, with her tight jeans and killer smile. I have two photos of her from that day. She had told me all sorts of shit about *her* parents, but she was still entangled with them, not estranged.

"My father is mean and demanding," I said. The waves were loud and the sun was hot.

"When I cried, as a *little* kid, four or five, he called me a girl. When I grew my hair long in high school, he called me a girl again, though I was big enough by then I could have whipped his ass.

"He wanted me to cut my hair, follow in his foot-steps, join the family business, like my mother had. But he treated her like shit, and for years, she cowered, and then she started throwing his crap right back at him. When she spoke up about how he treated her, or me, or my sister, he said that being soft did us a disservice, that it was a dog-eat-dog world and we had to be tough.

"I was not tough."

By this point, we had stopped walking and Lisa stood in front of me with her mouth wide open and her hands on her heart. She was such an intense listener that it seemed like her ears got bigger the more I talked.

"When the draft came," I continued, "I told my parents I believed the war was immoral, that I was going to resist the draft or go to Canada. Predictably, my father called me a girl. He sure was original.

"One day when my father was at work, I ran away and never looked back. I've been on my own since. Did I answer your question?"

"Oh honey," she said. "I'm *so* sorry." And she wrapped me in her arms.

She had never called me honey before, and I started crying and she murmured sweet things in my ear and I wept like a baby. Which was damn unsettling. I'd never been that exposed with anyone before.

We'd been going out for a month then, and I'd been wanting to have sex, but she wanted to wait. That night she invited me into her bed, and she was so appreciative that I "let her in" and so loving, it was too much. I left in the morning while she was sleeping, and escaped to the Bay Area, where I eventually found work with *News on the Run*. I wish she was here now to ask me her nosy questions.

She moved to Georgia for a graphic design program, and she wrote me twice, and I wrote back, but I never mailed the letter. I felt like I didn't deserve her.

I said that I didn't remember anything about my father except what I told Lisa, but the truth is that earlier this week, at Aquarius Harbor, watching the sword fight through my viewfinder, my father holding his own against spry and cocky Honest, I was *gobsmacked*. The sword fighting was a side of my father that I'd blocked out, because it was easier to hate *everything* about him.

When I was little, we used to play fight with swords and I loved that. The swords must have been plastic or wood, I can't remember, and maybe it was only a few times, maybe a dozen. But he played with me. That I'm sure of. He wasn't horrible every minute of every day. Now that I'm thinking about it, I remember he did magic tricks for me too.

I can't get the image of him lying in a pool of blood out of my mind. But that wasn't him. That was his lifeless body. It wasn't the man who jousted with me.

The floor rumbles under my feet and I snap my attention back to City Hall. Once again, the crowd is chanting, "Unlock the doors" and stomping their feet in rhythm.

This eruption happens in seconds and Tin blows her whistle, but that only exacerbates the situation. Now there are boos mixed in with the chants. This is great TV. I know gripping footage when I see it.

A couple audience members near the microphone stand up and bang their folding chairs on the floor. Tin holds up her arm and waits until the din dies down. She waits a long time and then she steps to the mic and doesn't speak for at least five seconds.

"I have a question," she says, "for Johnny Dash." She pauses again. "About Jazz, his cameraman."

Uh-oh.

I don't move a muscle.

"Jazz?" says Johnny, as he swipes two fingers in front of his throat to signal me to stop filming. I push the stop button.

"Look at him," Tin says, walking toward me. "Doesn't he *look* like he's in disguise, with his oversized sunglasses and bushy beard and headphones and baseball cap? Like he has something to hide."

She stops a few feet from my spot at the foot of the stage. I'm standing on the gym floor, resting the camera on the stage, which is four feet higher.

"Jazz," she says, "when we met earlier, in the hall, and I asked you about your camera, I stuck a strip of tape on the handle, and got a workable set of fingerprints, which we ran, and, lo and behold, you were in trouble with the law, right here in Sausalito, years ago, when you went by a different name—"

"No, stop!" I say. She reaches down and removes my headphones, hands them to me, then takes off my hat and sunglasses. I don't pull away.

"That name you used to go by," she says, "is Fenton Felton, *Junior,* son of Fenton Felton, *Senior.*"

I hear a gasp so loud it echoes off the gym ceiling.

Dawn jumps to her feet. "*Junior!* It's you."

My mother is not as quick to stand, but almost. "Fenti!"

Johnny shakes his head in disbelief. "*Junior? Fenton Felton, Junior?*"

I eye the exits.

"The doors are locked," Tin says, but I run anyway, tucking the bulky camera under my arm like a football, climbing the steps onto the stage, and disappearing into the wing behind the black curtains. But the camera is connected by a cord to Johnny's mic, which Johnny holds tight with both hands, and I get yanked back onto the stage.

I sigh, set the camera down. Dawn runs to me and wraps me in her arms. I sink into her embrace, though my body feels stiff and the headphones are caught between us and dig into my collarbone.

She retrieves her chair and hands it to me. I sit, bury my head in my hands. No one is chanting or stomping their feet now. They're all staring at me.

"Jazz," Tin says gently. "I am so sorry for your loss. It must be devastating, and crazy making, to witness your father's murder, to see his bloody body on the stage through your viewfinder."

Barney approaches me with the mic, but I pull my head into my shoulders like a turtle retreating into its shell. Tin waves Barney away.

"May I please have my hat and sunglasses back?" I say.

"Of course," she says, and I don my hat and glasses as soon as she hands them back to me. I study the headphones in my lap. The leather around the earpads is cracked and worn. "I imagine," Tin says, "that it's even harder given that you have been estranged from your father."

I don't respond.

"I understand you may not be comfortable sharing your story," she says, "but let me take a stab at it. Tell me if I have this right."

I'm angry that Tin exposed me, but I understand why. She needed to quiet the crowd, which is cooperative now, and she had to sacrifice me.

"You grew up here in Sausalito," she says, "and you left to get away from your father, then—"

"And my mother," I say. My mother, who has been inching toward me. Now she hesitates.

"You made your life elsewhere," Tin continues, "became a cameraman, and heard about this 'houseboat war' in your hometown, with your father and mother at the center of it, and you were understandably curious. You hooked up with Johnny Dash to see what was happening up close. But you came in disguise because you wanted to keep your identity secret."

My mother speaks, in a whisper, but I hear her.

"Did you call me Mom?" she says. "Do you know how good that makes me feel? Do you need a place to stay?"

"I said 'mother,' not 'Mom.' There's a difference." My voice sounds rusty, as if my jaws need oil.

"Couldn't we at least have lunch?" she asks. "What did your father do to you?"

I turn to Dawn. "It starts with lunch," I say, "and then she's going to want dinner." And I laugh. The same demonic laugh as my father's and I exaggerate it, which I've never done before. The crowd is stunned back into silence.

"That's right," I say. "I have my father's laugh."

"Would lunch, or dinner, be so terrible?" Dawn asks. "I mean, Dad's not around to poison—"

Tin interrupts. "We're going to pause this family reunion because I know *you*"—and here she spreads her arms to the far reaches of the gym—"want to leave. Here's what we're going to do. We have lots of people in line, but we're going to get you out of here in thirty minutes. My promise to you."

She turns to the young man at the front of the line. "You're next." I'm so relieved that I'm no longer in the spotlight and as I lift the camera back onto my shoulder, I imagine telling this story to Lisa. No one listens like she does.

TIN HOLLAND

[Sausalito's first woman police chief]

36

Who's Stalking Who?

I've never seen the man standing in front of the mic before. He has salt-and-pepper hair and wears a blue bowling shirt. I don't *know* most of the people in the audience, but I *recognize* many of them. Not him.

My brain hurts with all I'm juggling—I'm conducting an orchestra, but the musicians are here against their will and acting like two-year-olds. I've been imagining the crowd as if it's an individual, but that's not the case. In a second, one loud malcontent like the unlock-the-doors man can turn a cooperative audience into an irate mob.

I ask the next witness to introduce himself and share what he knows.

"I'm Dick Theria and Wednesday night, after the city council candidate debate at the Bar Whose Name We Dare Not Speak, I followed Fenton Felton—"

"You *followed* him?" I interrupt. "Because?"

"I'm a private investigator hired by the North Bay Bank to dig into Fenton Felton's finances. I heard he was living on his yacht, so I followed him to the yacht harbor."

Hic raises his hand, stands, and starts speaking. "Perhaps I can be helpful here," he says. "It was common knowledge that Fenton was having cash flow issues. He *had been* staying at Sally Cal's inn, but she kicked him out when he was six months behind in rent. Then he stayed in Tiburon at a hotel until his cash ran out. Overnight stays *are* allowed in the yacht harbor."

"I was not the *only* person following someone that night," says Theria. "As I followed Fenton, I saw him following Brenda, the waitress from the Dare Not, and he startled her when he stepped out of the shadows. I could tell she was angry, though I didn't hear their conversation. After Brenda left to walk home, Honest, the pirate, followed Fenton. I know this because Fenton turned around suddenly and yelled. 'What are you doing, stalking me?' and I thought he had made me. But it was Honest he was shouting at."

Theria stops. "It's tough to concentrate," he says, "when that scoreboard clock is counting down my seconds. I'll be brief."

"If you've ever been to a city council meeting," I say, "you know the reason for a timer. We'll pause it."

"Honest's voice was loud," says Theria, "so I could hear him tell Fenton Felton, 'I have a proposition for you.'"

"Did you hear anything else?"

"No, but half an hour later, Honest stumbled toward where I was hiding, as if he'd been drinking."

Honest jumps out of his chair and starts speaking. "Look, I knew Fenton Felton did not take my sister seriously, because she's a girl, a woman and all that, and I thought he might be more *willing* to listen to *me* pitching the compromise plan instead of Fate."

"*You* brought the plans to Fenton Felton without telling me?" Fate's eyes are popping, and she's in Honest's face, her nose an inch from his. "You who says compromise is failure?"

Honest backs away. "Why are you pissed at me?" he says. "Other than that you're *always* pissed at me. I was pitching *your* amazing plan, trying to save *our* homes."

He raps his fingers on his forehead and shakes his head. "Compromise is not *always* failure. I groveled to Fenton Felton, and he blew me off just like he did you. Why aren't you angry with *him*?"

"I am," she says, "but he's dead, and you're not."

I ask Honest and Fate to sit on the empty bench. They eye each other, then she walks around the bench and sits near the end closest to me. He climbs over it and sits near the other end. The gap between them is big enough for two people to sit comfortably. Lander hovers behind the bench, halfway between them.

"Tell me if I have this right, Honest," I say. "On Wednesday, after you participated in the city council candidate debate at the Dare Not, you followed Fenton Felton to his yacht and pitched the compromise dock plan that your sister presented earlier this morning. The compromise plan that incorporated Aquarius Harbor into the new marina. The plan you opposed. Is that right?"

"I didn't have the blueprint," he says, "but yes. I had Fate's sketches. Actually, it was Jude who made the sketches. Credit where credit is due."

"And what happened?"

"What I just said—he blew me off."

"But according to our witness, Mr. Theria, the private investigator, you were there for some time."

"There *was* whiskey."

"You must have exchanged more than a few words. Neither of you are tongue-tied."

"We had the same tug of war as always. I made the case for accommodating Aquarius Harbor instead of evicting us, as hard as that was for me, since I don't believe in compromise, but he was even more stubborn than me."

"Can you recall anything in particular that he said?"

"Nothing you haven't heard before," he says, "that we're low-life squatter scum, that kind of scorn. The only thing we agreed on was that the whiskey was smooth."

I write a note on my pad. "What is H hiding?" They must have talked about something.

I continue to look down at my pad, and I scribble a doodle in the hope that Honest or Fate will fill the silence, but they don't.

I turn my attention to the tall young man waiting at the mic and ask him to begin. He wears bell bottom jeans with patches and sports a goatee that barely shows.

"My name is Ted and I was sitting three rows behind Fate." He points to the chair where Fate was sitting before the melee and murder. There's an older woman sitting there now who leans forward in her seat intently, like a cat ready to pounce on a mouse.

"I'm tall enough to see over her shoulder," Ted says, "and she was writing notes on one of her index cards. Printing. All capital letters. But when Honest jumped up and insulted Fenton Felton, just before the lights went out, she immediately wrapped her index cards with a rubber band and sat on the edge of her seat, as if she knew what was coming next."

The man—or is he a boy?—shakes as he speaks, his sincerity so raw I feel protective of him. "I'm not suggesting she, or he"—he points to Fate and Honest—"*did* anything, I'm only doing my duty as a citizen to report what I saw."

I haven't focused on Honest as the murderer, because he couldn't have blown the fuse and even if he had an accomplice, I have a hard time believing he's angry enough at Fenton to kill him. But he's play-acting all the time, and I don't know who he really is.

I look at him and hold my gaze for ten seconds, then turn to his sister. "Fate," I say. "Did you know what was coming?"

"I didn't," she says. "I must have acted out of instinct. I don't remember. Honest was provoking Fenton the way he provokes me. I thought something might happen and I needed to be ready."

"Ready for what?" I ask.

She makes a face like I've asked a stupid question. "To protect Honest from his worst instincts, which I've been doing for what seems like forever."

"Did you know Honest was going to bait Fenton Felton?" I ask. "Before the melee and the murder?"

"No. He may have said something earlier, but I've learned not to believe most of what he says."

"And when did you rush up to the stage?"

"When they started wrestling and punching each other."

"You thought Fenton Felton might hurt Honest?"

"Or he might hurt Fenton Felton."

HONEST ABERNATHY

[Pretend pirate, houseboat resident, brother of Fate, boyfriend of Dawn]

37

One More Final Question, Part 1

I'm on the bench next to Fate, trying to sit still, but I can't stop my feet from bouncing. I forgot my foot powder this morning what with everything going on and my feet itch like crazy inside these tight boots. I squeeze my hands together in my lap and press my feet on the floor and try to look relaxed.

Also, Lander has ordered me to keep my mouth shut, and it's killing me.

Tin grills Fate about whether she knew what was coming before the melee and the murder. I clamp my teeth together so I don't say anything.

Fate says she did not know what was coming, but feared that I might do something reckless, like hurt Fenton Felton.

Why is she saying that? It's one thing to feud privately, but this is in front of everyone. If this is her way of saying that I did it, it's too obvious. She's too sharp not to see that.

Tin looks up from her notes. "Honest," she says, "I have one *final* question for you. When did you first learn that a barge had been sunk blocking the pile driver?"

She's so casual with her question, like she's asking me my sign. It's Aquarius, in case anyone cares. I don't put stock in the stars.

Lander shakes her head, but she knows I'm going to talk no matter what she says. Turns out she's not such a great lawyer, though, to her credit, she never claimed she was. I'm not under oath or anything and I have nothing to hide, that is, other than sinking the barge. That's probably when I got the athlete's foot, or rather feet. That night in the storm. My feet were soaking wet.

"Fate told me, Friday morning. She was up early. It was a sight to behold." I'm careful not to gloat, but the memory makes me giddy.

"You had no knowledge of the sinking of the barge before then? You weren't involved in sinking it?"

"No." I act incredulous but try not to overdo it. For a moment, I consider copping to what we did, because Tin is no fool, but I'm afraid of Fate's wrath. If we're going to admit to sinking the barge, and there are good reasons to do that, even if it gets us in trouble, I have to talk with Fate first. I mean, look how pissed she was to learn that I pitched Fenton Felton on the compromise plan. *Her* plan.

"You must have known that this would *infuriate* Fenton Felton."

I nod. "It did. I saw him that morning at the harbor. He was seething."

"And where were you Thursday night, when the barge was sunk?"

"At the Dare Not. I told you already. I tied one on. What did Brenda say, that I was 'drinking obnoxiously?'

That's why I wasn't up at the crack of dawn."

Tin does not care about the barge. *What* is she up to?

"On Tuesday," she says, "you were involved in a sword fight with Fenton Felton, is that correct?"

"It was on the TV news. No sense denying it."

"Like you denied sinking the barge."

"Oh, you're good, chief. Remind me never to play cards with you."

She smiles. It's hard not to like her, at least a little.

Tin is playing chess. I see the gears turn under her black service hat. She didn't wear her hat when the meeting started. She was like, I'm here to facilitate, not to arrest anyone. Now she's all official, questioning witnesses and everything, locking us in against our will, using the basketball clock as a timer.

"Tell me if I have this right, Honest. You were worried Dawn was going to break up with you. You were feuding with her father, who Dawn defied with a fierceness you could smell. Might you, *theoretically*, have tried to win her over by killing her father? Postponing your eviction?"

The crowd "oohs" and "aahs."

"Not that I think you did this," she says, "but I have to ask." She's accusing me of murder. *Theoretically*. This is preposterous. OK, I'll play along.

I stand. "OK, Chief," I say, "Don't tell Dawn, but—" now I crouch and whisper, "I don't love her *enough* to *kill* for her."

I know Dawn hears me, but I pretend otherwise. Her eyes dart from side to side. She thinks I'm making light of a dangerous situation.

Tin must know I'm not the murderer. I'm positive. She's got something up her sleeve.

"But Chief," I say, "*you* hated Fenton Felton.

Shouldn't *you* be a suspect too? You were on the stage with us."

I wink.

"Not that I think you did it," I say. "But I have to ask."

I pause and see everyone's eyes shift from me to Tin. Some immediately, some more tentatively. She holds my gaze with a neutral expression. I return the favor.

She milks the pause. Waits for me to say more. But why? I've thrown down the gauntlet. It's her turn. I sit back down on the bench.

"I did not *hate* Fenton Felton," she says, "but as I said previously, no one is beyond suspicion. If you uncover evidence incriminating me, I'll get it to the right people. But I know you're just teasing me."

Tin writes another note on her pad, makes us wait again.

"Honest, how did you come to live here, in Sausalito, at Aquarius Harbor? You lost your parents in an accident, do I have that right, and you and your sister moved here after that?"

What's this about? Changing the subject? Bringing down the temperature?

"Not right away," I say. "At first, I crashed with a friend in the Haight, but the Haight was getting mean. The Summer of Love was over, I mean, *over*, and I met some cool folks who were migrating here to Sausalito and living on houseboats. I had tinkered with boats in high school, and I'm mechanically inclined, and I found this decommissioned ferry for sale, that a friend in Vallejo turned me on to, and—"

"Where was Fate?" she asks. "When did she move here? I want a short story here, not a novel."

I glance at Fate, whose eyes are locked on me.

"Fate was in Michigan," I say, "in Kalamazoo, with our uncle, and she didn't like it, but she also didn't want to be placed with foster parents, so when I suggested she move here, to Sausalito, with me, she was game. I promised to build us each a cabin on the deck of the ferry. The berth rent was $50 a month, an excellent deal. I had *some* money from our parents' insurance, but I needed to make it last."

"You were Fate's legal guardian?"

"I was," I say, "until she turned eighteen, and I should have been stricter. She took advantage of the freedom she had. But how does this relate to the matter at hand? I don't understand."

"I think you do," Tin says.

But I don't. Or I don't *want* to. I wiggle my toes inside my boots, wishing I could take them off and scratch the bottom of my feet.

"This morning," Tin says, "*immediately* after Fenton Felton jumped on stage and accused Fate of stealing his berth plans, you followed him, insulted him, shoved him in the chest, and wrestled him to the ground. *Moments* before the murder."

"Those fights were theater," I say. "He knew that. I knew that. So do you."

"Your knife is the murder weapon," she says.

This has already been established. She's trying to trick me, but to what end?

"Someone must have pinched my knife from my scabbard," I say. "It was a *clean* pinch. I didn't notice it."

Before she responds, I know what she's going to say. She did trick me.

"Who *was* that someone?" she asks.

Oh shit! She's going after Fate.

38

One More Final Question, Part 2

When I ask Honest who swiped his knife, he swallows, licks his lips, and opens his mouth.

He doesn't speak. What can he say?

He knows.

Whether he knows because he sees that I know or because he came to this epiphany on his own doesn't matter.

He knows. I know.

But knowing is not the same as having proof.

There are no fingerprints on Honest's knife, the murder weapon. If the murderer is Fate, she wiped her prints off the knife handle with her dress, which is splattered with blood. Most likely *after* stabbing Fenton Felton, when the blade was in Fenton Felton's chest. That required careful execution and premeditation. In the dark.

Honest and Fate sit silently on the bench, all four of

their feet flat on the floor. Honest fidgets. Fate is still as a statue. The audience members are quiet, as if they're all holding their breath.

Since I became a police officer in Sausalito five years ago, I've watched the houseboaters in a variety of settings, from the Dare Not to the grocery store to their street theater and appearances on *News on the Run* and I've been especially intrigued by the relationship between Honest and Fate. At first, I thought they were a couple, until someone told me they were brother and sister. Which made far more sense.

My take was that they squabbled constantly and were also hopelessly dependent on each other. If either committed the murder, there's a good chance they collaborated.

But the stricken look on Honest's face makes me wonder.

"Honest, you and your sister have been working *together* to resist the eviction warrants that have been served on you, working *together* to protect Aquarius Harbor?" I ask. "Is that correct?"

He swallows. "Yes."

"You've also been living *together* for a long time, on the ferry you built cabins on. Cabins you built *together*. Do I have that right, you built the cabins together?"

"Yes, sort of," he says. "I did most all the building, the carpentry, the wiring and all, but Fate kept me on budget, kept me on deadline. I mean, I'm not a strict adherent of the eight-hour workday, so I needed nudging."

"Would it be fair to say that you and Fate are considered the *leaders* of the Aquarius Harbor Collective, in as much as a collective has leaders?"

"Brenda's been stepping up," he says. "Jude created these amazing cardboard protesters, drew the sketch of

Fate's plan from the blueprints. Dewey organized the dinghies. Mickey's contributing in all kinds of ways."

"Fair enough," I say, "but *you* Honest and *you* Fate have been working *together* to stop Fenton Felton from evicting you from your homes and building his new harbor. You worked *together* Thursday night in the rainstorm to sink the barge that blocked Fenton Felton's pile driver."

Before either of them can deny what they did, I shift gears.

"Fate," I say, "do *you* think your brother killed Fenton Felton?"

This, apparently, is what Fate *wants* me to think, that Honest is the murderer. Twice, she dropped hints. Not subtle hints. But she responds as if I slapped her.

"As many scrapes and screw-ups as I've rescued him from," she says, her voice cold, "I can tell you he is not a murderer. He believes in nonviolence. As do I."

"During the break," I say, "you called Lander, your lawyer, urging her to come here to City Hall, because, as you said to Honest, 'you're in big trouble.' Is it possible, *theoretically*, that calling Lander and expressing your concern, in front of all of us, might make it *more likely* that I focus on Honest as a primary suspect?"

Fate looks to Lander, who shakes her head. A tiny shake. But I see it. So does Fate.

"You're a smart young woman, Fate. Pretending to *protect* Honest while accusing him is awfully *transparent.*"

"That's not it," Fate protests. "Of course, I knew you'd focus on Honest, because of, you know, the knife, the sword fight, the poster, the insults." She looks down at the stack of index cards in her hand, wrapped in a red rubber band.

I jot notes on my pad. *Milk the pause. Give Fate more time. How could she pull this off?*

Fate meets my gaze, then looks down. I will her to fill the silence, but she doesn't.

"Watching you today, Fate," I say, "and over the past weeks and months, I understand your animosity toward Fenton Felton—he was unrepentant about evicting you from your homes, he refused to even look at the plans you devoted so much time to drafting, and today he accused you of *stealing* the plan, from him."

I continue, slowly, deliberately, trying to be curious instead of accusatory. I remove the mic from the lectern, grip it in my right hand, and pace, back and forth, in front of the bench. I study Fate. I study Honest. I study the other five persons of interest. I study the crowd.

"And yet," I say, "you act, *sometimes,* as exasperated with your brother as with Fenton Felton."

Fate looks straight at me, her lips pressed together tightly, her arms folded across her chest.

"Tell me if I have this right," I say. "You were afraid you were going to lose your home and community, you were furious with Fenton Felton *and* your brother, so you went for broke. You went for a two-fer. You killed Fenton Felton and then you framed Honest for the murder."

Even as I say this, I think, how is that even possible? She would have had to slip away from the melee, blow the circuit with the wire, steal Honest's knife, in the dark, and find Fenton Felton, also in the dark, in front of hundreds of witnesses.

I continue pacing. Beside the rank gym smell, there's also bleach, from the quick mop job this morning before the stage was assembled. The crowd is rapt.

"No," Fate says. "*No*. I didn't. I wouldn't."

Her denial is defiant. Not hesitant in the least.

I'm ready to pounce, but I still have no evidence.

I hate that this murder happened on my watch, while we were purportedly forging a peace plan. And I will take no pleasure putting this murderer behind bars. But this is my job and I relish, in my own never-going-to-get-giddy way, this high-wire act I'm performing. In front of hundreds of people, including Justine.

I pace back toward the lectern, milking the tension. Fate and Honest are so different it's hard to believe they had the same mother and father. Except the shape of their eyes, which are identical, though hers are baby blue and his a deeper blue with a hint of green. Swashbuckling Honest with his bombastic clowning and timid Fate with her index cards and her ridiculous typewriter on a harness. What a pair.

The harness! There it is in the first row, under the chair where she sat this morning. That's it. The evidence I've been hunting for. I feel a surge of relief.

It's time to pull the second rabbit out of my hat.

But not just yet.

"Fate," I say, "earlier I asked you if you knew what was coming before the melee and the murder, and you said no, but that you thought Honest might hurt Fenton Felton. That's pointing the finger in my book."

That's not a question, but it begs a response.

Fate breathes slowly. Honest taps his feet.

I wave away Barney, who's been holding the mic in front of Fate, and I approach her.

"Earlier, you said you were *protecting* Honest."

I hold the mic to her lips. "Yes," she says.

"Why?" I ask.

The gym is so quiet I hear the sweat dripping from my underarms.

"I promised my mother I would look after him," she says.

"When was that?" I ask. "That promise."

She hesitates. "In the hospital. Before she died."

"But Honest was eighteen then," I say, "an adult, and you were fourteen. If my math is right."

"He was reckless," she says.

I feel for Fate. For being orphaned. For growing up in the shadow of her showboat brother. For all the complicated emotions she keeps in check. For what is about to upend her life.

But the puzzle pieces fit together now. I have to go where the evidence leads me.

"You and your brother were in the back seat of the car when the accident happened," I say.

I'm pressing Fate on what happened ten years ago because she seems more willing to talk about the past.

"We were. It was a *crash*, not an accident."

"Not an accident?"

"No, I said mean things to my mother. That afternoon, before we went out. She was upset. We had another fight in the car, and she was turning her head toward me in the back seat yelling at me when the truck hit us. It was *not* an accident."

Honest leaps to his feet. "Dammit, Fate, stop blaming yourself for what happened to Mom and Dad." He waits until she looks up at him. "It's not *your* fault."

We could unlock the doors now and no one would leave.

"I was obnoxious that day too," he says. "And Dad was frazzled."

"That's right," says Fate. "He was. Because I was acting out."

"*You* were acting out? I was drunk in the middle of the afternoon. I was Mr. Big Shot High School Graduate. It's been going on eight years and you won't stop blaming yourself. It's almost like you *wish* it happened that way."

Honest cringes, like he's in pain, which gives me the willies.

"Mom was difficult," says Honest. "She'd already had two accidents. I fought with her on that drive too."

"You think everything is about *you*," Fate says. "The crash was about *me*. It was *not* about you."

Honest grimaces and shuts his eyes, then sits back down.

"Fate, I say, "what did you say to your mother the day of the crash?"

I expect her to dodge the question, but she's eager to speak.

"I told her she was a selfish bitch who cared only about herself and that she would rather crush my spirit than let me be who I wanted to be. I wished harm on her and it came true."

The audience gasps. I swallow my surprise.

"You must wish you had another chance to talk with your mother," I say.

"Only every day," she says, gazing into the distance. She looks so sad, lost in her tragic memories.

I pause to give her a chance to continue, but she doesn't.

"One more final question," I say, "What can you tell me about night-vision cameras?"

39

Catch One Catch All

Tin is asking me about cameras. It's a trap. She thinks I killed Fenton Felton.

I would remember that. My memory issues have plagued me for years, but I've never forgotten something that recent, that consequential, that deliberate. It's not possible. I would never take that risk. I was against sinking the barge. I wear a seatbelt. I don't smoke. I hardly drink any more.

I'll never forget the afternoon of the crash, so how could I not remember what happened this morning?

"Nothing," I say, my voice flat and throaty. "I don't know a thing about night-vision cameras."

"How about you, Jazz?" Tin says. "Can you explain how night-vision cameras work?"

I shiver, even though the gym is stuffy and warm.

"I can't see in the dark," he says, "but my night-vision

camera *can*. It transmits infrared light, which the human eye can't see, but the camera *does*."

I can't swallow. I can't breathe. My mouth feels like cotton, but then I do breathe, and regain some semblance of composure. The crowd is watching my every move.

"Jazz," Tin says, "You were filming when Fenton Felton and Honest Abernathy were fighting and the lights went out. Did you keep filming in the dark?"

"Damn straight," he says. "Things were getting exciting."

"Can you project that on the screen?" says Tin. "Your night vision footage?"

Tin stares at me.

I spring up from the bench and run. The doors are locked, but my legs have a mind of their own. I race to the side exit, barrel down the stairwell to the basement tunnels under the gym. Footsteps echo on the stairs behind me.

I have to hide. I know exactly where.

One night, the first year Honest and I lived in Sausalito, we broke into City Hall and played flashlight tag and catch one catch all in the stairwells and tunnels. I found a supply closet with a large linen locker inside it and I hid there. No one ever found me.

That's where I'll hide. The footsteps get louder, echoing off the walls. I make it to the basement, but the supply closet is locked.

I try the door next to it, which opens. Inside are cardboard boxes of toilet paper. One box is ripped open. There's barely room to stand. I close the door and twist the thumb lock in the center of the knob. Loud voices careen down the corridor. The closet smells of lemon disinfectant.

That night we broke into City Hall, I don't remember how we got in. Someone had a key, or picked a lock, or broke a window. The games that night were fun, but what made it so special was being included with a bunch of adult men when I was only fifteen. They were boys really, as flaky and immature as Honest, but back then I felt like I'd died and gone to heaven. The breaking and entering was a bonus.

Catch one catch all is a cross between tag and hide-and-seek that I learned to play on our block in Sacramento. One person is "it" and every person who gets tagged is also "it," so the number of people chasing you keeps getting bigger until everyone is tagged. But if your hiding place is good enough, like my linen locker, and no one finds you, sooner or later, someone shouts, "new game."

I remember the long and hot summer evenings in Sacramento when we played until dark—dozens of us— and when we chanted "new game," we would stretch the "new" for as long as our breath held out. Like coyotes howling. I never thought we had an idyllic life until we didn't have it anymore.

The clomp of feet and voices get closer. I hear Chief Tin say, "Who has the keys?"

She's one door away, outside the supply closet.

Tin assumes I'm guilty because I ran, but I panicked. I couldn't have killed Fenton Felton. I would remember if I did.

I don't know why I'm hiding in this closet. Just because no one found me when we played catch one catch all doesn't mean Tin won't find me today.

I hear Mayor Sally, too. She says there's a key closet next to her office. I reach to the hem of my dress where the blood has dried and the cotton is stiff. The room is stuffy, but a draft cools my ankles. A sliver of light seeps in under the door.

Why do I forget some things and remember others? I'll never forget the afternoon of the crash. It's seared in my mind. And I remember playing catch one catch all years before that.

I hear a knock. I feel the vibrations in my shoulder.

Someone grips the door handle, tries to turn the knob. It wiggles but doesn't turn. The hinges creak. The corner of the cardboard box of toilet paper digs into my calf.

What's strange is that it seems like the more I forget, the more vividly I see what's going to happen next. What I see now is that I'm going to prison. To a cell as small as this closet.

"Hello in there." It's Tin. "I may be talking to myself, but this is where I would hide if I were escaping." Her voice is calm and friendly, but that's part of the trap. "You've had some major tragedy and trauma in your life. I don't know if you remember me telling you this, but I'm also an orphan, a different kind. I want to help you. Whatever you did, you—" She stops. "Other people are coming now."

I can't open the door or let her know I'm here. She'll go away sooner or later. It's dumb luck that she knocked on this door.

She keeps talking, softer now, something about how they found the keys, how they are unlocking the doors one by one and coming this way.

The key turns in the lock and there's the kindly face of Tin.

"Hello Fate," she says. "You're under arrest."

She escorts me up the stairs with my hands behind my

back. If I keep my hands there, she says, she won't cuff me. Lander, at the entrance to the gym, says in my ear, "Don't say a word."

Tin leads me onto the stage. Now she's going to show the video and I'm afraid to watch it because of what I will see. But I also *want* to see it. To learn what I did. *If* I did anything.

Tin goes to the lectern and starts explaining to the crowd what happened. I interrupt.

"Aren't you going to show the video?"

"No," she says.

"I bet there is no video. No night-vision camera. You lied. You made it up. Running doesn't make me guilty. You have no proof."

Lander is waving at me, telling me to shut up, but I can't. "Besides, how could I possibly have stabbed Fenton Felton in the dark? How would I know where he was? It was a brawl, everyone tangled up."

Honest pops up. "It was *me,*" he says. "I did it. I stabbed Fenton Felton. Fate is innocent."

He presses his palms to his chest and squeezes his eyes closed like he's in pain. How could *he* have done it? I'm just coming to grips with the possibility that it could have been me.

"I had wire in my pocket," he continues, "to reinforce the harness for my drum. I took the wire and jammed the socket. I grabbed my knife and stabbed Fenton Felton and I wiped the knife handle on Fate's dress."

Honest is usually a brilliant liar, but now, when it counts, he's not convincing.

I don't know how I could forget stabbing someone. I remember bounding out of my seat when Honest and Fenton Felton started fighting, and running up the stairs to the stage, but no memory of what happened after that.

No, that's not true. I remember when the fuse blew because there was this hissing sound like a balloon deflating as the lights went out. It wasn't just the darkness, it was the stillness. The hum from the loudspeaker stopped too and there was a second of total silence before the crowd freaked out.

Seven Months Later

HONEST ABERNATHY

[Pretend pirate, houseboat resident, brother of Fate, boyfriend of Dawn

40

Did We Beat the Establishment or Did We Join It?

I arrive at the Dare Not early for the victory party and drink two beers before I sit down. We're supposed to be celebrating today, because our beautiful new harbor is finished, but Fate is behind bars and I'm freaking out because of what she told me yesterday when I visited her at the jail.

I wave to Jenna, my waitress tonight. "Another cerveza, por favor." She's already spurned my advances twice today. I can take a hint. "Changed my mind," I say. "Bring a pitcher."

I'm by myself because Dawn's running late. She'll get kudos galore tonight, which she deserves, but she's been so busy with the harbor project she's had no time for me.

The Dare Not is filling up. The bar is supposedly closed for our private party, but it's not really private because Dawn invited the whole community and the freeloaders are already here for the spread. Though it is a cash bar, so there's that.

Bobbing against the ceiling are dozens of colorful helium balloons, their strings hanging down just above my head. I yank a string and when I let go, the balloons bounce around like an open break shot in pool, but with none of that clackety-clack sound. A rainbow Aquarius Harbor banner is tacked to the back wall.

My legs are wobbly. I better pace myself with the beer.

Every new high-end berth in the harbor is already leased, and new tenants are moving in every day. The crazy thing is that Dawn kept the name Aquarius Harbor for the whole development, even though *our* berths, which were grandfathered in as part of the compromise, are tucked into the backside of a new levee and take up less than a quarter of the total space. The notoriety of Aquarius Harbor was too useful not to exploit—what with the eviction raids, the street theater, the civil disobedience, the murder at City Hall, not to mention Fate's upcoming trial. You can't buy that kind of publicity.

When Lander arrives, looking foxy in a frilly blue party dress, I wave her over and pour her a beer.

"How's Fate?" She knows I saw her yesterday.

"What I say is confidential, right?" I ask. "You're still *my* lawyer too?"

She nods.

I can't sit still. My whole body is shaking.

Though Lander helped with some legal hurdles facing the harbor project, her biggest contribution was landing a top-notch criminal lawyer to defend Fate.

"This is a nightmare," I say. "Fate maintains that she doesn't remember stabbing Fenton Felton, but she said, and this is blowing my mind, she said the *plan* to kill him *appeared to her,* fully realized, like it was projected onto a movie screen in her head. You know she's always making notes on her index cards? That's what she saw. A checklist of tasks on an index card. In the same block printing she does. The first task? 'Stick wire in outlet to blow fuse.' *Unbelievable,* but that's what she told me. Make me shudder just saying it out loud."

"Lower your voice," Lander says. She hunches her shoulders and squeezes her hands together. She's freaked out too.

Out of the corner of my eye, I see Dawn arrive in a bare-shouldered magenta dress. For months, she's been wearing these dreadful navy business suits and tying her hair in a bun so people take her more seriously as the manager of the new harbor. She looks *hot* today. Everyone is hugging her and toasting her. She does not appear to be looking for me.

Lander waves her hand in my face to get my attention. "Did Fate tell her lawyer what she told you? About this checklist?"

"No, no way. That would practically be a confession, an admission of premeditation. She shouldn't have told *me.* She says she didn't write this list, it *appeared* to her, *as if she wrote it,* but she didn't."

Lander studies me. "You're not yourself."

"*No,* this *is* myself. What you've seen before is an act, like everyone says. How can this be? I mean, I knew Fate was troubled, you know, traumatized by what happened to our parents. What happened to us. Years ago, I took her to a social worker in San Rafael to process things, but she stopped going and I didn't make her stick with it. I never thought she was this far gone."

Lander touches my hand. "This is not your fault."

"It is," I say.

There's a ruckus at the entrance as Johnny Dash runs in, his tie flapping over his shoulder, Jazz behind him, squeezing his bulky camera through the narrow entryway. We all know Jazz now, he's part of the scene. But when he's working, he's got that same behind-the-camera invisibility as before.

Johnny races toward me and I stand, as he screeches to a halt a foot from my frothy mug. I take a healthy slug and wipe the foam from my mouth on my sleeve like a proper pirate.

"This is Johnny Dash, *News on the Run,* live in *Sausa-leeto* at the Bar Whose Name We Dare Not Speak, for the victory party celebrating completion of a compromise dock plan for Aquarius Harbor, which includes seventy low-income houseboat berths for existing residents, who would have been evicted if not for the compromise. According to the deal, their berth rents will rise to market rates over six years.

"The architect of the compromise plan, Fate Abernathy, is behind bars awaiting trial for the murder of Fenton Felton at City Hall seven months ago. Here's Fate's older brother who's been celebrating for hours. Honest Abernathy, how does it *feel?*"

"Feels awesome," I say, "but I've been thinking—did we *beat* the establishment, or did we *join* it?"

Jenna returns with another pitcher, which I raise high. "A toast to the Aquarius houseboaters' groovy victory." The foam spills over the top of the pitcher onto my hand. "Far freaking out. We did it. We backed them into a corner with our compromise plan."

Dawn struts in front of me and grabs my beer pitcher.

"Don't you *dare* take credit," she hisses, "for the plan you *fought* every step of the way."

"It was an act," I say. "A negotiating ploy. To make Fate's plan *seem* reasonable."

"Remind me again what I ever saw in you," she says.

"My audacity, my confidence, my humility—"

Johnny interrupts. "Dawn Felton, you've been credited with getting this new harbor built. Any truth to the rumor that you're breaking up with Honest?"

"You'd humiliate me on TV?" I say.

"No comment," she says.

"*What?*" I growl. "Deny the rumor. I deserve that much."

Now Johnny Dash is gushing about how Dawn resuscitated her father's doomed project and built the harbor ahead of schedule and under budget. Dawn starts thanking everyone but the bartender and his baby brother, like she won an Oscar. Everyone except me.

There's more hubbub at the door again—Brenda's arrived with her newborn daughter—and everyone moseys to the front. Chief Tin is here too. No one's paying attention to me anymore.

Brenda told me she named her daughter Alice after her beloved late grandmother, and also the other Alice, Dawn's mother, who opened her house to Brenda and her baby and is now her godmother and honorary grandmother.

I met Baby Alice shortly after she was born, as did many others, but since Brenda's been living up in the hills with the two Alices, she hasn't been out and about much.

Baby Alice is wide-eyed and smiley and everyone exclaims how big she is. She's got blue eyes like Dawn and her father, but she looks more like Brenda.

Her skin color, her hair, the shape of her head.

Godmother Alice sets a platter of cheesecake on a table and admires it before slicing it. The cheesecake is in the shape of a houseboat with a miniature Aquarius Harbor banner on top, on toothpicks.

Alice hands a plate of cheesecake to Brenda and trades it for the baby, who burps loudly.

"She's going to be popular with the boys," I quip. That gets laughs.

Now comes a noisy, stinky fart and the crowd around Baby Alice backs away.

"Not all the boys," I say. More laughter. I drain my beer. I'm starting to feel better.

Later, when there have been so many toasts I can't stomach one more, I jump on my chair. "Enough of this self-congratulation. This compromise deal sucks. We got conned. Six years is not long enough to keep our berths affordable."

"Why? Because you're too lazy to find a job?" Dawn snarls.

"Lander, find a loophole. Dawn, you're turning into your father."

"No," Dawn says, glaring at me. "I'm running an honest business, and lazy squatters need not apply."

She laughs, and it's not her usual snarky laugh, but a full-bellied maniacal laugh, just like Fenton Felton's.

She holds her hands over her mouth in horror. "Oh no! NO!"

TIN HOLLAND
[Sausalito's first woman police chief]

41

If You Want, You Can Call
Me Your Girlfriend

"I want you to introduce me to everyone," Justine says.

We're walking down Bridgeway from her truck to the Dare Not on a sunny, blustery spring afternoon. Masts clank in the harbor. The breeze smells of fish and coffee. Justine is so excited about the Aquarius Harbor victory party we're about to join that she pulls my arm to get there faster.

I pull back. We're almost there. There's no need to rush.

"And no hey-everybody-this-is-Justine, that's not good enough," she says. "I want one-on-ones, especially with the murder suspects."

"I will see what I can do," I say. She is not making this easy for me.

Justine wears black jeans and black turtleneck, cool

as a cat, and over that a dazzling gold, black, and orange dashiki dress that's so attention-getting it makes me self-conscious. As if being tall, black, and butch weren't enough. She's so striking, and here I am holding her hand.

Last fall, two weeks after she invited me to the Castro to protest the Dan White sentencing, I asked her to dinner. I was in my pajamas at home, at my kitchen table, the phone cord taut. The murder of Fenton Felton at City Hall was waning into yesterday's news and my work as police chief was becoming boring again, the way I liked it.

She said yes.

But a qualified yes. "I don't hide," she said. "We go out in public. Are you fine with that?"

I said yes. Which may not have been *unequivocally* true then, but now, seven months and a dozen dates later, it is. That's not to say that I'm as comfortable taking Justine to this party as I'd like to be. But here we are, thirty seconds from the entrance to the Dare Not.

Justine and I have spent most of our time together in Oakland, where she lives and where there are two lesbian bars and a whole scene that does not exist in Marin. At first, I felt like an imposter, but I relaxed into a new way of being myself. Which was easier because no one knew me there. But here in Sausalito, *everyone* knows me, which is why I'm feeling uneasy.

"If you want, you can call me your girlfriend," Justine says.

"I'm not sure I'm ready for that," I say, dropping her hand and laughing. I'm also not sure if I'm joking.

She waits at the door, seemingly unfazed by what I said. She likes to tease me.

Through the window I see it's already crowded. I gird myself.

We slip in without fanfare, because everyone is huddling around Brenda and her baby. Justine and her colorful dashiki wrest attention from Brenda's baby for barely a blink.

When Alice picks up the baby, also named Alice, and grabs a champagne flute to give a toast, I spot Brenda walking over to the window alcove and plopping down in a chair with a sigh. I nudge Justine. We follow Brenda.

"Brenda," I say, "this is Justine, my friend." I squeeze Justine's hand, for a second, then let go when Brenda smiles and extends *her* hand.

We grab chairs and sit. "I find it interesting," Justine says, "that the first person you introduce me to is the only other black woman here."

That's *not* why I started with Brenda. "Brenda is one of the more sensible people in Sausalito," I say, "and—"

"Other than that I got myself pregnant with a married man who everyone hated," Brenda interjects.

"Let's just say, Brenda listens more than she talks," I say.

"I've heard about you," Brenda says, and Justine flashes me a grin with a question mark. "Well, only that you and Chief Tin reconnected at the Dan White protest and that you were the one at City Hall who shouted, 'Give the woman her damn fifteen minutes.'"

"It was ten minutes," Justine says, "but yes, that was me."

Justine must think I've blabbed about her with everyone. But Brenda's the only one. A year ago, around the time I became chief, I met Brenda at the Dare Not for the first time and got to know her, and one day she asked me if I was seeing anyone. I said no, because I wasn't, but I was touched that she asked. When the time came that I could answer yes, I shared my news with her.

"You know, we wouldn't be here celebrating without Tin," Brenda says.

"Really?" says Justine. "Do tell."

"She held us to our word. She reeled in Dawn, she reeled in Alice, she even reeled in Honest, got him to work a hundred hours of community service, cleaning up the harbor during construction, in exchange for reducing the charges for the barge-sinking."

Justine gazes at me again with that half-grin, as if to say, "you've been holding out on me," then turns back to Brenda. "She didn't reel you in too?"

"Brenda didn't need reeling," I say. "She needed the opposite. Someone to push her. Like you push me."

Brenda turns to me. "I didn't tell you that my father came for a visit, to see my daughter, his granddaughter. It was sweet." She shifts her eyes to Justine. "My father worked here, during the war, at the ship factory. He brought me here once to visit, when I was a teenager, but my parents were divorced, and I didn't see much of him."

Alice returns with the baby, hands her back to Brenda, and I introduce Justine to her, as "my girlfriend."

Alice pokes me in my ribs with the base of her plastic champagne glass. "Your girlfriend, huh? You are full of surprises, Chief Tin."

I feel embarrassed, but I don't sense any negative judgment.

I ask Brenda if I can hold Baby Alice.

She squirms when I take her, and I hold her to my chest and rock her side to side. She calms down. What a trooper this baby is.

"Look at you," says Justine. "Not only can you solve crimes, you hold a baby like you were born to it."

Alice calls Jenna over to order another bottle of champagne. "Speaking of solving crimes," she says, "I want to hear, Chief Tin, how you sleuthed out that it was Fate who committed the murder? I was there on the stage, studying carefully what everyone said and did, and Fate was the *last* person I suspected."

"You've heard my story already," I say. "And you've also heard those sensationalized versions that make me out to be a superhero when all I did was stumble into dumb luck."

"I want to hear it again," she says.

Alice has become a fan, and I notice how she uses our friendship as currency in politics. She won the election for city council handily, though Honest got more votes than anyone expected.

When Jenna arrives with the bubbly, Alice fills three plastic flutes to the brim and passes two of them to us. The baby is sleeping now, her head on my shoulder.

"Let me give you my short version, so I don't keep you from enjoying the festivities." I take a drink. The bubbles tickle my throat.

"The first clue," I say, "was how visibly angry Fate was—*multiple times* that day. It registered most viscerally for me when Fenton Felton claimed she stole the berth plan, the one we're celebrating here today. Fate was livid, justifiably so. The tendons in her throat were bulging."

I've told this story enough times by now, I know how to pace it. I understand how an actor on the stage feels, repeating the same lines night after night, as if each time is the first time.

As I continue with my story, the crowd in the alcove gets larger and I consider starting again from the beginning, but I said I would be brief. I feel the steady rhythm of Baby Alice's breathing, which is comforting.

"When I asked Fate why she was protecting Honest, she started talking about her parents' death, seven years ago, blaming *herself*. Not evidence, but Fate taking the rap for something that happened long ago, well, that convinced me I was on the right track.

"Other than the reenactment, after our break, I devoted most of my investigation to motives and state of mind. They all had motives. What little physical evidence I had pointed to Honest. His knife. The poster on the telephone poles. Picking the fight with Fenton Felton.

"At this point, I'm pacing back and forth in front of the lectern, and out of the corner of my eye, I spy Fate's typewriter, in its harness, under the seat in the front row where she sat before the melee and the murder.

"Wrapped around the harness is wire, reinforcing the straps holding the typewriter, the same kind of copper wire, with black insulation, that we found on the stage by the electrical outlet.

"With all the focus on the murder, I lost sight of the blowing of the circuit, without which the murder would have been seen by everyone. Someone jammed wire into the outlet. Could that wire have come from Fate's harness?

"I didn't know. So, I had to trick Fate into thinking I did."

I drain my drink and set the plastic glass back on the table.

"I sprang the night-vision-camera trap and she ran. Later, we compared the wire that blew the circuit with the wire from Fate's harness, and they matched, though it is a type of wire that's available at every hardware store. Fate is innocent until proven guilty."

Two people shout out questions, but there's yelling in the main room and we all get up and follow the noise. Honest is standing on a chair and Dawn is sniping at him about being too lazy to find a job. I hand Baby Alice back to Brenda.

Honest says Dawn is turning into her father, which is quite the cheap shot, and she denies that vehemently, and then laughs. But it's not her laugh, it's her father's maniacal laugh, coming out of her mouth. She shrieks, "Oh no! *NO!*"

I would shriek too.

DAWN FELTON

[Defiant daughter of Fenton and Alice, girlfriend of Honest]

42

My Worst Nightmare

I am horrified hearing my father's laugh coming out of *my* mouth.

I grit my teeth and squeeze every muscle in my body to stop myself from screaming.

But I hear the scream in my head. *"I am not my father!"*

I keep it inside.

Everyone stares at me—Brenda with exaggerated concern, Honest with embarrassment, my mother with amusement, Johnny Dash with excitement.

I am mortified beyond my worst nightmare and I search for somewhere to hide.

Brenda dings her glass with a spoon. "Another toast to Dawn, who made this victory possible by *not* acting like her father."

Jazz raises his arm high. "Here, here. You are *not*

Fenton Felton, Dawn. I'm erasing that clip." He sets his camera on a table and presses a button. "Honest is an *asshole* for saying that."

I'm tempted to grab the nearest pitcher of beer and pour the whole bloody thing down my throat, but that might make it on TV, so I fold my hands tightly and stare at them with my jaw clenched.

Behind me, a plate falls to the floor and shatters, but no one looks. Every eye is locked on me.

From the kitchen, I hear the strains of "Sultans of Swing," the song that's been playing from every radio in town this spring. I try to tap my feet to the beat to dissipate the tightness I feel everywhere in my body. It doesn't work.

Now Brenda is telling the story about how I sweet-talked the loan officer into refinancing our debt, which my father had not been able to do. Therefore, I could not possibly be like him.

I never laughed like that before. Why now?

The toasts keep on coming, but they don't undo the laugh. Everyone is trying too hard and that only makes it worse. Hearing the demonic cackle of my father come out of my mouth tears at me more than his death did, and I don't care what that says about me. That's the truth.

My mother tucks Baby Alice under one arm like a football and holds her glass high with the other.

"Dawn deserves all the praise she's getting," she says. "The new, safe, up-to-code, inclusive, and beautiful Aquarius Harbor is exactly what Sausalito needs. We've been through a dark, divisive, and tragic period and this new harbor is bringing us together, helping us heal."

I'm relieved to see so many faces turned towards my mother instead of me.

"As you know," she continues, "Dawn is going to Florida this summer for a diving certificate program, then graduate school in marine biology in the fall, and I'll be taking over as director of the new harbor and—"

The loud hiss and gurgle of the espresso maker stops her. Now Chief Tin raps her glass with a spoon and raises her arm.

"I'd like to take this opportunity to share some perspective. Johnny Dash may have been the first to describe the strife here as the 'houseboat wars,' but he was not the only one. The evictions were divisive and bitter, and we were fortunate the confrontations were mostly non-violent, at least until Fenton Felton was murdered at City Hall. At the meeting I convened and hosted. It was audacious for us, for me, to expect to find a resolution at that community meeting, and it was just as audacious to expect the community to come together after the murder.

"But you did, we did, and no *one* person made that happen. It was all of you and you should be proud. Now there's another platter of cheesecake and I've had more than my share, so go at it, and remove the temptation for me to get another slice."

A busboy sweeps the dish shards into a pan. I find the bathroom.

Honest is waiting for me when I get out.

"I'm sorry," he says. "Can we talk? Outside?"

He turns on his sincere puppy dog face, but he's been drinking since before I arrived.

"I've sobered up," he says. "I drank a cappuccino and a glass of fresh-squeezed orange juice." He steps back and beckons me forward, toward the front door. "Not at the same time," he adds.

When we get to the sidewalk outside the Dare Not,

he apologizes again. "What I said about you turning into your father," he says. "That was cruel."

"At least you know that." I hug myself with my arms. The fog is low and thick.

"You can't lose your shit about the laugh," he says. "It's like the color of your eyes. Yours are blue and so were your father's. So are Baby Alice's. Because you're related. You have traits in common. But you're nothing like him. And you deserve all the toasts you're received tonight and more. Don't let the laugh ruin your triumphant day. Also, no one's toasting you for this, but I never would have built a composting toilet if not for you."

"That was a wonderful present, a grand gesture of the highest degree," I say, "but I'm freezing. We need to go back inside."

"How about another grand gesture," he says, "giving you the shirt off my back?"

"No, no—" But he's already pulling his frilly white pirate shirt over his head.

"Lift your arms," he says.

After I slide my arms through the sleeves, he takes my hand and kisses my fingers. His undershirt is bright white, right out of a laundry commercial.

"I came here today," he says, "determined to redeem myself for falling down on the job of being Fate's guardian. Instead, I acted like a child. But you broke up with me on TV and everything. Or did you?"

"You know I'm leaving next month."

"You hurt me, so I hurt you. I know that's no excuse. But I'm turning over a new leaf. I've decided to go back to law school and then I'm going to fight to protect the redwoods or save the bay, I don't know. The important thing is to work for a purpose *larger* than myself. Not that protecting our homes at Aquarius Harbor wasn't a righteous struggle, but we were saving our own asses."

My first impulse is to say something sarcastic, but I don't. "That sounds promising," I say. "Plus, you'll be able to afford your berth."

He leads me by the hand back inside. "Oh, right," he says.

"You don't care about money, do you?" I say.

He shrugs.

Back at the table, I start to take Honest's shirt off, but he says to keep it, that it looks good on me, that he has a sweatshirt.

"Go have your grand adventure," he says. "Spread your wings. I'll write, I'll call, I'll visit."

43

Honest Climbs on a Chair, Again

Justine and I talk with almost everyone in the bar, even Sally, who comes out to join the party for ten minutes, then takes a cab home. I never get a chance to introduce Justine to Honest or Dawn—at one point, through the Dare Not's picture window, I see them outside talking, their faces close, their expressions tense. They don't look like they want to be interrupted.

As we gather our coats to leave, Justine gives me a hard time about meeting so few of the suspects.

She's playful, but I feel defensive anyway. "I told you," I say. "Three of them aren't even here. Mickey, the flaky blond quipster, disappeared after the murder. I heard a rumor he was some sort of spy or provocateur, hired by Fenton Felton to disrupt and discredit the houseboaters, but I doubt that. Though when I visited Fate in jail, I'm sure I told you this, she said Mickey was all set to throw a Molotov cocktail at one of the eviction raids, but she talked him down.

"He left no forwarding address, no paper trail, and Mickey Macgillicuddy is definitely a made-up name. That doesn't make him a spy.

"And Huck, Fenton Felton's hiccupping sidekick, he moved with his family to Santa Rosa. At first, he worked alongside Dawn and Alice on the harbor project, then there was a falling out. That's all I know.

"And Fate is not here for obvious reasons."

As we approach the front door, Honest climbs on a chair. *Again.*

He waits to speak until Jazz is in position with his camera and Johnny is set with his mic. He's not drunk like he was earlier, but his eyes are wide and wild.

"Fate, my younger sister, who designed the dock plan we're celebrating today, should be here getting toasted," he says. "Instead, she's in jail because she was arrested for the murder of Fenton Felton. *But she was not in her right mind.*"

He pauses and looks around the room. The Dare Not is as quiet as a library, except for the clinking of glasses behind the bar. We're all watching and listening. I put my coat over the back of a chair.

"I don't understand why Dan White, who killed two men in cold blood, gets off with manslaughter for binging on Twinkies and Fate can't get off for being traumatized by our parents' accident and then by me, her immature, insensitive brother and piss-poor guardian, who goaded her, dismissed her, told her to suck it up when she couldn't."

Lander, standing behind Jazz, waves her hands and zips her mouth with her finger. Honest sees her. We all do. But he keeps going.

"Fate didn't commit the murder. She wouldn't even go along with sinking the barge, because it was an act of violence. She only came along to keep me out of trouble, which she's been doing since our Mom and Dad's accident. Before that too."

Now Lander yanks on Honest's arm, but he shakes her off. "I'm not excusing what she did, what she allegedly did, but I beseech you all: Talk to your friends, write a letter to the editor, use your influence however you can to ensure she gets a fair trial. So she's found *not guilty* by reason of diminished capacity and—"

Finally, Lander pulls him off the chair and he stumbles to the floor. Jazz keeps filming. Honest springs up and brushes himself off.

Lander accosts Johnny Dash. "You can't use this footage," she says. "It will prejudice the jurors for Fate's case."

"That's up to my producer," Jazz says.

I nudge Justine toward the front door. I've had enough excitement for today. But Johnny Dash intercepts us and sticks his mic in my face.

"Tin Holland, you're the police chief in this bucolic hamlet and you arrested Fate Abernathy for murder. What do you say to a diminished capacity defense?"

Justine and I are not holding hands, but we're standing close to each other, clearly leaving the celebration together.

"No comment," I say. "It's not my role to prosecute or sentence Fate Abernathy."

"But you're off-duty," Johnny says. "What's your opinion as a private citizen?"

I take Justine's hand, squeeze it. "As a private citizen, I choose to be private and keep my opinions to myself."

When we climb into Justine's truck for the short drive home, I sigh. "Whew. I'm tired."

"I don't understand why," she says. "I mean, you came out tonight in your hometown as a lesbian, a lesbian with a girlfriend, on television, *and* you were toasted as a hero, *and* you have this poor young woman's fate in your lap."

"When you put it that way, it's no wonder."

"You also drank your share of champagne."

We clinch our seatbelts at the same time.

Justine laughs. I do too, but a second behind her and more at her laugh than our simultaneous seatbelt clicks.

I feel uneasy and I'm not sure why. With all the positive reaction to Justine being with me and all the praise I got for helping with the harbor and solving the murder, I should be happy and relaxed.

"You have a lot to think about," Justine says. "I mean, that was a train wreck in there, Honest rambling while the camera rolled, and if I were his lawyer, I would have tackled him and dragged him from the bar. I mean, he practically said she did it. But here we are talking about a diminished capacity defense and maybe Honest is not as crazy as all that."

"He's a clown, but he's not crazy at all," I say. "And you're talking about diminished capacity, not me."

"If you think Fate should get a lighter sentence, you should say so." Justine shakes her car key as she talks. "I would be harsher, it's true, but I don't know this woman except from the bleachers. You know her. You *like* her."

"I don't know her," I say. "As for liking her, I don't know. But I am sympathetic, her being an orphan, traumatized and all that. It doesn't mean she's innocent."

"Couldn't she plead to a lesser crime, make a deal? Save everyone a lot of trouble."

"Look at you, Ms. Bleeding Heart. That's for her lawyer to work out."

"I'm not a bleeding heart. Nor am I the police chief."

Now she starts the car.

"Fate has to pay a price," I say. "The sentence can't be *too* lenient. Sometimes I wish I hadn't tricked her into running. And *you*, you sure like to push me out of my comfort zone."

"I do," she says. "You're easy to tease."

"Take us home," I say.

THE END

AFTERWORD
What *Really* Happened

I told you in the prologue that this is what really happened, but obviously, that's not true.

Though *Pirates of Sausalito* is inspired by true events, it's a made-up story, invented first for a murder mystery play that I wrote and directed for the Tam Valley Players in 2023, and then adapted and expanded for this novel.

As the disclaimer boilerplate goes, any resemblance between the characters and persons living or dead is purely coincidental. With two exceptions: Sally Cal, a fictionalized version of Sally Stanford, and Donlon Arques, without whom the houseboat communities might never have come to be.

For a full rundown of those true events, and links to stories, photos, and videos about the houseboat wars, visit my website at *johnbyrnebarry.com/houseboat-wars/*.

Here are *some* of the things from the novel that really happened:

1. Houseboats first appeared in Richardson Bay in the 1890s, when San Franciscans started mooring simple cabins and elegant retreats on rafts and barges. One was constructed from four abandoned horse-drawn

streetcars. By the early 1900s, there were more than thirty vessels, though most were only weekend or summer residences.

2. In 1942, Bechtel opened a ship factory in Sausalito called Marinship, which employed 20,000 workers, who built 93 cargo ships and oil tankers in three years. After the war, boatbuilder Donlon Arques, who had worked in the shipyard himself, purchased the abandoned Marinship land, dragged old boats onto the tidelands, and rented them to soldiers returning from the war.

3. The "houseboat wars" were real. In the 1950s and 1960s, the waterfront became home to artists and bohemians, beatniks and hippies, who built or scrounged colorful, artistic, and sometimes dilapi-dated homes in an area that became known as "the Gates," named after the entrances to the ship factory. Today, Sausalito has streets named "Gate 5 Road" and "Gate 6 Road."

One resident described the houseboat harbor as "a warren of ramshackle junks, arks, hutches, rotting barges, battered ferry boats and abandoned hulls." Another said one extension cord supplied electricity to dozens of households. "If someone plugged in a hair dryer, everything would blow."

During the 1970s, there were multiple attempts by city and county leaders to clean up and clear out the houseboat community, citing public health violations, but the houseboaters resisted with civil disobedience, music, street theater, and legal—as well as question-ably legal—maneuvers.

Houseboaters in dinghies armed with oars pushed away police boats serving eviction orders, and protesters went limp when police arrested them. These confrontations were well-documented in photographs and video footage. Local TV news anchors like Dave McElhatton and Dennis Richmond reported live from Sausalito during these skirmishes.

4. After a pile driver was towed in, with a police escort, to build new piers, a lawyer for the houseboaters tried to get a Temporary Restraining Order (TRO) to stop construction. The TRO failed, but at high tide, in the middle of the night during a rainstorm, several houseboaters maneuvered a large barge into the harbor, and sunk it in the mud, blocking the pile driver. They painted "Midnight TRO" on the side of the barge.

5. Sally Stanford ran a brothel on Nob Hill in San Francisco from 1940 to 1949. *San Francisco Chronicle* columnist Herb Caen wrote that "the United Nations was founded at Sally Stanford's whorehouse," basing his tongue-in-cheek claim on the fact that many delegates of the founding conference for the United Nations were customers of Sally's and some of the negotiations took place in the brothel's living room.

    Sally moved to Sausalito in 1949, where she operated a hotel and restaurant. She ran for the Sausalito City Council six times, finally winning in 1972. She served as mayor from 1976 to 1980.

6. Dan White, a San Francisco police officer who was elected to the Board of Supervisors in 1977, broke into City Hall on November 27, 1978 and assassinated

Mayor George Moscone and Supervisor Harvey Milk, the first openly gay elected official in the United States.

White was charged with first degree murder, but was convicted of the lesser charge of manslaughter, and the night his verdict was announced, thousands of angry San Franciscans marched from the Castro to City Hall. This became known as the White Night Riot.

Dan White was released from prison in 1984 and committed suicide the following year.

7. There is no evidence that there were undercover agents or provocateurs in Sausalito during the houseboat wars. However, for more than fifteen years, until 1971, the FBI operated a counter-intelligence program (COINTELPRO) and infiltrated a wide variety of organizations, famously the Black Panthers and the Ku Klux Klan, but also peace groups committed to nonviolence.

   We know this because a citizens' group broke into an FBI office in Pennsylvania and turned over the files they stole to the media, which led to congressional investigations. In one case, an agent posing as a radical member of Students for a Democratic Society, trained students on using Molotov cocktails.

8. To stop developers from building a parking lot for a proposed high-end marina in a wetland area, community artists created more than two dozen cardboard "protesters" and set them up in front of bulldozers to block construction. These cardboard cutouts generated a great deal of media buzz, and remained for a week before they were run over by bulldozers.

9. Two houseboat "neighborhoods" reached a compromise with the city and county—the Napa Street Pier Co-op at Gate 5, today known as Galilee Harbor Community, and the Gates Co-op at Gate 6. Residents were allowed to stay, but had to bring their houseboats up to code and meet strict environmental standards. Today, both co-ops are officially designated as low-income housing.

However, only a fraction of the houseboaters took part in that program, which required significant investment. Many houseboat residents refused to participate or could not afford to.

10. Were there pirates in Sausalito during the houseboat wars? No and yes.

There were no pirates who attacked ships and stole from them. But there were self-proclaimed pirates, who dressed the part, who flew pirate flags. Critics and opponents of the houseboaters often called them pirates, claiming they were lawless. Journalists called them pirates as well. And there was one fellow who paraded around the waterfront with a parrot perched on his shoulder.

There are thousands of real people who live or have lived in houseboats in Sausalito, some of whom experienced the houseboat wars and have their own stories to tell. Some played pivotal parts, like sinking the barge to block the pile driver. Take a walk along Gate 6 Road at Waldo Point and you might meet one of them.

ACKNOWLEDGMENTS

Writing is solitary, which is mostly fine, but I can't imagine how I would have ever finished this book, or any of my books, without my writing groups. Over the past two decades, I've been in three writing groups and all have helped me improve my writing, my storytelling, and my editorial judgment. Equally important has been the support, encouragement, and community we've given each other.

For this book, I especially want to thank my current writer's group, which started at the Mill Valley Library ten years ago. It was a drop-in group that met twice a week—we wrote for an hour, and then in the second hour, we read brief sections out loud and shared feedback. When the pandemic came, we moved to Zoom and continue to meet twice a week. Thank you to Kate Moore, Gary Nelson, Rob Fisher, and Jon Tresan.

This novel was adapted from a play that I started writing as the pandemic arrived, and we had no idea how long it would be before live theater returned. I'd like to thank Susan Keller, Tommie Whitener, and Joel Blackwell, members of another writing group that I was part of for several years. They helped me with the script as well as this novel.

We finally performed the play in 2023 and, if I do say so myself, it was an entertaining and funny show. I'd like to acknowledge the actors and crew of the Tam Valley Players, our local community theater troupe, who brought the words and characters alive, as well as helping me to sharpen the dialog in the play. Nothing like hearing actors say the words out loud to learn what lines snap and what lines don't. The majority of the dialog in the play found its way into the book.

Thanks to Abby Young, Bill Leeman, Sean Pritchard, Jessica Bentley, Amy Apollo Ahumada, Carol Butler, Mick Mitrovich, Chris Nisi, Denise Kendall, Lewis Shireman, Karen Clinton, Tom Davey, Jeff Brown, Helen Russell, and Camille Esposito.

It's impossible to overstate how important my writing groups have been, but their feedback was mostly one chapter at a time over a period of years. That's why I recruited almost two dozen beta readers, who read an almost-final version of this novel, beginning-to-end, and gave me invaluable feedback.

Thanks to Francesca Graziano, Becky Parker Geist, Patrick Barry, Sean Barry, Michael Barry, Peter Deibler, Kate Rassbach, Roy Schachter, Rita George, Linda Hartman, Carole Raimondi, Abby Young, Denise Kendall, Carol Butler, Harriet Moss, Larry Clinton, Bob Schildgen, Ellen Kehoe, Mark Friedman, Susan Keller, Marcia Weisbrot, Lisa Maslow, and last, but not least, my wife Nanette Zavala, my toughest critic and strongest supporter.

DEAR READER

If you enjoyed this novel, please tell your friends and family and post a review online wherever you buy books. There are hundreds of thousands of books published every year, and it's a daunting challenge to get the word out.

You might also enjoy one of my other "page-turners with a conscience"—*When I Killed My Father: An Assisted-Suicide Family Thriller; Wasted: Murder in the Recycle Berkeley Yard;* and *Bones in the Wash: Politics is Tough. Family is Tougher.*

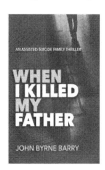  

Find out more at *johnbyrnebarry.com*.

I would also love to hear from you. You can reach me at *johnbyrnebarry@gmail.com*.

Made in the USA
Middletown, DE
19 April 2024

53184189R00172